WRETCHED RETRIBUTION

(Book 3 Of The Wretched Series)

E.G. MICHAELS

Wretched Retribution

TITLES BY E.G. Michaels

THE WRETCHED SERIES

The Wretched

Wretched Culling

Wretched Retribution

Operation Flashpoint (A Wretched Series Novella)

KYLE SIMMONS SERIES

Before The Clock Strikes

The Countdown

On The Clock

Time's Up

Every Minute Counts

On Borrowed Time

COLE HUTCHINSON BOOKS

Gone Too Far

PROLOGUE

Six Days Ago
Location: Bergstrom Biogenics

Gerald Giles had never been more terrified in his life. He tugged on the restraints keeping his arms secured to the treatment table. The straps quickly confirmed his fears: they were more than capable of keeping him from moving. Giles was not a physically imposing man. Despite regularly working out in the prison weight room, he hadn't managed to build up his physique. He'd been trying to get bigger physically for the last five years, but his muscles refused to grow much more. Maybe the blame lay partly on his lack of understanding on how to weight train like a bodybuilder or even a powerlifter.

Of course, Giles's area of expertise was something completely different. At one point, he'd been a prolific computer hacker with dozens of successful cyber-breaches that had gone undetected. He was one of the top cyber thieves in the world, maybe even the best one of them all. But that all changed the one time he made a mistake and got caught. Of course, hindsight was always 20/20. Deciding to steal three million dollars from the Sanlucci family had been a bad decision. The organized crime family noticed the missing funds and launched their investigation, which left nothing to chance. Several days later, their enforcers showed up at his nondescript home and demanded their money back with heavy interest and penalties. In the heat of the moment, he'd panicked, pulled the secondhand revolver he'd kept for personal protection, and shot one of the men. When the dust settled, he was in jail for murder and cyber crimes. The Sanluccis pulled an expected move and began calling in owed favors. Then he'd heard through the grapevine that they'd contracted several other hackers to track down every other cyber crime Giles had ever pulled. The district attorney's office must have thought Christmas came early that year when they found a manila envelope left under the office door. Inside there was a flash drive containing enough evidence to put Giles behind bars for one hundred years' worth of non-consecutive sentences. That was going to be a lot of years filled with the usual prison lifestyle and periodic attempts on his life. He'd been lucky to survive four attempts so far, but Giles knew he was on borrowed time. Sooner or later, he was going to wind up dead with a homemade shiv in his body, compliments of the Sanluccis.

That was why he'd agreed to do this study. He'd bought their story hook, line, and sinker. He was going to receive a one-time injection of an experimental medicine that could rapidly increase his muscle mass with no side effects. The idea of being much bigger physically meant his chances of fending off a future attacker might become considerably higher.

But now, he was regretting that he ever agreed to participate in this scientific study. Heck, he was kicking himself that he hadn't told Dwayne Haas what he'd recently discovered. Giles glanced over at the man, who was also confined. Haas was a huge, violent man that few other people ever wanted to cross. They had somehow formed an unlikely friendship, but one that had benefited both men. Haas kept Giles safe from harm. Giles used his extensive computer skills to hack the prison library computer and create a private Internet access portal that Haas could use to avoid any security software or Internet blockers the prison had installed on their computers. With this unrestricted access, his friend could view whatever he wanted online. Considering some of the things Giles had cleaned from the browser history, Haas was regularly viewing things that would likely land him in solitary confinement for weeks or months at a time.

Giles heard a sound and turned his head toward it. He saw Doctor Bergstrom coming toward him with a large syringe in his hand. Giles felt his heart begin to pound a little faster.

"Hey, Doc, what's this stuff do again?"

"It's a healing agent," Bergstrom said with a fake smile. "It accelerates your healing speed."

"I thought you said it would build up my muscles really fast."

"You're right," Bergstrom said. "My mistake. It's a healing agent."

"Uh-huh," Giles said skeptically. His gut feeling told him that the doctor was lying. "I don't have any injuries right now."

"That won't be a problem," Bergstrom answered. "We'll give you this medicine. After we know it's had time to spread through your whole body, we'll create a substantial wound on your body."

"Wait, what do you mean *substantial?*"

"Something that will be easily noticeable," Bergstrom said. He began to prep a needle in plain view.

Giles felt a wave of fear come over him. "L-like a cut on my arm?" he stammered.

"You'll see."

"Doc, you didn't answer my question. I want to know—" Giles let out a yell as the needle slammed into his exposed arm. "Damn, Doc, you could have warned me first."

"It'll take a few minutes until you begin to feel the effects," Bergstrom said with a detached clinical voice. "Until then, it's best if you just lie still and relax as best as you can."

Giles struggled to lift his head, and as he did, the room began to suddenly blur. "Doc, I don't feel—" Giles began to say. The next thing he knew, everything had gone black, and he was unconscious.

Giles awoke with a start. He lifted his head and began to take in his surroundings. He wasn't sure how long he'd been unconscious, and the idea that he may have lost a significant amount of time brought a feeling of fear coursing forward. There was something wrong with his eyes. Giles blinked and tried to focus on a nearby table. He tried blinking once more, and there was no change in his vision. Everything he looked at appeared to have a reddish tint to it. Giles heard another inmate scream.

"We're losing him," Bergstrom shouted. "Somebody get me the crash cart."

Giles tried turning toward the doctor's voice, but something was in his line of sight. He felt a rush of annoyance sweep over him, and he instinctively reached toward the impromptu barrier. There was a brief moment of resistance, and then he felt something give a moment before his arm swung free. His eyes fell on his newly-freed arm. There was some type of leather binding dangling loosely from his arm.

How? How did that happen? Giles thought to himself. He glanced at his other arm and saw it had a similar, yet still intact, restraint. Giles gently pulled his arm against the binding and it held firm. A voice in his head sounded out. It began urging him to push harder, to fight against this thing trying to keep him from getting off the gurney. Giles felt a surge of power rise up from seemingly his toes toward his shoulders, and he yanked his bound arm firmly. The binding snapped as if it were made out of tissue paper, and his arm swung freely. Giles sat up, reached down, and grabbed the restraints holding his legs still. He yanked on one, and it broke with a loud snap. He stared at the newly-broken restraint, trying to figure out what had happened.

I don't understand. Is this some kind of dream? he thought. Restraints weren't supposed to be so easy to break. Especially for a guy like him. Giles reached over and grabbed the remaining binding and gave it a hard pull. It immediately tore, and his hand swung up easily.

Giles swung his feet off the table and onto the floor. As he went to put his weight on his legs, his knees buckled and he crashed to the floor. The room quickly spun counterclockwise, then clockwise, before righting back to normal. He blinked twice and looked again. Everything in the room still had a reddish tint. Giles shook his head and looked around to see his surroundings. The room had quickly turned into a chaotic scene.

"Somebody restrain him," Bergstrom screamed.

Giles spun toward the doctor's voice and braced himself for a potential assault. As he turned, he saw a staff member rush to grab another inmate.

Beeks. Something is wrong with Horatio, too, Giles thought. He saw Beeks fire a single punch toward the man's chest, and a moment later, the orderly flew backwards and landed in a broken heap. Two more orderlies rushed toward Beeks.

Should I help Beeks or not? Giles mentally thought.

Giles heard a new noise and turned his head toward it. He saw an open door was slowly closing again and made an immediate snap decision. Beeks could handle himself. Especially since the man had never been particularly friendly toward him, either. If it weren't for Haas, Giles would have likely been on the receiving end of Beeks's prison yard bullying tactics.

Where is he? Where's Haas? Giles mentally thought. He scanned the tables. There were three empty tables and two dead inmates still strapped to the table in the room. Beeks was in the midst of a battle with the staff, but Haas was nowhere to be found.

He must have gotten free. A wave of happiness surged forward, and Giles immediately made a decision. He moved toward the still-closing door as quickly as he could. After two steps, he felt his body instinctively drop on all fours and began bounding toward the door. It was a strange reaction, but then Giles struggled to explain any of the new things he'd seen and felt in the last couple of minutes.

Giles slammed into the door, and it swung back open once more. He pushed through the doorway and into the corridor. There was a glimpse of movement at the end of the hallway, and Giles blurted out, "Haas, wait!"

Except that it didn't sound like words. More like growls and yips. But yet, he understood what he'd tried to say.

What the hell had Bergstrom done to them?

He rushed down the corridor, and as he rounded the corner, something slammed into him, knocking him off his feet. He saw a raised hand full of claws and immediately growled, "Wait!"

"Giles?" a tentative voice rumbled.

"Yes," Giles answered. "Haas. Are you okay?"

"No," the man answered. He gestured toward his body. His physique had grown even larger, with large patches of hair covering most of the surfaces. "Look at me."

"It's the medicine," Giles replied. "See?" He held out one of his own arms for inspection.

"Leave me alone," Haas growled. He turned his back toward his friend and began to slowly move away. As he did, Giles saw there was some type of strange plating on the back of the man's arms, back, and neck.

"Dwayne, wait," Giles said calmly. "Stop."

"Why?"

"You're not alone."

"Really? Look at me," Haas demanded. "They've turned me into some kind of freak."

"I know. So am I. Come with me. We'll figure it out together."

"Where? Where can we go, looking like this?"

"I know a place, not far from here," Giles said. "We'll start there and figure it out together. All right?"

"Is it safe?"

"Yes," Giles said. "You can trust me."

"Okay."

Giles motioned for Haas to follow him. As they approached an emergency stairwell, the door suddenly swung open. Giles saw a security guard step into the hallway. A low growl came out of his throat.

"Freeze!" the man shouted. He began to reach for something on his hip.

There was a blur of motion past Giles' shoulder and he saw Haas crash into the man, knocking the guard to the ground. The man's body landed in the still-open doorway, acting as a human door wedge. Giles watched in horror as his friend pushed past the man's defenses, latched onto his exposed throat with his teeth, and tore it open. There was an immediate arterial spray, and Giles watched in fascination as it happened. A moment later, a wave of insatiable hunger overpowered his ability to think, and he found himself joining his friend.

A few minutes later, their hunger had been sated. The two former humans descended down the stairway and escaped into the night. Neither one was ready to talk about what had happened or what they had done. All they could do was follow an instinctive feeling to get as far away from Bergstrom Biogenics as soon as possible.

CHAPTER ONE

Present Day

Location: Somewhere in Delaware

The windshield wipers made a rhythmic swishing as they moved the steady rain hitting the windshield out of the way. Malcolm Foster continued to actively scan the roadway ahead for any would-be threats. Of course, thanks to the steady rain, even the Reapers were wisely staying under cover. Foster couldn't help but think of the last time he'd driven in a rainstorm like this as a cop. He'd been an active Philadelphia police officer then. Even now, he might even still be considered a cop. Of course, once Reapers showed up, everybody's previous occupations were rendered null and void. The entire law enforcement structure in most cities had been obliterated in a matter of hours. It had quickly become a free-for-all where only the strongest and savviest people had a fighting chance of staying alive. Foster ran a hand through his dark hair. He usually kept it high and tight to prevent perps from grabbing a handful during an arrest. But like many things, he'd put keeping his hair perfectly groomed on the back burner and focused on trying to help his group of survivors stay alive.

It was easy to assume the Reapers were a bunch of mindless creatures. But experience had taught Foster that wasn't always true. There seemed to be some governing force controlling their actions. Sometimes they seemed to follow a packlike mentality. Other times, they seemed to be wisely following orders.

Take the current weather. They were in Delaware, traveling along US Route 1 South. There had been a handful of the creatures along the roadway, but as the rain began, they moved as one to retreat to a nearby building or covered structure. Of course, it could be just as likely as simple common sense. Even dogs and cats knew when it was time to get the hell out of the rain. There was so much they didn't know about the Reapers. Well, except they were bigger, faster, and stronger than humans. And if that wasn't bad enough, it was extremely hard to kill the damn things, too.

"Do you think they're going to be okay?" a voice said, interrupting his thoughts. Foster glanced over quickly and saw Derrick Sams sitting in the passenger seat. Sams was a former Army Ranger and the resident smartass of their group. While he was known for offering periodically bad jokes, the man had proven himself repeatedly as an extremely capable fighter. And if Foster was being honest, Sams' humor wasn't too far off what Foster frequently heard among other police officers. Most of the time, he found it was easy to get along with Sams.

"I think so," Foster said. "At least, the grandparents had the right idea."

"What was their deal?" Sams asked. "I was a bit preoccupied when you were dealing with them."

Foster chuckled. "You mean you were getting treatment for your sore butt and legs," he corrected. "For a so-called bad-ass Ranger, you sure spent a lot of time moaning about some bumps and bruises."

"I wasn't moaning."

"Uh-huh. Nut up, Army."

"Whatever," Sams muttered. "Next time you can be the one to have a bunch of bricks and rocks fall on you."

"I'll keep that in mind," Foster said. "I just think it's funny."

"You think it's funny that I got hurt?"

"Sort of. You know, for all your jokes about cops being flatfoots, you were the one that got caught by that trap."

"Yeah, yeah," Sams said. "Laugh it up while you can."

"All kidding aside, I'm glad you weren't seriously hurt."

"Wait a minute. Now you're being nice to me. What's your endgame here?"

"What are you talking about?"

"You're not going to try and kiss me, are you?"

Foster laughed. "No chance in hell."

"Come on, man. You know I'm the best-looking guy in the group."

"That's one man's extremely-biased opinion," Foster replied. "Last time I checked, that doesn't do a damn thing for me. Not that there's anything wrong with that."

"No argument here," Sams said. "Hey, you gonna fill me in on the kid and her grandparents, or what?"

"Right. So after I helped you get your sorry, bruised butt back to the house, Nick called on the walkie-talkie. He said that Olivia's grandparents had shown up. Turns out they were from the Pottstown area."

"How'd they know to come down?"

"You know, it was the damnedest thing. One of Olivia's little brothers got worried about their mom. He managed to get a call through on their mom's cell phone."

"Somebody must have been looking out for them."

"I'll say. Cell reception has been spotty at best for days," Foster said. "Not only did the call get through, but Grandma and Grandpa actually answered it. Turns out both of them were still alive and well. They managed to hop in their gas-guzzling SUV and make the trip from Pottstown to Olivia's house."

"That must have taken them a while."

"I wouldn't be surprised if it took them three times longer than normal."

"Well, it is a hassle having to navigate around all of the car wrecks and wandering Reapers," Sams pointed out. "Especially if you're trying to avoid wrecking your ride."

"No argument here. I didn't actually meet Olivia's grandparents. Nick and Lizzy did."

"Gotcha. So should I ask them the story instead?"

"Only if you want the full version," Foster said. "If you like, I can give you the quick and dirty version."

"Might as well tell me what you know," Sams replied. "It beats listening to all of the radio stations that aren't broadcasting anything but canned messages."

"Yeah, I miss listening to music on the radio, too," Foster said. "Okay, the quick version it is. Turns out Olivia's grandparents have a place up in the Poconos."

"Poconos?"

"It's a group of mountains. Pretty rural. A few hours from here."

"Good to know."

"Yeah, so her grandparents have a place near Jack Frost Mountain. They scooped up their daughter, the three grandkids, and packed them up in their SUV. They hung around long enough to thank Nick and Lizzy, and then they were on their way."

"You think they made it there okay?"

"Hope so," Foster said. "I hate to think otherwise. Lizzy did make it a point to slip Olivia her cell phone number."

"Nice thought, but I'm not sure how much that'll help," Sams said. "Especially since we're heading in the opposite direction."

"Yeah, I hear you," Foster said. "Speaking of calls, I should probably put one in to the rest of the group." He checked his rearview mirror and saw a Hyundai Tucson and Toyota Land Cruiser following him closely behind.

After much discussion, they'd settled on Charles, their elderly sage and former priest, driving the Tucson with their resident physician, Amanda, riding along. The two of them were definitely the least experienced fighters in the group. They'd compensated by putting the former Army Ranger Nick Walker and his wife, Lizzy, in the Land Cruiser. The married couple was happy to act as rear guard for their makeshift convoy. Knowing Nick as well as he did, their marital vows had likely included regularly practicing at the shooting range, as both of them were quite skilled with guns.

Foster was currently driving a Chevy Suburban. He'd worried a bit about the Reapers recognizing the vehicle again after some of the previous encounters where he had run over or away from their attacking packs in the early days.

Fortunately, they'd caught two lucky breaks. The first break came on one of their scavenging runs when they found several cans of spray paint. One hour and a hack repainting job later, the vehicle was now a dark green. Of course, that was before it had started to rain. Now Foster could only hope the new paint would turn out to be waterproof, too. If not, there was a good chance their vehicle could be quickly recognized by the Reapers again.

The second break had been earlier today. They had passed an Arby's Restaurant on Route 202 South and spotted a small gun shop. The sign out front proudly announced they bought and sold guns. The group had decided to investigate after seeing the front door had been smashed in. There were bullet casings scattered through the floor and a long, dried blood smear near the cash register. It was where someone had likely tried to make a last stand and failed. Most of the store had been cleaned out, but when they investigated further, they had found nearly one hundred loose rounds of 5.56 ammunition sitting in a bucket in the back room. It was enough ammo to fill a few extra magazines for their AR-15s, which was greatly appreciated. The hundred rounds was a drop in the proverbial bucket of what Foster would want them to have. The world they lived in now meant in order to feel fully protected against any future Reaper attacks, you'd want a full arsenal of weapons and ammo to repel the hostiles. Even so, the extra ammo was still an improvement in the right direction.

"It's getting pretty dark," Sams said. "Any thoughts on pulling over and letting everyone grab some rest?"

"Sure," Foster said. "We'll look for a rest stop. Some place off the main highway that probably has been overlooked by the Reapers."

"Let's hope so. I don't know of too many places they haven't found yet."

The walkie-talkie chirped aloud. "Foster, you there?"

"Yeah," Foster answered. "What's up, Nick?"

"We should start thinking about finding a place to stop before it gets too dark."

"Sams and I were just talking about the same thing."

"Charles said there's a rest stop coming up soon. Some place called Smyrna."

"Yeah, that might work," Foster said. "We might be able to find some supplies there and hole up for the night."

"Affirmative on the supplies," Walker said. "But I doubt we'll want to sleep outside the vehicles. If it's like any other public rest stop, then it's going to be difficult to find a secure location. Too many entrances and exits out of each of the buildings."

"Good point," Foster said. "All of us could really use a solid night of sleep."

"Since I know where the rest stop is, did you want me to take the lead?" Charles asked. "It might be easier that way."

Foster glanced at Sams, who nodded once. "Sure," Foster said. "Just stay close so you don't lose us."

"I will," Charles replied.

Sams chuckled. "What you meant to say is, 'stay close so we have a snowball's chance of rescuing you if you get into trouble.'"

"No need. Charles already knows that," Foster said. "Besides, when have you ever known the man to be a risk-taker?"

"Good point."

Foster watched as the Tucson sped up, passed him on the left, and moved back in front of him. The vehicle slowed down enough to maintain a twenty-foot cushion between them. The Tucson's right turn signal went on, and Foster did the same. He glanced at the road sign approaching and saw they were nearing exit 119A. Foster checked his rearview mirror and saw Walker had followed his lead and was preparing to exit the roadway, too.

As their caravan of vehicles exited, the road eventually straightened out and Foster saw a new sign signaling they were now on Route 13. There was a road sign, which mentioned a Wawa convenience store and a McDonald's were farther ahead.

"Any chance he's stopping for a Big Mac?" Sams asked.

"Not likely," Foster said. "I can't imagine anyone is still working in a restaurant these days."

"That's too bad." Sams chuckled. "I wouldn't mind having one again. Chalk that up as another thing the Reapers managed to ruin for everyone."

Foster saw Charles pass a Shell gas station and then signal he was moving into the left lane. The Tucson slowed down enough to make a left turn. Foster followed suit, and as they pulled into the parking lot, he saw a sign that announced they had reached the Chauncey O. Simpson Memorial Rest Area. Foster parked and turned off the engine.

He began to look through the Suburban's windows to check out their surroundings. There was some type of camping area to his left and an enclosed area to his right. In the distance, there appeared to be at least one tennis court that he could see. There didn't appear to be anything moving in the growing darkness. Foster strained to hear any telltale growls or moans and heard nothing but silence.

Foster cued the walkie-talkie. "It's really quiet," he said. "I don't see any signs of activity."

"A Reaper-free rest stop," Sams said from the passenger seat. "I can't believe it."

The walkie chirped, and then he heard Walker say, "Yeah, maybe. But we need to stay on our toes."

Foster pressed the transmit button. "Looks like that building has glass windows. But without getting out and checking it, I can't be certain if that's the only vulnerability." He released the button and waited for Walker's reply.

"If it's like a lot of rest stops, there's probably a bunch of glass windows and doors," Sams added. "They would make it easy for Reapers to spot us and decide to charge through."

"I'm not thrilled about trying to explore in the dark," Walker answered. "I think it might be best for us to wait until morning in the vehicles."

"I agree," Foster transmitted. "Everybody stay in the vehicles. We maintain some type of security. Maybe two people staying on lookout and switching it up every two hours. If they spot any Reapers coming our way, they wake the rest of us. Then we deal with the hostiles or just drive out of here." He released the transmit button and waited.

The walkie chirped in response, and Foster heard Walker say, "Sounds like a plan. I'm going to switch vehicles before one of my eardrums falls out." There was a loud thud in the background, and then Walker said, "Why'd you punch me?"

"Because you were being a jerk," Lizzy said. "Not everybody likes riding in a truck in dead silence for hours."

"Like I said, Lizzy is looking forward to talking with her best friend," Walker said calmly. "I'm going to make that happen. This is Walker, signing off."

CHAPTER TWO

Horatio Beeks had once heard the line "It's good to be the king" in a movie. The movie's name escaped him at the moment, but it was quite fitting for describing his current life. It seemed like almost yesterday that he was just another death row inmate who had nothing to look forward to except when the powers that be decided it was time to execute him.

Unlike some of his prison peers, Beeks had given up a long time ago the idea of ever being able to atone for all of his sins. There were far too many criminal things he'd done in his past. He had serious doubts that any divine being would be willing to forgive everything he'd ever done wrong. He couldn't blame them, either.

The humans had begun to call his children Reapers. He actually liked the name. It made them sound as dangerous as they actually were.

The transformation had left him bigger, faster, and stronger than ever before. He had even gained the ability to heal from nearly any injury. And he'd gone from being a death row convict to the leader of millions of personal minions.

Of course, a crown never rests easily on any king's head. Beeks was constantly worrying about potential threats to his Alpha position at the head of his giant pack.

But right now, that was the farthest thing from his mind, because he was staring at an underling groveling in front of him. The soldier was doing everything it knew how to demonstrate its loyalty and appease its master. Especially since both of them knew he'd failed to complete his mission.

"What do you mean, you lost them?"Beeks asked in a low growl. "You were supposed to follow them and see where they were going."

"I-It was more than a few humans, my Lord," the soldier stammered. "They used those machines to move away quicker than we could follow."

"They're called trucks, you idiot," Beeks taunted. "Maybe you can remember that the next time your fur-covered head sees a pack of humans."

"Y-yes, my Lord."

"Did you think to call ahead? Tell anyone else in the family that you needed help?" Beeks snarled. "We had Foster and his group cornered. And you let them escape."

The soldier said nothing and slunk even lower on the floor.

"He was afraid of them," a new voice said. A moment later, it added, "My Lord."

Beeks turned toward the voice to see who dared to interrupt. It was one of his soldiers. Beeks studied the minion. It held the appropriate revered position, and yet it still emanated a strong, confident vibe. Beeks couldn't help but wonder why this soldier wasn't cowering in fear like most of its peers.

Beeks turned his attention back to the minion kneeling in front of him. "Is this true?"Beeks growled.

A whimper came out of the throat of the cowering soldier. A small yellow puddle began to form under its legs.

"You disgust me," Beeks said. "Get out of my sight."

"Yes, Master." The soldier yelped and began backpedaling away while still staying bent over. As soon as it reached the open doorway, it turned and fled the room.

Beeks turned his attention back to the soldier who had spoken out of turn. The minion was still holding the proper position without any reluctance or fear.

"What is your name?"Beeks said softly.

The soldier began to answer in a series of growls and grunts.

"Not your former name," Beeks said. "Your new name."

The soldier said nothing.

"You have not been given one yet. Have you?"

"No, my Lord."

"Very well," Beeks said. "I shall call you... Achilles."

"It is a nice name," the soldier said politely. "Thank you, my Lord."

"Rise, Achilles," Beeks said. "Let us speak frankly."

The soldier stood upright and looked Beeks directly in the eyes.

Beeks felt a brief moment of uneasiness as he saw those yellow eyes staring back at him so intently. He was far more used to his minions doing everything they could to avoid making direct eye contact with him.

"Achilles," Beeks said slowly, "this is an opportunity for you to gain status in the pack. Do you understand me?"

"Yes, my Lord."

"Go with some of your other brothers and sisters. Find these humans. Find this one who answers to the name Foster."

"Yes, my Lord," Achilles said. "I will not let you down."

"And once you find them?"

"Yes, my Lord?"

"You are to report in," Beeks continued. "Do not engage. Is that clear?"

"As you command, it shall be."

"Good. This Foster, he is a very important human," Beeks said. "I do not want him killed by any hand except my own."

"You promised," a voice roared out loud. "And now you break your word?"

Beeks and Achilles turned toward the new arrival. Several other soldiers dropped their heads at the arrival of the new red-eyed elite soldiers. Beeks growled in frustration. Malice had arrived with a flourish, his red cape flowing freely behind him. The last thing he wanted was to be upstaged, and his elite soldier had managed to do exactly that.

"Fos-ter is mine," Malice said loudly. "Do you understand that, mutt?"

"His name is Achilles," Beeks interrupted. "And he is to follow my orders, not yours. Do you dare challenge my command?"

"Not at all, my Lord," Malice said, flashing what might pass as a pasted-on smile. "I stand corrected." He turned his attention to Achilles and flashed his fangs. "Do you understand our master's orders?"

"Yes, I do," Achilles said. "I have no quarrel with you, Malice. I only seek to serve our master."

"Then I suggest you go do what he asked," Malice countered. "Go on, mutt. Before our esteemed leader grows tired of your mongrel presence and decides to end your filthy existence."

Achilles turned toward their master, nodded once, and then quietly stood and left the room.

Malice waited until Achilles left before he dropped onto one knee.

Beeks turned his attention toward his elite soldier and stared fiercely into its eyes. He glared until he felt Malice look downward uncomfortably. Beeks felt a small burst of pleasure. Malice might feel comfortable bullying others lower in the pack order, but he was not ready to challenge Beeks as Alpha.

"I am reporting as ordered, my Lord," Malice said with a throaty voice.

"I'm glad to see you haven't forgotten how to show me the proper level of respect," Beeks said. He chose his next words carefully. "It sets a good example for the others in our family. It tells me that you still recognize your place."

"Yes, my Lord."

"But I do not like hearing you talk that way to Achilles."

"My Lord, he is just a mongrel."

"I don't care," Beeks said. "He is someone I believe has great potential. Achilles could quickly become someone we can count on to handle some very important things for us."

"We don't need him."

"Really? As much as I value you, you cannot be in multiple places at once."

Malice glared at the floor in silence.

"If you think I'm wrong, then say so."

"We don't need him to find Fos-ter," Malice said between gritted teeth. "I gave you my word."

"Yes, you did. But I have something else that I need you to focus on. In the meantime—"

"I want Fos-ter," Malice roared.

"Enough," Beeks shouted. He reached out telepathically, grabbed Malice's mind, and squeezed hard.

The soldier screamed in pain and dropped to both knees, clutching his head. A small amount of spittle began to form in the corner of his mouth, and his body began to spasm in pain.

"You will do as I order you to do," Beeks snarled. His voice continued to rise. "I have given you my word. You will have your chance to extract your revenge. Foster will pay for killing your brother. But you are part of a bigger family now. You answer to me. You do my beckoning for as long as I let you live."

Malice groaned in pain and began to instinctively pull himself into a ball.

"Do you understand me?" Beeks roared. He released his hold on Malice's mind and heard the soldier immediately gasp in relief.

Malice wiped the spittle from his chin and slowly shifted back into the proper position.

Beeks waited until he did before he spoke again. "I've gotten word that there are some others who are like us. They appear to be organizing their own packs. I need you to find out more about them. I want to know where they are. I want to know if they are a threat to our family. And once you do, then you are to report what you find to me. Only me. Is that clear?"

"Yes, my Lord."

"In the meantime, I will have others looking for Foster and his group."

"But, my Lord—"

"Find them. Not capture or kill," Beeks said. He lowered his voice in what he thought might sound a bit more soothing to his agitated soldier. “You will have your chance. I gave you my word. Remember?”

“I remember.”

“Do not test me,” Beeks warned. “Foster and his group are a handful of humans. This other family might be thousands of soldiers who could be a direct threat to our family.”

“I understand, Master.”

“I hope you do. I’m counting on you.”

“I won’t let you down, my Lord.”

“See that you don’t,” Beeks answered. “You’re dismissed.” He waited until Malice left the room before he let his mind wander off to another thought which was trying to capture his attention. He quickly realized it would be best to work the situation through his mind if he could do so without any interruptions. He glanced at the trio of guards still remaining in the room. He reached out and touched all of their minds at once.

“I need some privacy. I want you to stand guard outside this room. Do not let anyone enter until I tell you otherwise,” Beeks mentally commanded.

A series of yips that sounded almost like yesses answered him back. The guards moved as one and stepped outside his throne room.

Beeks let out the breath he hadn’t realized he had been holding. He began to think back to that fateful night. A night when he went from being a death row inmate to the leader of millions.

There had been four other patients in the room with him. Two of the men had died during the experiment. A third, Dwayne Haas, was a block mate of his. Another man whom he knew simply as Giles was in the room. In the frantic craziness that ensued, Beeks hadn't seen either one of them leave the room.

Since then, he hadn’t been able to determine their whereabouts. It was almost as if the two of them had disappeared off the face of the earth. Were they the ones rumored to be organizing their own families? If that was true, could they be planning some kind of attack on his family? There wasn’t any way to know right now, and that bothered him deeply.

Maybe they were planning to challenge his position as leader of his own pack. He believed it was the largest group of Reapers in the United States.

But it would be foolish to assume that. He couldn't rule out that someone else, or even a group of other red-eyes, could have amassed an even larger mass of soldiers and were planning on smashing his family into submission.

Well, he couldn't allow that to happen. He couldn't let someone else rise up and challenge for his place. Not when the future was so bright and so many things were lined up in his favor.

This was his destiny. His calling to be the leader of millions and eventually billions. All would come to worship and adore him. Maybe it would be out of fear. Maybe it would be out of admiration. Either one was fine as long as they never forgot he was their unquestioned master.

Beeks began to laugh. His old high school guidance counselor had once told him that he'd never amount to anything in this world. Well, he was proving that old fart wrong. If he could find that man, he'd personally tear his heart out of his chest and make him watch as Beeks ate it in front of him.

Undisputed leader of the entire world. The very idea made his heart swell with pride. It was a beautiful dream to have, and each day he moved one step closer to achieving it. And if anyone was foolish enough to get in his way, then he would kill them without losing a minute of sleep.

CHAPTER THREE

It was almost daylight when the walkie-talkie chirped to life. Foster immediately awoke with a start.

"Foster, you there?"

Foster pressed the transmit button. "Yeah. What's up?" he asked.

"It's light enough that we should be able to see the interior of the stores pretty easily," Walker said. "We can grab any supplies we find while things are quiet."

"Okay. Sure."

"You don't sound excited."

Foster stifled a yawn. "I would be, if you told me there was a pot of coffee waiting for us."

"There might be somewhere around here, but who knows how long ago it was made."

"Figures."

"Even so, it can't hurt to take a look," Walker said. "They probably sold food and beverages. We might even find some packages of coffee."

"True."

"Plus, we don't know what things would be like closer to Rehoboth."

"Gotcha. I'm on my way," Foster said. Out of habit, he checked the mirrors and scanned his surroundings. He put his hand on the door handle and was getting ready to step out of the vehicle when he heard Sams blurt out, "Did somebody say coffee?"

"Morning, Derrick."

"Uh-huh. It would be an even better one if we had some fresh coffee to drink."

""There's zero chance of hot coffee right now," Foster said. "We don't have any way to brew it inside the vehicles."

"Can't blame a guy for wishing," Sams grumbled. "I'd kill a Reaper with my bare hands for a fresh cup of joe."

Foster saw Walker approaching the Suburban and opened the door a bit more.

"If wishes were horses, then the beggars would ride," Foster said. "I doubt there's a Reaper barista on the premises."

"With all of the shit we've already seen, I wouldn't doubt it."

"He does have a point," Walker said. "Heck, you already had a Reaper messenger. Way I see it, we can't rule anything out at this point."

"You want me to come with?" Sams asked.

"Not right now," Foster said. "Nick and I should be able to handle checking out the stores. If you can stay on lookout with the vehicles, that would be a big help."

"Great. Civilian babysitting," Sams grumbled. "With my luck, you guys will find a fucking mountain of Tastykakes and soft drinks while I'm here twiddling my thumbs."

"Or we find nothing but a bunch of trash and dead bodies," Foster countered. "We've talked about it. The three of us are the best shooters of the group. At least one of us needs to be on protective detail at all times."

"Blah, blah, blah." Sams mimicked someone talking with his hand as he spoke. "See if you find me something with some caffeine in it, will ya?"

"I'll keep an eye out," Foster said. "Call us if anything uninvited shows up."

"Copy that. Designated babysitter is now on duty."

Foster and Walker began walking away. As they did, Foster heard his friend chuckle softly.

"What's so funny?" Foster asked.

"I just realized I had the transmit button held in while I was holding it," Walker said as he waved the walkie-talkie. "If Lizzy was listening, then I'm sure she'll have something to say about the babysitting comment."

"You think Derrick will be sporting some new scorch marks on his body when we get back?"

"I wouldn't bet against it," Walker said. "Come on, let's go see if we find anything useful in these stores."

"Hold up," Foster answered. "We don't know if any of the rooms will be without working lights. Let's take the rifles with the night-vision scopes just in case."

"Works for me," Walker said.

Foster backtracked to the Suburban. He opened the driver's side door, reached behind the seat, and grabbed the suppressed AR-15 rifle with the Eotech Optic sight. He checked the magazine was firmly seated and then trotted back to meet Walker. As he did, he saw Walker had the same weapon already in his hands. The former Ranger motioned for Foster to lead them out.

It turned out the first building they reached wasn't a store after all. Foster felt a feeling of disappointment spread over him, and he shoved the emotion back down. It was far too soon to chalk this rest area down as a complete waste of time. Even so, the fact this building turned out to be a tourist information center instead was definitely a letdown. The center had tall glass walls on three sides, and a dedicated glass revolving door allowed access into the open space.

"Definitely not any fresh coffee in there," Walker said. "I don't see anything of interest. You?"

"Two water fountains," Foster replied. "If they work, it could be an easy way to refill water containers."

"That's a big if. Especially if there's no power. I wonder what's behind the brown door?"

"Sign says conference room."

"Huh. Probably doesn't have anything we can use in it, then," Walker said. "I say we skip checking it out."

"Works for me. I'll stay on point."

Foster slowly moved past the information center's entrance and toward an upcoming inverted *L*-intersection. He proceeded to the edge of the intersection and did a quick visual sweep.

To his left, there were women's and men's restrooms. There was a freestanding ten-foot-high brick wall intermixed with ground-to-ceiling white circular columns. The brick barriers had a pair of vending machines on one side. The pillars did not. The structural mixture ran parallel to the restrooms for most of the sidewalk. The entire ensemble of restrooms, overhead roof, and freestanding wall formed a makeshift tunnel with periodic gaps to allow people to move about easier.

To his right, there was a short pathway which led to a perpendicular path containing an identical layout of bathrooms and freestanding partial walls. Foster looked straight ahead and saw a decorative fountain about thirty yards in front of him. The fountain was enclosed with a pretty bed of flowers. Foster wasn't the least bit surprised it was no longer working.

"Coming up on your left," Walker announced. He stopped near Foster and took in their surroundings.

"Thoughts?" Foster asked.

"There's some vending machines against those freestanding walls. Might be something we can use in them. But this is a death trap waiting to happen," Walker said. "There's no good place to fall back besides the restrooms."

"The soda machines aren't lit."

"Fountain's not running, either," Walker answered. "How long you think they've been without power?"

"No clue."

"The beverages should be okay as long as they're still sealed."

"Yeah, good point. Might as well take them all then. Between you and me, I'm grabbing the bottled water first," Foster said. "It has more possible uses than a can of soda does."

"No argument here. I don't like soda."

"The restrooms could have hostiles sleeping in them," Foster said. "We need to clear them, too. How do you suggest we do it?"

"I'll clear the first one while you stay on overwatch outside the entrance door. We'll switch roles for the next restroom. If either one runs into trouble, they can call out and the other can be there in a few steps."

"That works," Foster said. He took up an overwatch position just outside the women's bathroom. Walker darted inside, and Foster heard stall doors being pushed open. A moment later, Walker emerged from the exit, still looking through his rifle's night-vision scope, and took up position next to him. Foster moved forward, passed his friend, and went into the men's restroom. It was nearly pitch black inside. He silently said thanks for remembering to bring his rifle with the night-vision scope on it. He'd hate to have to attempt to clear this area without it. He scanned the room through the night vision and saw nothing out of the ordinary. As he moved through the men's room, he came upon the glass exit door. He pushed on the horizontal bar, and it swung open easily. Foster stepped outside, letting the door close quietly behind him. The two men repeated the process for the remaining set of restrooms before moving back in front of the fountain.

Foster activated his comms. "Sams, come in."

"Yeah, what's up?"

"Restrooms are clear. If anybody wants to use them, send them our way, but tell them to bring a flashlight."

"I'll pass the word," Sams said. "Any coffee?"

"Afraid not. There's no stores here. There's some vending machines we're going to try cracking open."

"Copy that. I'll ignore any glass breaking I might hear."

"That works. Foster out."

"How are you planning on cracking those machines?" Walker asked. "Breaking the glass?"

"Nope. I'll use this." Foster reached into his backpack and pulled out a tubular lock pick.

Walker let out an appreciative low whistle. "Where did you get that?"

"Found it on one of our recent scavenging trips."

"Looks handy."

"Yeah, I wish I'd had it at the airport because it would have made getting into those machines a lot easier."

Foster moved to the vending machine door, inserted the pick, and in less than one minute, the lock disengaged. Foster grabbed the edge of the machine and swung its door open, revealing the snacks inside.

"You made that look easy. You know if you ever decide to have a life in crime, you've already got a head start."

"Nope. Crime doesn't pay." Foster chuckled. "You know, I can't tell you how many times people lock themselves out of their house or car," Foster said. "There were guys on the force who were even quicker than me at popping a lock."

"That's a vending machine, not a car."

"Same concept, different device."

"Uh-huh. Let's clear this machine and move on to the next."

The two men had managed to clear three vending machines when Foster heard the comms come alive.

"Foster, come in."

"What's up, Sams?"

"I'm seeing hostiles approaching. Approximately a dozen of them about four hundred yards out. So you may want to pick up the pace."

"Copy that," Foster said. He turned toward Walker. "Time to go."

"What's going on?"

"Sams has hostiles incoming."

"Reapers?"

"Likely, but I can't rule human assholes, either."

"Gotcha," Walker said. He grabbed one last handful of packaged food and stuffed it into his backpack. He quickly slung it over his shoulders and brought his rifle up into a low ready position. "You want to take point?"

"Sure," Foster said. He brought his rifle up and began working his way back toward the vehicles. He saw Walker moving a few steps behind and knew he didn't have to double-check that his friend was covering his back.

Foster began moving back toward the vehicles, and as he approached the L-intersection, he saw a trio of Reapers coming from the opposite end of the rest area. "Ten o'clock," he called out as he skidded to a stop near one of the vending machines. He brought his rifle up and began aiming.

"Got them. Keep moving," Walker yelled before he began firing.

Foster saw one of the Reapers get drilled in the face. The bullet's impact stopped it in its tracks, and the monster collapsed in a heap. Foster heard two more shots sound out behind him a moment before one of the Reaper's heads exploded into a bloody mess.

The remaining Reaper continued to rush in and launched itself at Foster. At the last moment, Foster twisted sideways to avoid its charge. The monster slammed headfirst through the vending machine's glass display. The impact momentarily dazed the Reaper, and Foster made it pay. He brought his rifle up to bear and fired once, scoring a headshot and killing the trapped monster instantly.

"I said keep moving!" Walker yelled. "Sams needs our help."

Foster picked up the pace and began a quick jog toward the vehicles. As he moved, he continued to actively scan for any potential threats.

"More incoming!" Walker shouted. "We're drawing a party."

Foster risked a glance over his shoulder and saw five more Reapers had come rushing around the corner of the farthest restrooms. They were still about four hundred yards away but were charging toward them. The Reapers split away from their pack and veered around to the opposite side of the decorative walls and pillars. Foster heard Walker swear out loud and doubled his efforts to find the incoming Reapers weaving in and out of sight. He spotted one emerging from a wall and rushed a shot, scoring a hit to the creature's leg. The Reaper stumbled, collided into a pillar, and fell onto the ground. Foster saw the monster stagger up to its feet. He fired once, drilling it in the head and putting it down for good. He heard gunfire to his left and saw another Reaper drop in front of him. The creature had managed to get within a hundred yards before Walker nailed it with a headshot.

"Move it, Foster!" Walker shouted.

Foster glanced back toward the vehicles and saw Sams, Lizzy, and Charles firing at four different Reaper packs charging toward them.

"Hurry," Amanda shouted. The doctor was positioned behind the driver's side of the Tucson and had joined the firefight, too.

Foster quickened his pace. He sighted through his rifle's scope on a Reaper that had stopped its charge short. The creature moved from a hunched-over position to an upright one and began to pound its chest. Foster saw the Reaper begin to open its mouth, and he immediately fired. He saw his bullet exit the back of the creature's mouth, and the Reaper dropped before it could utter a sound. Foster continued moving toward the vehicles, firing twice more before he reached the side of the Suburban. He pulled next to Sams and continued to fire at incoming hostiles.

"Why is it every time you leave, I end up in a gunfight?" Sams yelled.

"You're welcome to go scavenging next time instead," Foster yelled back.

"And miss out on all the fun?"

"Covering!" Walker shouted. "Fall back to the vehicles."

A pair of Reapers managed to reach the passenger side of the Suburban. As they began to climb up onto the hood, Foster and Sams fired as one. The demonic duo collapsed dead on the corner of the SUV.

"Get in," Foster yelled. "I'll cover you." He saw Sams backtrack, and a moment later heard the driver's door open and close. The Suburban's engine began to turn, and then he heard it roar to life. Foster continued to fire and move backward until he reached the rear door. He fired twice, scoring a double-tap to the neck of a nearby Reaper. Foster yanked the door open and jumped in. As soon as his butt hit the seat, he lunged back, grabbed the door, and pulled it shut a moment before the Suburban began moving.

"Did everybody get out?" Foster yelled.

Sams shouted, "Hold on."

Foster saw a bloody Reaper, standing wobbly on its feet, a moment before the Suburban's front end slammed into it. The creature pinballed sideways and crashed somewhere out of sight as the vehicle continued to accelerate.

"Did everybody get out?" Foster yelled. "Is everybody okay?"

"I don't know. I think so," Sams said. "Can you shut it for a minute while I try to get us the hell out of here?"

Foster immediately went silent. He looked out the side window and saw hundreds of Reapers flooding the rest area from the opposite direction. He turned his attention to the front window. As they headed to the rest area exit, Foster saw a small white building. There was a bloody Reaper perched on top of it, gesturing for its packmates to follow them. Two seconds later, the scout was growing distant in the rear view, and they were pulling away from the rest of their pursuers.

"Holy shit, that was close," Sams said.

Foster felt the Suburban continue to accelerate. "Too close," he admitted. "I'd say we got lucky."

"Nothing wrong with lucky," Sams answered. "It beats good but dead every time."

"Give me the walkie," Foster said. "I want to find out about the rest of the group."

Sams reached across the front seat, picked up the walkie-talkie, and offered it to Foster without taking his eyes off the road.

Foster pressed the transmit button. "Give me a sit-rep," Foster said. "Anyone hurt or missing?"

"Lizzy and I are fine," Walker answered. "No injuries."

"Amanda and I are uninjured," Charles replied. "Although, with the way the good doctor is currently driving, I'm not feeling confident about our chances of avoiding an accident."

Foster chuckled. "We're clear of the packs now. Might be a good idea for all of us do a more reasonable speed. Sams and I are uninjured, too."

"Glad to hear everybody is present and accounted for," Walker said. "Next stop, Rehoboth Beach."

CHAPTER FOUR

It had been several days since their transformation at Bergstrom Biogenics. Giles and Haas had slowly made their way from the city of Brotherly Love to someplace far less populated. There had been several stops along the way when the need to feed had become unbearable. Each one of them found a victim and ate without pity or remorse. Eventually they had come to an abandoned warehouse in Delaware. It was a place Giles knew about from his previous life. The building would serve as a temporary home for them and their growing pack.

They hadn't planned on having a pack. It was purely by accident that they discovered how to transform humans into their own loyal followers. There was so much about their new abilities that neither one of them understood. If he was being completely honest with himself, Giles had a feeling they had barely begun to tap their full potential.

"I feel like we're hiding like rats," Haas growled. "We should be out there adding more numbers to our packs and expanding our territory."

"I disagree," Giles said. "It's likely the humans are hunting those of us who have turned."

"That's not what I've heard. Some of the newer followers had images in their mind. Things they saw on television or in person that suggest there's a lot of transformed ones out there."

"Transformed like us? Or the mindless minions we can create?"

"They're not mindless."

"Really?" Giles challenged. "Watch this." He mentally reached out to his followers in the warehouse.

"Stand on one leg and hop in place," he commanded.

Dozens of minions began bouncing up and down on one leg.

Giles motioned to the followers. "I rest my case."

"All it means is they will follow our command," Haas said. "That's not a bad thing for us."

"If you say so."

"We should be out there. Gathering more followers. Using our combined power to control things. Maybe collecting followers that someone else created."

"Controlling someone else's soldiers could be a problem. We don't know who's leading them," Giles countered. "They could be looking for war."

Haas chuckled. "Scared of the boogeyman again?" he said. "I'm telling you, we don't have anything to be afraid of."

"Are you sure?"

"Not totally, but—"

"Then we have to assume there are others like us and prepare accordingly."

"Look, we've seen with our own pack that most humans don't turn like us."

"Uh-huh," Giles said. "Don't get cocky. Just when you think you are the biggest bad-ass in the world, someone else comes along and takes you out."

"Maybe. But it won't be any of these things. They lose their ability to think and act and do like us," Haas said. He pointed to the still-hopping followers. "Can you make them stop? It's distracting as hell."

"Sorry," Giles said. He quickly sent a mental halt command, and the minions immediately stopped bouncing.

"We need to find out who's in charge of these larger packs," Haas said.

"I agree," Giles said, "but we need to be careful on how we do it. We do not want to be forced to submit to a much larger group."

"Yes, that would be bad."

"I still think we need to stay out of sight for now and learn what we can from the shadows."

"We need more soldiers," Haas growled. "Our current plan doesn't give us many new ones to choose from."

"Perhaps I will pay my friend a visit. See what he can do to supply more candidates to us."

"Be careful," Haas said. "I don't trust your friend."

Giles chuckled. "Your instincts are good. He's a liar and a crook. But he's predictable. More importantly, he's scared of what I'll do to him if he double-crosses us."

CHAPTER FIVE

They'd managed to put three miles of distance behind them, and so far nothing seemed to be pursuing them. Foster heard his walkie-talkie chirp, and then Walker said, "Let's switch up the order."

"Any particular reason why?" Foster asked.

"Good operational practice. It will also give you two a break," Walker replied. "No point in you having to act as point man the whole way."

"He's getting bored," Foster and Sams said in unison.

Foster chuckled softly. He counted to two, then pressed the transmit button and said, "Sounds good. Charles, you'll pull over behind me and let Nick pass. Once he does, follow him and I'll take rear guard."

"Understood," Charles said over the walkie.

Five miles later, the four-lane roadway had transformed into more of a rural environment. There were cross streets nearly every block and a scattering of different businesses along each side of the road. The area looked like it had been hastily abandoned. Foster could only imagine how busy this area must have been at one time. It was just another sign of the lifestyle they used to enjoy that the Reapers' arrival had taken away from them.

Up ahead, Foster saw Walker begin to slow down and stop at the top of a hill.

"Problem?" Sams asked.

"Maybe," Foster replied. "I don't think Nick would have stopped in the middle of the road for no reason."

The walkie-talkie came alive. "Guys, it's a family," Lizzy said. "It looks like they're in trouble."

"I'm not sure if it's a good idea for us to stop," Foster said. "They could already be infected. Once we stop, then we could be in danger, too."

"We need to do something," Lizzy argued.

"Can they be saved, or is it too dangerous?" Charles asked.

"Walker, tell me what you see," Foster said.

"Disabled minivan. Looks like it's missing a tire. Four Reapers around it."

"Can we easily remove the threat?" Foster asked.

"Not sure. I'm going to roll past it slowly and see if that's enough to draw them away."

Foster watched as Walker's Land Cruiser began moving forward slowly. A moment later he saw the Tucson begin moving, too.

"Dammit, Charles," Foster muttered under his breath. The elderly man had mistakenly followed Walker. Now Foster felt committed to keep their caravan bunched closely and maintaining a protective rear guard. He took his foot off the brake and followed the other two vehicles.

As he began to pass the disabled vehicle, he saw four Reapers still crowding against the driver's side doors. Suddenly, a child appeared in the windshield and began to wave frantically.

"Oh, hell," Sams moaned a moment before the walkie came alive again.

"They've got kids in there," Lizzy shouted. "Malcolm, we need to do something."

"What do you think?" Foster asked.

"I think it's a terrible idea," Sams said, "but I'm not sure the rest of the group will agree with me. If there's a chance they haven't been infected and we do something, then that's some bad karma shit to not help."

"Yeah, my thoughts exactly," Foster said. "Guys, let's see what we can do to help."

"Nick thinks it's a bad idea. I told him I don't agree," Lizzy said. "We need to help those kids."

"Guess who's gonna get a lecture later," Sams said under his breath. "It's gonna be good old Nicholas."

"Not your problem or mine," Foster said. He cued the walkie as he began to apply the brakes. "We need to draw them away from the minivan. If you have hollow-point ammo, use that." The specialized ammunition was known for not passing through the body of its intended target and hitting something else behind it. Using hollow points should allow them to minimize the chances of accidentally hitting the minivan.

"Glocks only?" Sams asked. "I hope we don't get into an extended firefight. I only have one extra magazine of hollow points."

"Four Reapers versus six shooters," Foster pointed out. "If we're lucky, we'll end this fast."

"Malcolm, I'm not sure what type of ammunition we have," Charles said. "I'm not sure how to check."

"I'll explain later," Foster said. "Why don't Amanda and you guard our rear and keep anything from jumping us from behind?"

"Now it's four against four," Sams said.

"I still like our chances," Foster said. "Especially with Nick and us being part of those shooters."

"Great," Sams said sarcastically. "Walker and I are gonna have to bail everyone else out of this mess."

"It's not a mess," Foster countered. "Have some faith, man."

"Uh-huh," Sams muttered as he pulled out his Glock and checked the magazine load.

"Pull up partially," Walker said. "We'll use the SUVs as cover."

"What?" Charles asked.

"Pull halfway up next to Nick's passenger door," Foster said. "I'll pull up on the other side. The vehicles will make it harder for the Reapers to reach us."

"Oh," Charles said. "Why didn't Nick just say that?"

Sams swore under his breath.

"Game on, Derrick," Foster said. "Let's go, Army." Foster stepped on the brakes and brought the Suburban to a skidding stop near the Land Cruiser's driver's side. The passenger side door flew open and he saw Sams jump out. Foster grabbed his rifle, slung it over his shoulder, drew his Glock, and followed the former Ranger. He saw Sams move toward the back end of the vehicle and mirrored his position on the opposite side.

Foster studied the scene in front of him. The Reapers were hovering between the disabled vehicle and their current location. It was almost as if they were unsure who they wanted to attack.

Time to force their hand, Foster thought. He brought his Glock up to a shooting position, aimed, and fired once at a Reaper farthest away from the disabled minivan. He wanted to ensure that his bullet was less likely to strike any of the people still trapped in the minivan. The bullet struck the Reaper center mass. It wasn't a killing shot for a Reaper, but then Foster hadn't been trying to hit a long-range shot with his service weapon. The creature let out an angry roar, slammed a fist twice against its chest, and immediately charged toward him, with its packmates following closely behind.

"Well, that pissed him off," Sams said calmly.

Foster turned his attention to the battle forming in front of him. He shifted his aim and let the lead Reaper get closer. When the monster was approximately twenty yards away, he fired once more. This time, the bullet flew true, striking the charging Reaper in the nose. The creature's head snapped back, and it collapsed, dead.

Foster shifted his position, aiming at the next closest Reaper, only to see it drop as someone else's shot struck the monster in the face. Foster heard Sams fire twice, and another one of them dropped in place. Foster saw the remaining Reaper, and he shifted his aim toward it. As he did, the monster dropped onto all fours and began bounding toward him.

Foster heard a chorus of shots ring out as he saw the incoming

Reaper take damage to its shoulder, neck, and chest. The monster stumbled and fell awkwardly onto its right arm. There was a loud snap as its elbow dislocated and the creature howled in pain. The joint was visibly deformed, and Foster fought back the bile rushing up his throat. He sighted on the disabled Reaper and fired once, striking the monster in the eye. This time the creature stayed down for good.

Foster quickly scanned the area in front of him, looking for potential hostiles. Suddenly, there was a burst of gunfire behind him. Foster spun around in time to see a series of bullets stitch up a charging Reaper's body from its chest up into its face. The creature's jaw sank inward, and it dropped ten feet from Foster's position. He saw a visibly-shaken Charles holding his rifle.

"Nice shooting, Padre," Foster said.

"I-I had to," Charles answered. "It was going to attack Derrick and you."

"You did it a kindness," Foster said. "The person it used to be wouldn't want to have killed another human."

"Clear," Walker shouted.

"Clear," Sams answered back. "Foster, you want to talk to the trapped civvies?"

"I'll do it," Walker said. "It was my wife's idea for us to stop, so I might as well finish the mission."

"Sounds good," Foster said. "Sams, you take a right flank of the vehicle. I'll take left. We'll cover Nick in case we get any unwanted company. Everybody, keep your eyes open. Call out if you see any hostiles coming our way."

The group sprang into action, and Foster watched everyone move where he had directed. It amazed him how well they worked as a group since they had only met a few days ago. He watched as Walker slowly made his way to the disabled vehicle.

Walker tapped on the glass and asked, "Is everyone okay?" A woman inside the vehicle continued to sob uncontrollably.

Foster glanced at the carnage near the rear tire. It appeared to have been a man at one point, and he guessed the Reapers had torn him to shreds.

"I'm sorry about your friend, ma'am," Walker continued, "but we need to know, is everybody in your vehicle okay?"

"My husband," the woman blurted.

"Right," Walker said. "Sorry about your husband."

"We got a flat tire," the woman sobbed, "and Gerald got out to try and fix it when those things attacked. They weren't supposed to do that." She began crying even louder.

Foster looked at the scene playing out in front of him. Walker looked like he was completely unsure what to say to the stranger who had watched her husband get torn to pieces. "Want me to give it a try?" Foster asked.

"Absolutely," Walker said. He motioned for Foster to switch places with him and began heading toward him.

Foster backtracked until he reached the driver's door. He did a silent count of three before he spoke. "Ma'am, my name is Officer Foster. I'm sorry for your loss."

"They weren't supposed to attack us."

Foster paused for a moment before continuing. He wasn't sure why the woman kept repeating that crazy idea, but he still needed to find out if they were okay. "Unfortunately, ma'am, sometimes they seem to have a mind of their own." He looked at the car. The damaged tire was lying on the ground. The Odyssey was still jacked up, with a perfectly intact spare leaning against it. Foster said, "Is anyone hurt in your car?"

"No, we're fine."

"Nobody got bit?"

"I said we're fine."

"Ma'am, it's really important you answer my question," Foster said. "Did anyone in the car get bitten by a Reaper?"

"No, my children and I stayed in the car the entire time."

"Okay, I'm glad to hear that. Do you have someplace you can go?"

"We have friends we're staying with."

"I see," Foster said. "Well, tell you what, if it's okay with you, I'll replace your tire for you, and then you and your kids can go on your way. I'm sorry about your husband. Do you have far to go?"

"No. Maybe twenty minutes."

"Foster," Walker hissed under his breath. "A word."

Foster took three steps toward Walker and met him halfway. He waited to hear what his friend had to say.

"Are you sure it's a good idea for them to be traveling by themselves?" Walker asked in a low voice.

"Would you rather take them on in our group?" Foster countered.

"Lizzy might."

"That's not what I asked you."

Walker sighed. "No, I'd prefer they don't join us," Walker muttered. "We don't need three more mouths to feed right now. Especially ones we don't know a thing about."

"I agree," Foster said in a low voice. "That's why I offered to help them on their way."

"We just need to make sure they're going to make it okay."

"What if we escort them part of the way?"

"That might work," Walker said. "Rock, paper, scissors on who changes the tire?"

"No need," Foster said. "I already offered to do it. It's part of the territory of being a police officer."

"Copy that," Walker said. "Sams, we're on overwatch while Malcolm changes the tire."

"Better him than me," Sams said. "I hate working on cars."

Foster walked back to the minivan and said, "Ma'am, I'm going to change your tire now. Can you keep your family inside the car?"

"Y-Yes, I can."

"Great."

Foster rolled his sleeves up and set about replacing the damaged tire.

Ten minutes later, Foster had replaced the tire and double-checked to make sure all the lug nuts were secure. He lowered the minivan carefully with the jack.

"Ma'am, if you can pop the rear hatch, I'll put your jack and other equipment inside it."

The woman was back to sobbing, so Foster repeated himself a bit louder.

He saw the woman lean over and grab a lever. Foster heard the latch pop open, lifted the rear trunk, and slid the hydraulic jack and its handle in the back, tucking it securely before closing the trunk again.

"All done," Foster said.

"Thank you. We're going to go now."

"You said you have friends nearby," Foster said. "Do you want us to go with you and make sure you get there safely?"

"That won't be necessary. Really. Thank you for changing the tire."

"Are you sure?"

"Of course. It's only a few minutes. I'll just keep the doors locked and won't stop for anything. You've already done too much. Thank you, Officer."

"You're welcome," Foster said. He heard the vehicle's engine start and took a step away to watch as she pulled away. He watched the vehicle go to the next street corner, hang a right, and then it quickly drove out of sight.

"Well, that was strange," Walker said.

"You're not kidding," Foster replied. "Most people would welcome having a few extra guns making sure they got to their destination in this kind of shit storm."

"Yeah. No doubt."

"Well, nothing we can do about it. It's not like we can force them to let us drive them."

Walker said nothing.

"I meant in a following the letter of the law kind of way."

"Right," Walker said. "I agree."

"All right," Foster said. "Mount up, everybody. Let's get the hell out of here."

"Thank you, boys," Lizzy said. "They may not have made it without our help."

"You're welcome," Foster replied. "I just hope that they make it to their friends safely."

"I'd like to think so," Lizzy said. "But I suppose it's best if we get going ourselves before it gets much darker."

CHAPTER SIX

The Reaper crept carefully into the throne room and immediately dropped onto one knee. The creature immediately lowered its head and stared at the floor like it had been instructed to do when in the presence of its master. It had learned from the mistakes of others before them that their master didn't tolerate less than the expected etiquette when you entered his private chambers.

"Yes, what is it?" Beeks snarled. "Can't you see I'm busy?" He stood up from his throne and began to pace in front of it.

The Reaper uncontrollably gulped and began to answer in a series of growls and yips.

Beeks stopped moving and turned toward the reporting soldier.

"You're taking too damn long to get to the point," Beeks growled. He mentally reached out and grasped the soldier's mind.

The minion stiffened in pain and let out a low yelp of pain.

Beeks ignored his soldier's outburst. It didn't matter what the minion thought. There was only one Alpha in their world, and only their opinions ever mattered. And until proven otherwise, Horatio Beeks was the uncontested leader of millions of his own personal minions. He turned his attention back to the minion's exposed mind and began quickly sifting through its memories to get the information he was seeking.

"Are they sure it's Foster?" Beeks said aloud.

"Yes, my Lord," the soldier answered in a series of growls and yips. "It has been confirmed by more than one pack member. It's a place with much grass and shiny surfaces that our packmates can see through."

"It's called glass, you idiot," Beeks snapped.

"S-sorry, my Lord," the soldier stammered. "There is much glass here. I'm afraid the ones who gave the initial report have been unreachable since."

"What?"

"I-I've tried, but they don't seem to be answering me. I can't find them. The rest of the pack isn't sure if Fos-ter is still there. They're searching the area, but so far they haven't seen him yet."

"You're disappointing me," Beeks growled. "Must I do everything myself?"

The soldier unconsciously let out a small yelp of fear.

Beeks reached out mentally. *"Malice, where are you?"*

"Not far from the den. Do you need me to return?"

"No. Change of plans. Others have seen Foster."

"Excellent. Where is he?" Malice asked.

"Close. But we're not sure if he's still there."

"Can you share the thoughts with me? It will help me find him."

"Hold on." Beeks reached into his memory, found the images he had retrieved from the still-kneeling soldier, and sent them to Malice. He saw his soldier look at another minion. That creature was smaller in stature, and Beeks immediately reached out and grasped its mind, too. Accessing two different minds while mentally communicating with Malice was stretching his powers a little more than he would have liked. But it was the best way he could think of to be able to see any telltale signs that Malice wasn't properly behaving.

A minute later, he heard Malice's voice inside his own mind.

"My Lord, I will take some of my soldiers and head to Fos-ter's last-known location. We will kill anyone who is foolish enough to be with him."

"No, you will not. You are to observe only. Do not engage him on your own."

"My Lord—"

"I mean it," Beeks mentally interrupted. *"If you find him, you are to report to me. Then I will send additional soldiers to you so that you'll be guaranteed to succeed."*

"And by that time, he might have gotten away," Malice argued. *"My Lord, I have one hundred of our finest soldiers with me. I'm sure that Fos-ter does not have many in his group. We will crush him and all who are foolish enough to not flee."*

"You mean, like you did the last time?" Beeks challenged. *"Oh, wait, that's not what happened last time. If my memory is right, the last time you ran into him was outside the airport. And what happened? You lost nearly all of your troops. You had to come scurrying back to me with your tail between your legs."*

"My Lord, we did not know Fos-ter had additional soldiers with him. It was—"

"I don't want excuses," Beeks mentally roared. *"I want results. Do you understand me?"*

"I want him to answer for what he's done. I want him to beg for his life before I take it from him."

"You answer to me," Beeks commanded. *"Do you understand?"*

Beeks reached out mentally and began to squeeze his commander's mind. He felt Malice's knees begin to buckle and then a moment later the sensation of ground under them.

"Yes...my Lord," Malice gasped.

"If you were not so valuable to me, I would end you right now. I will not tolerate your back talk and disobedience. Especially in front of the other soldiers."

"My Lord, I-I did not mean to upset you."

Beeks felt the soldier's body continue to be wracked with pain. He felt Malice begin to curl up into a tight circle, clutching his head.

"I expect more from you, Malice. You need to stop disappointing me."

Beeks mentally pictured his hold on the soldier's mind releasing like he was opening his fist. He switched to another soldier's eyes and watched as Malice slowly picked himself off the ground and moved into the proper half-kneeling position. He was content with what he saw and withdrew his hold from both minions' minds. Now that Malice had received a proper attitude adjustment, Beeks fully expected him to do as he had ordered.

A wave of hunger came over Beeks. He motioned for an underling. The minion scurried forward, dropped onto one knee, and stared at the floor.

"I'm hungry," Beeks said.

"What would my Lord like?" the minion asked.

"A cow," Beeks replied. "Take several packmates with you and get me one."

"Yes, my Lord."

"And make sure it's still mooing when you bring it to me."

Malice picked himself up and knelt on one knee as his master expected. He checked the area around him. None of his soldiers were looking his way, and Malice felt relieved. It would have been incredibly embarrassing if he'd lost control of his bladder. He wasn't going to be like so many other soldiers who pissed themselves when their master applied his mental hold on them.

"Wait here," he growled at his pack. A series of yips answered him. Malice stalked toward a nearby brick building and rounded the corner. He waited until he was out of sight of his soldiers before he pulled his arm back and punched the building as hard as he could. There was a loud bang, and the wall collapsed inward. Malice felt an immediate shot of pain. He looked at his hurting limb. He saw that his hand and wrist were visibly broken and hanging off-kilter.

He was not a little weakling. He was Malice. Even before his transformation, he had been a killer and someone that many others feared. Now he was even bigger, stronger, and meaner. He didn't care what his master said. He didn't need Beeks to send more soldiers to do his own dirty work. If the opportunity presented itself, he would take care of Foster himself.

Malice watched as his hand and wrist reset itself and began to heal. He turned, and with the swish of his cape, he stalked back to his soldiers. It was time to find and kill Foster.

CHAPTER SEVEN

President Mary Vickers strolled into the conference room with what she hoped was a confident leader-of-the-nation type of walk. It wasn't hard to blame her for not being quite sure how a president should carry themselves. Until recently, she'd only been the Secretary of Health and Human Services. But once the Reapers arrived, the chain of succession quickly fell apart. In a matter of hours, she was the last person remaining. Especially after President Marshall chose to cede his position rather than risk being used as a political hostage. It had to have taken tremendous personal humility and courage, knowing that he was likely to die as soon as the Reapers learned he was no longer the commander-in-chief. Vickers missed her friend terribly. There were so many things she wished she could ask. She knew if he were here, he'd probably be able to confidently tell her how she should handle the dozens of problems and crises she was currently dealing with. If she let herself even consider the magnitude of what she was trying to handle with practically no staff to speak of, it would quickly reach overwhelming status. But right now, she didn't have time to have a panic attack. The tattered remains of her country were counting on her knowing the best way to handle every problem they were faced with.

At least she felt safe now. It had been the right call to leave Camp

David and move her skeleton crew and herself to the *USS Eisenhower*. The nuclear carrier was stationed far enough off the coast of Virginia where no Reapers could reach them.

Vickers glanced over her right shoulder and saw Special-Agent-In-Charge Malory Nash standing alertly at the doorway. If anyone was still feeling their way around their position, it was the former Deputy Special Agent. Nash had received an unexpected in-the-field promotion when the rest of President Marshall's detail was killed. As it stood, Nash was in charge of her presidential protective detail, which right now consisted of a motley group of random Secret Service agents and security personnel from Camp David, along with a few naval military police requisitioned from the *Eisenhower*. It was just an absolute hodgepodge of personnel from a wide range of backgrounds and training. The very idea made her flinch, but it was the best they could pull together under the circumstances.

Vickers moved to the front of the conference room table and sat down slowly. A telephone had been placed at the end of the table near her, and she stared at it expectantly.

"We're early, ma'am," Agent Nash said.

"How early?" Vickers asked.

"Two minutes," Nash answered. "Don't worry, he'll call."

"Yes. I suppose he is quite punctual like that, isn't he?" Vickers quipped. "I've never known the general to be late for anything."

"Ma'am?"

"It's kind of annoying, isn't it?"

"Well, I really couldn't say," Nash answered. "I only recently met the general."

"Yes, I suppose so. It's just the two of us here in the room for now."

"Madam President, I'd say it comes with the territory."

The phone began to ring, Nash began to reach for it, and Vickers shook her off.

"I think I still remember how to answer my own phone," Vickers replied. "You've got enough on your plate already."

"Yes, ma'am."

Vickers picked up the phone and answered.

"Hello, President Vickers, please," a male voice said smoothly.

"Speaking."

"What a pleasant surprise," General Weindahl answered. "I'm not sure I've ever had the commander-in-chief answer their own phone."

"I think it's safe to say things are quite different from the old status quo."

"Indeed. Is everything still to your liking there, ma'am?"

"As much as one could expect, under the circumstances," Vickers said. "The doctor tells me that the motion sickness should probably begin to pass in a few more days. I guess I'm just not used to being on a boat after all."

Weindahl chuckled. "And you wonder why I haven't rushed right out there myself, Madam President."

"Are you saying that you get seasick?" Vickers asked. "I'm surprised to hear a four-star general and the leader of our entire military force could suffer from such a common ailment."

"I will neither confirm nor deny such a statement."

"Uh-huh. I'll take that to be a yes," Vickers said. "Having said that, I meant what I said before."

"Ma'am?"

"General, you might be the most important person remaining in our armed forces. Our country would be in dire straits if we were to lose you to enemy combatants."

"Ma'am, I doubt there's many places safer than the Pentagon these days. I'm not worried about my safety here, and there's no reason you should be, either."

"We've been extremely lucky the Reapers haven't attacked the Pentagon yet," Vickers pointed out. "We can't expect our luck to continue to hold. Eventually, they will attack your location."

"If they do, we will be ready to defend it," Weindahl replied. "I have round-the-clock drone surveillance watching for any Reaper activity that might be heading here."

"Rasheed, do I need to make it an executive order? Quit dragging your feet, and get your ass someplace offshore."

Weindahl sighed loudly. "No, ma'am. You do not. I will make arrangements to move to another location before the end of today."

"Okay, let's not waste any more time. Shall we get on to our meeting?"

"Of course, Madam President."

"How are we proceeding with Operation Flashpoint?"

"It's still in the planning stages, ma'am," Weindahl said. "Based on our available personnel, we're not going to be able to hit every Reaper location at once."

"Why the hell not?"

"To be honest, ma'am, we're fighting this thing on multiple fronts all at once. We have other cities reporting Reaper attacks."

"What cities?"

"The latest ones are Houston, Salt Lake City, and San Jose. There's reports of Reapers approaching Seattle and Los Angeles as well."

"Jesus, our boys are stretched thin."

"Paper thin, ma'am," Weindahl answered. "Our military effectiveness has dropped dramatically. Quite frankly, we're trying to stop them from spreading any further through the rest of the country if possible."

"You didn't mention Hawaii or Alaska yet," Vickers asked. "Are they still safe spots?"

"For now."

"Care to elaborate?"

"Of course. Hawaii is probably going to stay safe for the foreseeable future. The key will be to block anyone else coming onto the islands."

"You mean to avoid potential infected that haven't turned yet?"

"Yes, that's right. Alaska can try to do the same thing, but if the Reapers manage to work their way through Canada, they could eventually reach Alaska. Of course, we don't know how resistant these things are to cold weather."

"Alaska's idea of cold weather is vastly different than ours."

"Indeed."

"I still don't understand how they could've spread as quickly as they did in some areas."

"I'm not sure I understand your question."

"If the Reapers are traveling on foot, then how did they reach some parts of the country faster than others? I mean, it's not like these things hopped on a train or plane to go cross-country."

Weindahl frowned. "Not intentionally," he said slowly. "But we're finding that the rate of infection varies from person to person. We're not sure why. It may have to do with the size of the individual or the strength of their immune system. The key point is not everybody turns right after they're bitten."

"Wait, what?"

"Let me try phrasing it a bit differently. Some people turn in a matter of minutes. For others, it takes them hours to succumb. It's possible that someone who could have been bitten by a Reaper got on a plane or in the car and traveled to another area before they started to turn."

"This is a nightmare."

"Indeed. We believe that's how this infestation has leapfrogged to some parts of the country rather than following a gradual progressive trail."

"Did Marshall shut down mass transportation?"

"No, ma'am. There were certain parts of the country that were locked down as they reported, but President Marshall failed to give that official announcement in time."

"Any idea why?"

"I'm not sure, ma'am. This infestation happened extremely fast. President Marshall didn't have much information to make his decisions on," Weindahl said. "We still don't know much about these things. But I did take the liberty of shutting down the airports in the reported outbreak areas myself after the president's demise."

"That's a good start. I think we should also shut down all modes of public transportation nationwide. All public airways, too."

"Even the areas where no outbreaks have been reported?"

"Absolutely. We need to get ahead of the Reaper outbreaks. If it hasn't already been done, declare a national emergency. If you feel the American public needs to hear it directly from me, then I'll do it."

"With all due respect, we believe these Reapers have some type of intelligent higher command. Someone who's giving direction as to where they should go and what they should do next," Weindahl said.

"They've already gone after President Marshall. If you were to identify yourself as the new commander-in-chief, then that would make you a target for them."

"It feels like I'm hiding like a coward."

"Consider it a strategic retreat, Madam President. We can still do a public service announcement on any remaining radio stations and television stations."

"Are you sure?"

"Of course. We will get the word out. We can contact the major transportation agencies and give them the order to halt services."

"People aren't going to like it."

"Americans have bigger things to worry about right now, Madam President."

"How are we doing with panicking and looting?"

"Not well. The National Guard has been fully deployed in most areas and is struggling to maintain peace and order. They've had some defections, but those numbers are better than originally expected, under the circumstances."

"Well, that's something which might resemble good news," Vickers said in an exasperated voice. "Do we have any idea how this infection works? How they're controlled?"

"I'm not sure I understand the question."

"Quit stalling, General. Is there anything other than what's in these action reports? Any ideas on how to stop the Reapers?"

"Not at this time, ma'am."

"Do we have anyone who can look into their biology?"

"I'm not sure I understand what you're asking me, ma'am."

"A weakness," Vickers demanded. "I want to find a weakness for these bastards besides a bullet in the head. Do we have anyone looking at a tissue sample or blood sample of these Reapers and figuring out what makes them tick?"

"Well, ma'am, not exactly."

"That's unacceptable. I have a second priority mission for you. Tell your staff to find a secure location that has biomedical staff and equipment. Someplace offshore, where these things can't get to. I want them working on determining how these Reapers are created."

"We already know how they were created," Weindahl said. "It was Project Dionysus."

"One project created tens of millions of them?"

Weindahl said nothing.

"I get that Doctor Bergstrom created the initial Reapers. A patient zero. But what the hell happened after that? How do we stop the infestation from continuing to spread? Do they have a weakness we can target? Or something that we can develop that will make our personnel resistant to their attacks?"

"Like a vaccination?"

"Yes, exactly."

"With all due respect, ma'am, I'm not sure that the smartest scientists in the world could come up with one in time."

"It's worth a try."

"Even if they did, it wouldn't keep the monsters from mortally wounding or killing our soldiers in close combat situations."

"In other words, you could be immune to being turned into a Reaper, but if you get your throat ripped out, you're going to bleed to death instead."

"I'm afraid so."

"But at least it would stop our soldiers from being turned into enemy combatants. We still need to try, General."

"I agree, ma'am."

"We also need to see what kind of armoring we can give our soldiers to better protect them."

"We could try existing materials, like body armor, riot gear, and Kevlar."

"My thoughts exactly. It's best if our soldiers can kill these things with a bullet to the head. But if things get up close and personal, our men need a better shot of winning in hand-to-hand combat. Some kind of body protection might help level the field."

"The results haven't been favorable in hand-to-hand combat situations," Weindahl said carefully. "Reapers are enhanced former humans. They are bigger, stronger, faster. Likely faster reflexes, too. We're starting to get reports that some Reapers have developed some type of armoring on their bodies."

"What?"

"Some type of natural protective shell on a backside of their bodies."

"What exactly was Bergstrom messing with in his laboratory?"

"I wish I knew, ma'am."

"Well, have your own team of eggheads figure that out."

"Yes, ma'am."

"And get me a better game plan."

"We expect Operation Flashpoint will deliver heavy enemy casualties."

"Do we know for a fact that burning these things will kill them?"

"They're living, breathing organic things," Weindahl answered. "I'm confident they'll burn to death."

"Uh-huh. Let's say Operation Flashpoint doesn't kill 100 percent of the enemy. How do we kill the surviving ones faster and safer from there? Especially without taking every inch of our country and burning it to a crisp?"

"I don't have an answer for you on that yet, Madam President."

"I'd like you to find one."

"Yes, ma'am."

"And General?" Vickers said. "I want a list of the cities we're going to hit first before the end of today."

"As you wish, Madam President."

CHAPTER EIGHT

As Foster drove into Rehoboth Beach, he saw the northbound side of the road had several vehicles blocking it. It was a stark difference from the southbound lanes, which were completely clear. Foster shifted his eyes back to the roadway ahead. He was surprised by how normal-looking it seemed.

"No car wrecks or dead bodies," Sams muttered. "Weird, huh?"

"It's almost like nothing has changed much here," Foster said. "Very strange, indeed." Foster led the rest of his group slowly down Route 1, taking note of the different stores and landmarks. A number of the resort town's stores appeared to be open. Foster finally bit the bullet and pulled into one shopping center near a twenty-four-hour Wawa. He headed to the opposite end of the retail strip and parked in front of the end store, which proudly announced they sold beef jerky.

"Why are you stopping here?" Sams asked.

"I have a feeling we're missing something," Foster said. "We need more information. Tell the rest of the group to hang back. If you want to come in with me, that would be great."

"Copy that." Foster heard Sams repeat their plan over the walkie to the rest of their group. Foster stepped out of the Suburban, closing it carefully to keep the noise to a minimum.

"I'm not sure how much of the group are beef jerky fans," Sams said. "Personally, I could take it or leave it."

"I'm shopping for information, not food," Foster said softly. "Just follow my lead, and don't correct me on anything I might say. Got it?"

"Uh, why is it your lead?" Sams asked. "Why isn't it my lead? In case you hadn't noticed, I'm more of a people person than you."

"Simple. Cops are used to lying, especially when questioning suspects. Soldiers are used to telling the truth. We need to gather information, not share it."

"Gotcha," Sams said. "Well, then you go right ahead and take the lead, Mr. Professional Liar."

Foster chuckled softly and moved toward the store's entrance.

The two men walked into the beef jerky store, and as they opened the door, a small bell announced their presence. A thin middle-aged man stood behind the counter and greeted them with a warm smile.

"Oh, newcomers. Welcome," the man said. "My name is Craig McCullers. I'm the owner of this establishment."

"Nice to meet you, Mr. McCullers."

"Oh, please. My daddy was Mister McCullers. Call me Craig."

"Right," Foster said carefully. "Craig, how did you know that we're new?"

"When you have been here as long as I have, you get to know most of the people," Craig said. "Especially in the off season."

"Gotcha," Foster said. "We're just kind of wondering what's going on here?"

"Where are you boys from?"

"Farther north," Foster said. "We're headed toward Virginia and decided to stop here for food and fuel."

"With everything going on out there, I'm afraid we don't have much in the way of fuel. It's been difficult to get fuel trucks and other supply trucks here," Craig said. "I suppose you still can get a good meal, though. As long as you don't mind things like eggs and bacon."

"No bother at all. You're talking about some of my favorite foods," Foster said with a smile. "I noticed the northbound lanes have a bunch of debris on them, but southbound doesn't."

"We've had some volunteers who have worked on keeping at least one part of the road clear," Craig said. "But like I said, with fuel being hard to come by, most folks aren't driving if they don't need to. To be honest, it's quite easy to get around Rehoboth on bike or by foot."

"Good point," Foster said. "But haven't you had any problems with the Reapers?"

"Reapers?"

"The monsters that some people are getting turned into," Foster said slowly. "Maybe you've seen them on the news?"

"Oh, right. Those things. Nope, they've been no trouble at all here."

Foster felt his jaw go slack. "Really?"

"Yes, really," Craig replied. "We've had no problems with those Reapers whatsoever."

"How is that possible?"

"Well, the credit should go to the Disciples of the Divine."

"I'm sorry," Foster said. "I'm afraid since I'm not from this area, I'm not familiar with them. Who are they?"

"A group that God has directly spoken to. They're led by a wonderful man, Ezekiel Morgan, who has the ability to communicate with these things. He's able to direct them and control them."

"That sounds pretty amazing," Foster said. "Any idea how he does it?"

"He doesn't do anything. It's God's divine power at work. Ezekiel is a man of great faith. A good number of people that have seen his abilities have decided to follow him."

"Sorry, I must be a little slow," Sams said. "Why would they follow him?"

"It's simple, really," Craig said. "Ezekiel and his Disciples help to control the monsters and keep them from attacking our citizens. You know, the Disciples of the Divine have a prayer circle later tonight. Perhaps you'd like to attend and learn more?"

"Maybe," Foster said. "To be honest, we're kind of bushed from being on the road all day. We're hoping to find someplace to grab some sleep."

"Of course," Craig said. He looked disappointed but quickly flashed a smile before saying, “I recommend the Cutler Inn. It's kept clean, and it’s part of this area the Disciples of the Divine help keep safe.”

“Sounds perfect,” Foster said. “Where is it?”

“Well, you go down about three blocks, hang a right, and it’s about two blocks farther down. You can't miss the big sign near the street.”

“Great. Thanks for the information,” Foster said. “With all that has happened recently, it’s nice to see folks who treat strangers kindly.”

“It’s the right thing to do.” Craig beamed. “My daddy taught me to always treat others proper. Enjoy your evening, gentlemen.”

“Same to you,” Sams added. He moved to the front door, opened it, and let Foster step outside before closing the door behind him. As soon as the door closed, he said in a low voice, “You're not planning on going to that hotel, are you?”

Foster motioned for Sams to wait until they got back in the vehicle.

The two men climbed back into the Suburban.

Sams waited until both doors closed to blurt out, “Please tell me you're not thinking about staying at this Cutler Inn.”

“No chance in hell,” Foster said. “At least, not without a lot of backup.”

“Man, I’m so glad to hear you say that. That guy was giving me the creeps. I bet that hotel is nothing but a trap. Probably grab naive travelers and brainwash them.”

“Could be,” Foster said. “Besides, we already have a place to stay. I just didn't want to tip off our hand.”

“Well played, Deputy Donuts,” Sams said. “You might have a bright future as a professional liar.”

“Uh-huh. So, when we were in the store, did you notice anything out of the ordinary?”

“Besides the obvious cult love fest old Craig has?”

“Besides that.”

“What about a beef jerky store having absolutely nothing on the shelves?” Sams answered. “Or the fact the owner didn’t even try to sell us anything?”

“Yeah, it seemed a little weird to me, too.”

“Dude, that was beyond strange. I’m just glad you didn’t keep talking with the guy. He was starting to creep me out talking about these Disciple characters."

"Me too." Foster chuckled. "Come on, let's get going before it gets any darker."

CHAPTER NINE

Captain Angel "Vas" Vasquez of the 134th Fighter Squadron and the "Green Mountain Boys" fame banked her F-35 Lightning II and did another pass over the battleground below her.

Based out of Burlington, Vermont, she'd been providing air support to Fort Devens in Massachusetts for nearly twelve hours now. It was far longer than she probably should have been in the air, but that was a moot point. They were in the fight of their lives against the Reapers, and from what she could see from overhead, it wasn't going well. She'd run her GAU-22/A, a four-barrel version of the 25 mm GAU-12 Equalizer cannon, until it was dry. Of course, 182 rounds of ammunition didn't go far in trying to kill the hundreds of Reapers that were attacking Fort Devens. The military base acted as an armed forces training center for approximately 650 Army Reserve, National Guard soldiers, and Marines. If it fell, the U.S. military would lose hundreds of badly-needed soldiers and another active base.

Before the Reaper outbreak, Vasquez's unit was part of the Vermont Air National Guard 158th Fighter Wing stationed at the Burlington Air National Guard Base. Most of the time, there hadn't been much to do besides operational paperwork and training exercises to try and stay sharp. Since then, they'd become an active part of the

United States Air Force by order of the President of the United States. It was a dramatic shift in routine, and as much as she hated to admit it, she was loving every minute of the war that had shown up on their doorsteps. She felt like she was on top of the world when she was inside the cockpit of her F-35. Especially those times where she could drop the hammer down and push her baby toward its top speed of Mach 1.6. Traveling at nearly 1,200 miles per hour, it absolutely challenged her to use every reflex, skill, and instinct she had as a fighter jock.

She was approximately two miles away from the base, and there was still a jaw-dropping amount of monsters heading toward Fort Devens. Vasquez fired her last pair of air-to-surface missiles and watched them smash into the middle of the Reaper pack. A moment later, there was a blinding flash of light, and a shockwave leveled dozens of Reapers that had been caught in its path. A huge cloud of debris, dust, and smoke rose upward, but the F-35, moving more than seven hundred miles per hour, had long passed it.

Vasquez prepared to bank left and come back for another pass when an alert sounded out. A split second later, a second one began going off, too. She glanced at the corner of her helmet screen, turned off both alarms, and swore softly under her breath. She was out of munitions and low on fuel too. She had no choice but bow out of the fight and return to base.

The comms in her helmet came alive. "Green Mountain Boy Seven, come in."

"You got her," Vasquez replied.

"Any chance you can pin the ears back on some more of these varmints for us?"

"No can do. I'm down to spitting at the enemies, and I'm on bingo fuel," Vasquez said. "I'm not sure if spitting will hurt them at all, but I'm willing to give it a shot. But unless you boys want to carry my plane back to base, you're gonna have to keep up the good fight without me for a little while."

"Roger, bingo fuel and Winchester ammo. We're a little too busy to lug your air chariot back to Vermont right now. But we'd really appreciate it if you can hurry back and lend us a hand again."

"I'll do my best. Keep up the good fight, Army."

"Will do. Thanks again, Mountain Boy Seven."

Vasquez took the F-35 up another four thousand feet in altitude, dropped the hammer, and the plane immediately responded. She took it to Mach 1.2 and held the speed constant. There was no point in taxing her plane any more than being in the air for nearly half of a day had already done. At her current speed, she'd reach base in a matter of minutes. Once she landed, they'd rearm and refuel her plane. She'd lobby to be allowed to jump right back into action, but she doubted she'd get permission. Her commander would likely point out that Vasquez was already four hours over her maximum flight time and ground her until she got some long overdue rest. Vasquez said a silent prayer that Devers could hold out until she or one of her squadmates could return to provide some much-needed air support.

CHAPTER TEN

The radio was playing softly in the background, and Amanda sat quietly, deep in her own thoughts. She glanced over at Charles and saw the older man was still focused on the road ahead. She liked him, but sometimes it was difficult to find things they had in common. Amanda mentally scolded herself. There were far worse people she could be stuck with in a moving vehicle than Charles.

She turned her attention back inward. The whole situation with Malcolm was confusing to her. On one hand, it was something new and exciting. Heaven knows, it had been far too long since she had a man who truly captured her attention and held her interest. Amanda blamed it on her work. The long hours and the hectic work of being an emergency room physician were definitely a big reason for her lack of a love life.

But if she was truly being honest with herself, that wasn't the whole truth. Amanda often hid behind her work because she was uncomfortable talking with most men. The fact of the matter was a good number of men she met were more focused on her appearance or the shapeliness of her body than her brains. The brains were definitely an issue for some guys. She could tell pretty quickly the ones who were intimidated by a smart woman. Some of them didn't even try to hide that they didn't like talking to someone as intelligent as her.

Amanda couldn't help the fact that she was extremely bright. She'd graduated from medical school with honors. And let's face it, you don't get into med school and graduate from medical school by being a moron. But all that seemed to change with Foster. Malcolm seemed comfortable in his own skin. He treated her and talked to her like she was an equal. He had a way of making everyone feel like they belonged in their group.

Which was pretty amazing in the first place. Just when the world seemed to come crashing down unexpectedly, a group of people somehow had found a way to come together and work smoothly. Maybe it was the collective need to survive. It was a strange type of friendship between all of them, but there was no mistaking the bonds that had formed. Each person in their group eagerly looked out for each other, even if meant making personal sacrifices along the way.

With Malcolm, she couldn't help but feel conflicted. He'd been distancing himself from her ever since the sewers. She still wasn't sure why she kissed him. Was it the stress and the emotion of being rescued? Or was it something more?

Her head kept telling her that she'd overreacted and grabbed onto the first available guy. But her heart was saying something else. That maybe this could be something more. Of course, the timing was absolutely terrible. They were in the middle of the fight of their lives. These creatures were attacking and killing millions of people. Every time they turned around, even more monsters were popping up.

The idea of starting a new romance while all of them were fighting to stay alive seemed like crazy talk. But for every single reason that her head could provide for why she shouldn't be thinking about love right now, her heart kept giving just as many rebuttals. Amanda wasn't sure what to do. She couldn't remember ever feeling so confused about something in her life. And this confusion was the very reason she had to make a very important decision. For now, she wasn't going to pursue anything with Malcolm. There were more important things to worry about right now than what might make her heart happiest.

"My Lord," Malice thought carefully. He had noticed his master seemed to be quicker to anger lately, and he didn't want to upset him if he could avoid it.

"Yes?" Beeks mentally sneered. "*What is it?"*

"We have reached the rest stop as ordered. There is no sign of Fos-ter anywhere."

"What? Nothing?"

"Master, there are signs they may have been here. There are machines which have been broken open and smell like they once contained food. There are bodies of some of our soldiers here. I see a trail of tire marks leading away from here."

"Which way do they head?"

"It appears to be away from our den and toward several small towns."

Beeks thought over what Malice was telling him. His elite soldier was currently south of Beeks's current position. If he were to head farther south, he'd likely reach several beach resort towns in a matter of hours. Of course, the tire tracks could be a decoy. It was possible Foster was still in the area. Beeks wrung his hands in anxiety. He felt a headache slowly creeping forward from the back of his head.

"I want you to hold the position," Beeks said, "*in case Foster or any of his group circle back there."*

"Are you sure? The tracks lead-"

"That is all for now," Beeks said.

"Y-Yes, my Lord."

Beeks severed the mental connection with Malice and reached out to Achilles.

"Achilles, where are you?" Beeks mentally sent.

"We have passed the rest stop where Malice and his soldiers are," Achilles said. "*He had warned me to stay away while he hunted Fos-ter. I thought it better to avoid a confrontation with my packmate and search the surrounding areas instead."*

Beeks silently seethed. That wasn't what he had told either of his top commanders to do. He would have to bring this up with Malice. It was unacceptable to have him overruling Beeks's direct commands.

"You probably made the right call," Beeks said carefully. "*In the future,*

please tell me if Malice gives you a different command than what I have given you."

"Of course, my liege."

"Are there any signs of Foster? Or this other pack?"

"No, my Lord, but we are nearing a town. There are signs here."

"Show me."

A mental image flashed in front of Beeks of what Achilles could see. The sign said: WELCOME TO REHOBOTH BEACH.

"Good. Search the town for Foster and this other group. Report back to me your findings. If you don't find anything in that town, then check the next town. Keep looking until you find one of them. I know either Foster or this other group has to be in the area."

"Yes, my Lord. As you command."

CHAPTER ELEVEN

Ezekiel Morgan brought his hands together in a final prayer motion. Inside the Disciples of the Divine chapel, his congregation let out a rousing cheer and began applauding eagerly on cue. He nodded and made what he thought would seem like a solemn gesture. Ezekiel slowly backed away from the altar, turned, and headed through the curtains. As the fabric closed behind him, he moved toward a small flight of stairs that were partially hidden from view. He quickly made his way back to his private chambers. He had formed this cult several years ago, and its membership had positively exploded since the Reaper outbreak had begun.

As he approached the remaining door between the hallway and his private sanctuary, he spotted a man standing outside.

"Has anyone gone in there?" he asked his most trusted guardian.

"No, my grace," Joseph answered. "Everyone else is still in the chapel. None of our followers wanted to risk missing your sermon."

"Excellent," Ezekiel said. "I'm afraid the sermon took a bit more out of me than I expected. I'd like to rest in my office. Please see that no one is allowed to disturb me."

"Of course," Joseph said. He bowed deeply and opened the door to the inner sanctum. He stepped to the side and let the pastor enter his private chambers.

Ezekiel made a beeline for his desk and flopped into the chair behind it. He glanced at the door and saw Joseph was still standing there. Ezekiel mentally counted to twenty, waiting to see if Joseph would leave or speak up. As his loyal subject continued to stand silently in the doorway to his study, he finally blurted out, "Yes. What is it?"

"I'm sorry to disturb you while you are in your study." Joseph swallowed deeply before continuing. "We've had an incident."

"What kind of incident?"

"One of our congregation was attacked outside of town."

"What? Who?"

"Gerald and his family."

"What happened?"

"They had a flat tire," Joseph said. "Gerald was attacked and killed by a Reaper."

"That's impossible. They're lying."

"That was my initial thought, too," Joseph said carefully. "But I've questioned his widow and children extensively. I believe they are being truthful."

"This isn't supposed to happen," Ezekiel stammered. "The Lord has promised us protection."

"I know that, sir," Joseph said. "The thing is, Gerald's family may have been killed too if it wasn't for another group of humans intervening."

"What?"

"There were six of them, led by a police officer."

"A cop?"

"Yes, that's right. After they killed the Reapers, the police officer changed their tire and sent them on their way."

"What did she tell them?"

"Nothing."

"Are you sure?"

"Positive. I asked her more than once," Joseph said. "All they did was change a tire. They did offer to travel with her to make sure that she got back here safely."

"What'd she say?"

"She told them *no, thank you*. And they listened, it would appear."

"This is not good," Ezekiel said. "I want increased security in town. Keep an eye out for any newcomers, especially this cop. Can she describe him?"

"Yes, sir. I wrote it down here for you." Joseph handed Ezekiel a piece of paper.

Ezekiel glanced at it and said, "Sounds pretty standard for a police officer."

"Yes, that's right. But these men had assault rifles."

"Interesting. Well, thank you for bringing this to my attention, Joseph. I will get to the bottom of this as soon as possible."

"Are you going to talk with him?" Joseph asked carefully.

"Well, of course," Ezekiel said smoothly. "The Lord has tasked me to talk directly with these things by providing one who is able to communicate with me."

Joseph stared blankly at the floor.

"Don't worry, Joseph. I will fix this. I promise. Do your best to keep our followers calm, ease their minds that we still offer safe passage here against the evils of the world."

"I-I can do that, sir."

"Excellent," Ezekiel said. He clapped his hands together for emphasis. "Now, if you don't mind, Joseph, I have some things I need to take care of. If you could see yourself out."

"Of course, sir."

CHAPTER TWELVE

Beeks sat on his throne, fighting a growing sense of boredom. It was probably his own fault that he had nothing to do besides manage his growing empire. It had only been a few days ago when he was on the front lines, transforming or feeding off humans. But now, with the millions of soldiers at his beck and call, he no longer needed to do any of those things. For somebody who was used to being an action taker, the transition to glorified couch potato was not an easy one to embrace.

There was a commotion by the entrance to his throne room, and he saw his two guards step forward and block someone from entering. Beeks looked to see who it was.

"Let him in," Beeks growled.

His guards immediately parted, letting a filthy-looking Achilles stagger into the room. The soldier was absolutely covered in dirt and blood from head to toe. His clothes were in shambles, but the soldier didn't seem to notice as he immediately dropped down to one knee to report.

"What is it?" Beeks said.

"I have come to report my findings, my Lord," Achilles said in a series of growls and snarls. "I could not find Fos-ter. But I found something else which I believe my Lord would want to know. There are others who are like you."

"What? Tell me more."

"T-They are not far from here," Achilles stammered. "I believe their pack is much smaller than ours."

"How do you know they aren't part of our family?"

"When I tried to approach them, they did not respond to my calls. They chose to attack us. It wasn't easy, but my packmates and I were able to escape and make our way back here."

"Were you followed?"

"I-I don't think so."

"You don't think? Or you know?"

"I'm sure of it, Master," Achilles said. "As soon as I left their territory, they didn't pursue me."

"Where are they?"

"They appear to have settled south of here."

"This is taking too long," Beeks said impatiently. "Hold still." He mentally reached out and accessed his soldier's mind. Beeks began to review what Achilles had seen. His soldier immediately stiffened under his mental probing.

There had been another pack which had prevented Achilles and his soldiers from entering a town. *Interesting.* They had acted like a border patrol and not a pack of territorial, mindless animals. *Very interesting indeed.* Beeks continued looking through his loyal soldier's mind, taking care to review each mental image like it was a delicate photo. When he was finished, Beeks slowly mentally retreated from Achilles' mind. As he did, the minion's body began to relax.

Achilles had spoken the truth. The soldier hadn't seen any sign of Foster. It didn't mean the pesky human was dead or no longer in the area. As Beeks was painfully aware, many of his minions were easily distracted and often needed more than one reminder about what their mission was. Beeks glanced through the images he had found in the soldier's mind once more. Achilles hadn't managed to spot any other Alphas, either. Once again, it didn't mean there wasn't one in the area. Beeks was definitely feeling a bit confused. The behavior of this other pack was very unusual. The most likely reason was that they were following the directive of their Alpha. But why would their Alpha simply tell their soldiers to repel intruders and not kill them?

If there was another red eye in the area, it might be someone Beeks already knew. A name rose from the depths of his memory. Dwayne Haas. The man was nearly as large as Beeks himself. He had acted as a bodyguard for a smaller inmate. Some nerd that Haas had decided to protect from the rest of the inmates. Giles. That was the geek's name. They had both been in the same prison with him. He had seen both of them strapped to a table at Bergstrom Biogenics. They could have escaped, too.

Would the two of them have decided to partner up together? It was possible, but Beeks found it hard to believe. Especially with the powers that you gained as a red-eyed Alpha. Why would you ever want to share your place at the top of your own pack with anyone else?

Beeks felt a wave of anxiety come over him, and his throat began to tighten. What if the two of them were planning to make a move against him? What if they were hiding out someplace, scheming on how they could overthrow Beeks and take over his family?

From what Achilles reported, there was no way they could match up pack against pack. Beeks had millions, and if Achilles' report was accurate, they did not.

But what if his loyal soldier was wrong? What if Achilles had only seen a tiny fraction of Haas's and Giles's combined forces?

Beeks couldn't rule it out. He immediately clenched his fists in a vain attempt to keep his anxiety in check.

Two other Alphas. They would likely overpower any of his ordinary soldiers. Maybe he could neutralize them by putting dozens or hundreds of his minions against them, but he wasn't sure it would work. Especially if these other Alphas had thousands or even hundreds of thousands of soldiers at their command. He couldn't risk losing everything he had built. Not now, when he was so close to gaining complete, unquestioned control over the entire United States.

Beeks dug his claws into his hands, trying to stave off a looming panic attack. He had one other red-eyed soldier at his command. Not a true-born Alpha like him, but Malice was still a powerful soldier. Of course, Malice was a hothead and completely consumed with avenging his fallen brother. Could Beeks trust him to step in front of this new threat to protect his master?

Beeks wasn't sure.

It was quite possible Malice would be too distracted chasing after that bothersome human, Foster, to protect his master. He wasn't completely convinced if Malice crossed paths with Foster again that he'd win, either. After their last encounter, Malice had been forced to tuck tail and retreat. The next encounter could end with Malice crippled or dead.

The more Beeks thought about it, the more convinced he became that he was extremely vulnerable. He needed more loyal soldiers that could act as his field generals and carry out his orders without question. He could really use some bad-ass personal bodyguards, too. Someone who would literally step in front of a bullet in order to protect him. He had to assume that Haas and Giles were going to attack at some point. If the roles were reversed, that's what Beeks would be planning to do.

Beeks turned and studied the soldier kneeling in front of him. Achilles hadn't been a member of his family very long, but he had already demonstrated more than once that he had courage and loyalty. Maybe he hadn't considered Achilles in the right light.

Beeks moved closer to the still-kneeling soldier.

"Bend your neck to the side and hold still," he mentally commanded.

Achilles tilted his head to the side as ordered.

Beeks grabbed Achilles by the shoulders, leaned in, and bit him on the neck.

The soldier yelped in pain.

"Hold still, my son," Beeks commanded. *"You have earned this."* Beeks focused his attention on what he was doing. He began to add some of his life force to his loyal minion's.

A moment later, Beeks opened his jaw, stepped back, and stared at Achilles.

The soldier lifted his head up, opened his eyes, and stared with his new red eyes for the first time.

Beeks smiled.

"Rise, my son. You have earned a new place in my pack."

Achilles rose and looked expectantly at his master.

"You will join your brother Malice in helping me to protect our family."

"I will not fail you, my Lord," Achilles said.

"I know that," Beeks mentally said. *"Get a feel for your new abilities. I will call for you soon. You're dismissed."*

"Yes, Master."

Beeks watched Achilles leave the room. He sat slowly onto his throne. The transformation had forced him to use some of his own personal life essence, and he was feeling a little weak right now.

But now he had another red-eyed soldier besides Malice. Two made Alphas. With the looming potential threat developing to the south, he needed the newly-enhanced Achilles now more than ever.

CHAPTER THIRTEEN

It had taken them far longer than Foster ever imagined to reach Gregory Powell's house. It was nearly dinnertime as Foster watched Charles slowly approach the front door. The former priest seemed unusually nervous about visiting his son, and Foster couldn't help but wonder if there was some unexplained reason why.

Charles leaned forward and knocked twice on the front door.

"Remind me again why he didn't call his son and say we were in the neighborhood?" Sams asked.

"He did," Foster replied. "Call went straight to voice mail." He watched Charles pause for a silent count of three and then knock twice more.

A curtain slid sideways, and a face quickly peeked out. The curtain dropped back in place, and the sound of a lock disengaging sounded. The front door began to slowly open. A young, slender dark-haired woman peeked around the door, glanced at Charles, and then the rest of the group.

"Lauren, what a nice surprise. Can you let us in, please?" Charles asked. "It's not safe for us to be out here for long."

"Where's Mom?" Lauren said. There was a noticeable hard edge to her voice.

"Your mother didn't make it. She asked me to make sure that we—"

"Then you're not welcome here," Lauren said before she slammed the door shut.

Charles stood there in shock.

"Daughter-in-law?" Foster asked.

"Daughter," Charles said. "I wasn't expecting her at my son's house. Lauren and her husband live in Virginia Beach."

"Knock again," Foster said. "Maybe we can reason with her."

"I doubt it. Once Lauren sets her mind on something, nothing short of an act of God will change it. I guess we should go, then."

"Bullshit," Foster said. "We don't have time for this nonsense." He stepped up to the door and knocked twice firmly.

The door flung open, and he saw Charles's daughter standing there.

"I thought I told you—"

"I'm a cop. I've got five other people's safety, including your father, that I need to worry about. I don't care what bad blood there might be. I need you to curb that shit and let us in right now."

"You can't talk to me that way."

"Watch me," Foster said. He lowered his shoulder and pushed past the petite woman into the house.

"Wait, what are you doing?" Lauren said. "Randy, help me."

A tall string bean of a man rushed into the room, holding a shotgun in his hands.

"Don't shoot, I'm a cop," Foster said as he dropped his hand onto his holstered Glock. "I'm here with Charles Powell and several other survivors."

"What?"

"Hi, Randy," Charles said. "It's okay. Please lower the weapon."

"Lauren, are you okay?" Randy yelled. "What happened?"

"They just barged in here. They don't belong here," Lauren said. She pointed toward her father. "Especially him."

"Let me guess," Foster said. "You're the son-in-law. Where's Gregory?"

"Who the hell is this guy?" Randy demanded. "Is somebody gonna answer me?"

"My name is Malcolm Foster. I'm a cop from Philly. I brought your father-in-law along with a bunch of other people here. We just need a place to stay for the night. We don't mean any trouble."

"Don't want any trouble?" Lauren shouted. "He damn near knocked me to the floor. Baby, do something."

"Lauren, can you please stop yelling?" Charles asked in a soothing voice.

"I can yell if I want to," Lauren shouted back.

"Randy, point that thing someplace else," Foster warned. "Or we're gonna have a problem."

"Evening, Charles," an older male voice said. There was a casual Southern drawl to it, and Foster's eyes followed the voice to an elderly man walking into the room, leaning heavily on a quad cane. "Seems like it's a bit nasty out there tonight."

"Hello, Randall," Charles said. "Yes, it is. Especially with those monsters wandering around. I brought some friends."

"I see that," Randall said. He glanced at Randy and said, "Boy, put that damn thing away. Your momma would roll in her grave if she saw you being so rude to your kin."

"He's not my kin," Randy grumbled.

"He's your wife's father," Randall lectured. "That makes him kin. Seeing that we're enjoying the hospitality of his son's home, the least you can do is act like you were raised with some manners."

"Yes, Pa," Randy mumbled. He lowered the shotgun and then added, "Sorry, mister."

"Randy, don't just stand there." Lauren pouted. "He swore at me."

"Now, honey, there's no need to get so upset," Randy said. "Especially since they made sure your dad got here safely."

"Fine," Lauren said. She started to the staircase, stopped, and then spun toward her husband. "You know what? Maybe you should sleep on the couch tonight." She pivoted back toward the stairs and stomped upstairs.

"Lauren, wait—" Randy called after her. He paused for a moment and then looked around him to gauge everyone else's reactions. "You'll have to forgive my wife," he said softly. "She's got a bit of a temper sometimes."

"She's been known to hold a bit of a grudge, too." Charles chuckled.

"Yeah, you could say that," Randy admitted. "I'm sure she'll be over it by morning."

"I took the liberty of locking the front door," Sams said. "Everything all right in here?"

"Yes. Randy, meet Derrick Sams," Charles said smoothly. "Randy is my son-in-law."

"Hey, nice to meet you," Sams said as he offered his hand, which Randy accepted. "Got any food, man? I hate to ask, but it's been a long trip to get here."

Foster saw someone new quietly enter the room. The sweatshirt-wearing man looked like a younger version of Charles and Foster immediately guessed it was his son.

"Seeing as this isn't my house, it's probably best to ask my brother-in-law," Randy said. He turned towards the newest arrival and said,"Gregory, meet Derrick."

"Call me Sams," he said. "Great to meet you."

"Likewise," Gregory said. He nervously pushed his sleeves up towards his elbows, turned his attention to Charles, and added, "Hey, Dad."

Charles stepped forward and embraced his son in a full body hug.

"Umm, I hate to break up this bonding moment," Sams said, "but I'm ready to eat the staircase railing."

Gregory broke the hug and took a step back. "I'm afraid we ate dinner about an hour ago. There's nothing left to share. We do have some apples in the kitchen."

"Wait, did you say apples?" Sams asked. "Awesome. Lead the way, Sir Gregory."

Foster watched Gregory and Sams leave the room. He heard Charles making some introductions, but he was having trouble focusing on the names being dropped. There was far more going on between the former priest and his daughter than anyone else was willing to talk about. He could only hope the bad blood didn't run so deep that it could jeopardize the group's safety.

CHAPTER FOURTEEN

Foster waited a few minutes before following Gregory and Sams into the kitchen. As he entered the room, he saw some movement behind him and noticed Randy had joined them. Sams was happily eating an apple at a small kitchen table as Gregory looked up expectedly.

"Thanks for getting my dad here," Gregory said.

"You're welcome," Foster answered. "If you don't mind, I have a few questions."

"No trouble at all."

Foster took a slow calming breath and let it out before beginning to speak. "I noticed the center of town seems to be almost normal," he said. "But your area is more like every place else we've traveled in the last couple of days. Can you think of any reason why that is?"

"Yes, there's a very good reason. Let me explain," Gregory said. "When news about the Reaper outbreaks started coming in, many of the locals chose to hunker down. This is where we live year-round."

"What about leaving town?" Foster asked. "Maybe heading toward your folks' place?"

Gregory grimaced. "The outbreaks started around Philadelphia. Reading is about sixty miles away from Philly. I figured it was only a matter of time until the Reapers reached there, too."

"So you decided to hunker down here," Foster said. "I saw some abandoned Army vehicles on our way into town."

"Of course. The Army tried to repel them and failed. They were hopelessly outnumbered," Gregory said. "Law enforcement didn't last long against the Reapers, either. I was sure the town was doomed to fall. But then something strange happened. The Reapers started acting differently."

"How so?" Foster asked.

"They started leaving humans alone. Well, at least certain people they did. The rest of us, they would attack on sight."

"Really? Any idea why?"

"Actually, I know why. A new group emerged. They call themselves Disciples of the Divine."

"Yeah, we ran across some of them earlier in town."

Gregory nodded. "They're headed by this guy, Ezekiel Morgan," he said. "He claims that he can control the Reapers."

Sams looked up from his nearly-finished apple. "Do you know if he really can?" he asked.

"Honestly, nobody's sure," Gregory admitted. "There are people I've known for years that swear this guy has complete control over these things. It seems that way because he has managed to take command of them. He's ordered the Reapers to protect his followers and certain parts of town. The people who are part of his group are kept safe. Everyone else is not."

Randy shifted nervously from one foot to the other. "It doesn't sound like much of a choice for the people who live here," he said. "When did you join his group?"

"I didn't. At least, not yet, I haven't."

"Well, why not?" Randy asked. "Seems like an easy way to keep your family and you safe."

"Believe me, I thought about that," Gregory said. "I've spent a lot of nights tossing and turning about what to do. But I just can't do it."

"Sorry, I don't understand," Foster said. "Like Randy said, it sounds like an easy way to protect your family from the Reapers."

"They're a cult," Gregory blurted out. "And before you ask, it's because of the things they say and do. Every single one of them swears that Ezekiel is God's direct messenger. They actively look for people to join their group."

"I noticed a store owner wearing an armband," Foster said. "He kept raving about the Disciples."

"Sounds about right," Gregory said. "I'm surprised they didn't try to get you to stay at one of their places or to attend one of their get-togethers."

"Oh, they did. But I stalled them for now," Foster said. "Just curious. Do all of their members wear an armband?"

"Yes," Gregory said. "I wear one too when I go out scavenging or shopping."

"Maybe I'm a bit slow, but if you ain't a member," Randy said slowly, "then how did you get yours?"

"Pure dumb luck," Gregory said. "I came across one of their members who no longer needed it. I had gone into this little thrift store on the main drag. The owner, Mr. Jones, was one of the Disciples. When I walked into the store, I found him dead on the floor. Looked like he'd had a heart attack and I was the first person to find him. There wasn't anybody else in the store, and there wasn't anything I could do to help him. So, I took his armband and got out of there as quick as I could. I didn't want anybody questioning me on how the poor man had died."

"Smart move," Foster said. "Odds are, they would've assumed the worst and probably locked you up at the police station."

"Probably," Gregory admitted. "I try to avoid going into the Disciple-controlled areas. Mostly out of fear that they may spot me and realize I'm not really one of their group. But especially if I see any of their Guardians."

"Guardians?" Sams said. He carefully set down the remaining apple core and picked up another apple. "What are they?"

"The Disciples' version of enforcers," Gregory said. "They do any of the nasty work that the cult needs to be done."

"Any way to tell who they are?" Foster asked.

"Sure. They're armed," Gregory answered. "Mostly bats and metal pipes. The more trusted enforcers will have guns."

Sams took a bite of the apple and swallowed it quickly. "I'm surprised nobody has shot these enforcers as soon as they show up," he said. "I'll take our guns over their bats any day of the week."

"Sounds good in theory," Gregory said. He rubbed the back of his neck. "Except the few people I know who had guns to defend themselves wound up having Reapers attack their house instead."

"It does sound like the Disciples and Reapers are somehow working together," Foster said. "I'd love to know how the hell they manage to control the Reapers."

"Screw that," Sams said. "I'd rather have a bunch of those armbands instead. We could sneak right through their territory and get out of town before they realize what happened."

"The armbands are tough to come by," Gregory admitted. "I got lucky getting one myself. I'm not going to lie. There's been a few times where that armband has allowed me to travel safely during the day. But short of killing a bunch of Disciples, we won't be able to get enough bands for everyone."

"Gregory, can you use the bands at night?" Foster asked. "It would be a lot harder to be spotted moving about."

"No way." Gregory shook his head vigorously. "We don't go out."

"Ever?"

"Never. If you're not a Disciple, it's not safe. We hide in the basement here and stay quiet."

"Isn't it a bit crowded for six people to sleep in your basement?"

"I guess," Gregory said. "Beats sleeping where anyone outside can see you."

"So why not cover the windows?"

"Tried to, but it took all of the lumber I could scavenge just to cover the ground floor windows. I haven't had a chance to collect any more nearby."

"Seems like it should be a priority to me," Sams said. "Any uncovered windows could be a place Reapers could enter."

"More than food?" Gregory said. "Or medicine? It's just been my son Henry and I since this mess started. I've been the only one able to go out and scavenge."

"What?" Foster demanded. "Nobody else has been helping?"

"We just got here the day before yesterday," Randy blurted out.

"Plus I wasn't feeling well, and Lauren needed to keep an eye on the children."

"Randall would probably be willing, if I asked him," Gregory offered.

"But he needs a quad cane to get around," Foster said. "Which doesn't make it easy to run if you get into trouble."

"Absolutely," Gregory said. "So that's why every night we hide in the basement, hoping we don't draw any attention from the nighttime patrols."

"Wait, didn't Lauren storm upstairs a few minutes ago?" Sams asked.

"Just to the top of the stairs," Gregory said. "The only windows upstairs are in the bedrooms and bathroom. We keep those doors closed all the time. Lauren likes to sit at the top of the stairs, sometimes in the dark, because it's quiet."

"The powder room in the basement means nobody has to go upstairs for a night-time bio break, either. You've been lucky none of you have been spotted here yet," Foster said. "Tell me more about these patrols."

"Well, if it's not the Reapers, then it's the Disciple Guardians themselves," Gregory said. "Because if they find you, they're going to force you to make a decision."

"What kind of decision?" Foster asked.

"Simple." Gregory frowned. "Join the Disciples of the Divine, or join the Reapers."

CHAPTER FIFTEEN

Foster made his way up the basement stairs. His nose picked up the scent of freshly-cooking bacon, and he felt his mouth begin to drool. He made a beeline for the kitchen and saw that Gregory was standing over the stove.

"Good morning," Gregory said. "How'd you sleep?"

"Morning," Foster said. He thought about the uncomfortable sleep sitting on one side of the basement sofa. With twelve people sleeping in the basement, he'd felt like a sardine stuck in a small tin can. They definitely needed to cover the second-floor windows and make the bedrooms a sleeping option in the near future. "Slept okay. You got any coffee?"

"Over there," Gregory said as he pointed to the coffeemaker sitting at the opposite end of the counter.

"Thanks."

"Might as well enjoy it for now. I figure I'm going to run out in another day or two, unless I find some scavenging."

"Good to know. I'll tell everyone to be on the lookout for more," Foster said. He glanced over at the table and saw a young boy sitting there with an iPad in front of him, playing a video game. "And who might you be?" Foster asked.

The young boy said nothing.

"Sorry, he's a little shy. This is my son Henry," Gregory said. "Henry, please say hello to Mr. Foster. He's a friend of Grandpa."

"Hi," Henry said. The young boy appeared to be completely absorbed with playing a video game on the electronic device. There was a half-eaten bowl of cereal in front of him.

The kitchen door swung open, and Foster saw a young teenager come walking in the door who was the spitting image of Lauren. The girl had a cell phone in her hand and was typing madly away. She glanced up and said, "Uncle Gregory, your Internet here sucks."

Henry stood up from the table, turned, and left the kitchen without taking his eyes off his iPad the entire time. The young girl flopped down in the newly-vacated seat.

"Stinks," Gregory corrected. "Emily, you know how your Mama feels about you cursing."

"Yeah." The teen looked up from her phone, spotted Foster, and then blurted, "What's your deal?"

"You were sleeping when I got here last night. My name is Malcolm Foster," Foster said. "I'm friends with Charles."

"I'm Emily," the teenager said. "But if I were you, I wouldn't mention Grandpa around my mom too much."

"Really?" Foster asked with a practiced surprised tone. He wanted to see what additional information the teenager might unknowingly volunteer.

"Uh-huh. Let's just say she's not a big fan."

"Gotcha," Foster said. He began to pour himself a cup of coffee. "You want a cup?"

"No way. I don't know why adults drink that crap."

Gregory chuckled. "I used to say the same thing when I was your age."

"Really? What changed?" Emily asked.

"Became a dad. I started drinking coffee when Henry was just a baby, and haven't stopped since."

"I started drinking it once I became a cop," Foster said. "Got any cream and sugar?"

Gregory pointed to some creamer packets and sugar that were on the counter, and Foster proceeded to fix his coffee.

"Oh shit, you're a cop?" Emily blurted out.

"Language," Gregory warned.

"Don't worry. I'm only a police officer in Philadelphia," Foster said with as warm of a smile as he could manage after only one sip of his first cup of coffee of the day.

"Cool. Hey, can I see your gun?"

"What would your mother say?" Foster asked.

"She would throw a complete shit fit."

"Emily Elizabeth," Gregory warned. "Language."

"Sorry," the teenager mumbled.

"Then the answer is a definite no," Foster said. "No point in making your mom mad if we don't have to."

"Ah, hell," Emily muttered. She glanced at her uncle and said, "What? That's not a curse word."

He turned his attention to Gregory and asked, "Where have you been looking for supplies?"

"I've been trying to stick to the areas that aren't under Disciple control. A good amount of those houses have been abandoned."

"Really? I didn't think that would be the case. Has there been much in the way of casualties?"

"A few," Gregory said. "There's been a lot of people who have joined the Disciples of the Divine. There's also been a handful who refused and were handed over to the Reapers. Next thing you know, there's even more Reapers."

"Do you know if they were definitely turned into Reapers?"

"Let's just say I've got a pretty good feeling. One of our neighbors was this widower, Larry Johnson. Nice enough elderly man, except if you upset him and then he'd be grumpier than all get out. Well, one day, Larry was confronted by the Disciples. I was close enough to hear the whole thing, but lucky for me nobody saw me."

"What happened?"

"They asked him to join the Disciples. Old Larry didn't just refuse. He started screaming at them to get the hell off his property. I still remember Larry wearing his favorite purple hat. You know, the football one with the bird on it?"

"Baltimore Ravens?" Foster asked.

"Yeah, that's it. Later that night, I heard some noises coming from the direction of his house. It was just Henry and me, and I needed to worry about keeping him safe, so I just took him down into the basement a little earlier than usual. The next day, I went to check on Larry. His front door was open, and there was nobody in his house. Just a long blood trail from the kitchen all the way to the front door. Later that day, I saw one of these Reapers walking around wearing the same clothes as old Larry. Same exact hat, too. Except there was this dried-up blood trail from the side of his neck all the way down his shirt. Last time I saw Larry, he was in perfectly clean and normal clothes. Now, I could be wrong. Maybe somebody else borrowed his hat and clothes right before they got turned into a Reaper. But I tend to doubt it."

"I tend to agree with you. It sounds like your neighbor was probably turned against his will," Foster admitted. "I gotta be honest. I think you've been pretty lucky here so far. We've probably should start thinking about ways to make this place more secure."

"To be honest, with all the people that are here now, we're pretty much busting at the seams," Gregory said. "This is just a small house. And since this all went down, Lauren showed up with her husband, her father-in-law, and Emily. Then you brought your group. That's twelve people to feed and bunk up in this place. We were already pretty crowded with just the three of us. I-I mean, the two of us."

"You said three."

"I was married."

"Was?" Foster questioned. "Is your wife gone?"

Emily stood up and began heading toward the living room.

"Are you leaving us already?" Foster sarcastically.

"Yeah, this is boring."

"Okay, catch you later," Foster said. He waited until the teenager was out of the room and then said, "You were telling me about your wife?"

"She met a guy on her job."

"Left?"

"Yeah, about two weeks before all this shit went down."

"Have you heard anything from her?"

"Nope. I'm not expecting to, either."

"Why's that?"

"She took our car and moved to DC with her new beau. Last time I heard, that place got overrun pretty quickly."

"You're probably right," Foster said softly.

The kitchen door swung open, and Randy walked in. "Huh? You're still here?" he blurted out.

"Where else would you expect me to be?" Foster asked.

"No, I didn't mean no harm by it," Randy stammered. "I just figured you'd be out doing some kind of top-secret mission or something."

"Well, I still might," Foster said. "How did you and your family get here?"

"By their boat," Gregory interrupted. "Sorry, I guess Randy should tell you himself."

"Okay," Foster said slowly as he drew out the word. "Randy, why don't you tell me about it."

"What do you mean?" Randy said.

"Your boat. How big is it?"

"Big enough."

"Okay, let me ask a different way. How many people do you think you can fit on it?"

"Well, you guys gotta see her, 'cause she's a real beauty."

"I don't doubt it," Foster said. He looked expectedly at Randy. "Could all of us fit on your boat?"

"How many people we got here?" Randy asked. "Ten?"

"Twelve," Gregory corrected.

"Hmmmph. My boat is rated to hold ten people," Randy said. "It might feel like we're stacking lumber, but I think we can fit everybody on board. I'm just worried about it being too much weight in the boat."

"Keep in mind, we do have two kids and three women in our group," Foster said. "All of whom are smaller and weigh less than the rest of us."

"Yep, that helps. Sleeping arrangements might be a little tricky," Randy said. "Everybody couldn't sleep at the same time."

"So we rotate bunks."

"I guess. We still have to worry about how much additional stuff we bring on the boat. I don't want to find out what might happen if we have too much weight. But that's not even the biggest worry."

"What's that?"

"Fuel. We're definitely going to need it before we leave here."

"Can we fuel up at the marina?"

"I'm not sure. It was dark when we arrived. I saw some of those things near the marina pump. To be honest, I was more worried about keeping my family safe. I knew we couldn't ask Gregory to come pick us up."

Gregory flinched uncontrollably.

"Sorry man," Randy stammered. "I didn't mean to pull at an old wound. It's just Lauren told me about your wife and-"

"It's okay," Gregory said softly. "You're right. I didn't have a way to come and get all of you."

"Right," Randy said quickly. "Anyways, we found an abandoned car and just hauled tail out of there."

"You got lucky to find an available vehicle so close to the marina."

"It barely qualifies as a vehicle," Randy quipped. "Thing had four bald tires, and one of them went flat on the way here. Had to limp the car here the last mile and a half. If God hadn't been looking out for us, we would've had a parade of Reapers following us to Gregory's doorstep."

"Well, the good news is my group has three working vehicles that we came here in. Plenty of space for getting everybody in there and getting to the boat. But if you don't mind, I'd like to go with you and take a look at it."

"Why?" Randy asked suspiciously. "We're perfectly safe here."

"For now," Foster said. "We need to consider the fact that your boat might be the best option for all of us to get someplace that is completely Reaper-free."

"I doubt any place like that exists."

"Sorry, I disagree," Foster insisted. "I've heard from multiple sources that they won't cross large bodies of water. We get somewhere like an island or at sea, and we no longer have to worry about Reaper attacks."

"Sounds interesting," Randy said, "but you still didn't tell me why you wanna go to the marina with me."

"Mostly to check the area and see how many Reapers might be stopping us from fueling up at the marina itself. If it's only a couple, then we might be able to eliminate them and fuel up at the marina."

"It would be a lot easier," Gregory pointed out. "Lugging fuel to the boat sounds like a serious headache."

"Yeah, it would be," Randy said softly.

"What kind of fuel does your boat need?" Foster asked.

"Gasoline. We can throw it in the tank and run it. Bad news is it takes a lot of it to run her."

"How much fuel are we talking about?" Foster asked.

"My boat has an eighty-four-gallon tank."

Gregory let out an appreciative whistle. "That's a lot of fuel. I sure hope we don't have to haul it."

"I agree. Fueling at the marina is definitely the way to go," Foster said. "Gregory, I need you to think of an alternate place nearby to get fuel. A Plan B, if we can't get it at the marina?"

"Sure. There's a number of gas stations in Rehoboth," Gregory said. "Anything in particular you have in mind?"

"Yes. Some place that would be low-traffic," Foster said. "A place only locals would likely use. That way, we'd be less likely to run into any large groups of people or Reapers there."

"Yeah, I know of a station that would work. If you need it, let me know, and I'll give you directions."

"Great," Foster said. "Randy, what kind of storage room do you have on your boat? How are you situated on food, water, medical supplies? Do you have any ammunition?"

"We have practically none of that stuff. I only have a few shells for my shotgun too," Randy said glumly. "With those monsters running around, I sure wish we did."

CHAPTER SIXTEEN

Ezekiel delivered another rousing sermon in front of what seemed like a packed chapel. The energy in the room seemed nearly contagious, and he drew strength from his flock's adulation. He brought his sermon to a close, and his followers rose as one, clapping and cheering their leader's gospel.

Ezekiel made what he thought was an appropriate gesture before exiting the stage. He couldn't wait to get back to his private chambers. One of his guardians had recently found several unopened bottles of a high-end bourbon. He didn't know where they had found it. He really didn't care, either. For all intents and purposes, everything the Disciples owned was his. And right now, he couldn't wait to enjoy a glass of the latest addition in his growing liquor collection. He quickened his pace, and his loyal assistant, Joseph, did the same.

As they reached the door of his private sanctuary, he heard Joseph say in a low voice, "I made sure your chambers were kept empty."

"Thank you, Joseph," Ezekiel said. He stepped into his office, turned, and slowly closed the door. He waited until he heard Joseph's footsteps fade away before he took a step toward his liquor cabinet. As he did, there was a loud noise behind him. Ezekiel immediately spun around and did an immediate double take. "You scared me," he scolded.

Giles let out a low rumble that sounded like a laugh.

"What do you want?" Ezekiel demanded.

"We need to talk."

"I'm not sure it's a good idea for the two of us to be seen together."

"We're the only ones in this room," Giles replied. "Who's going to see us?"

"That's not the point," Ezekiel said. "You know when you first showed up, I almost didn't recognize you. Pretty amazing for two guys who grew up on the wrong side of town together."

"And did time together, too," Giles rumbled.

"That's true, but you stuck with your life of crime," Ezekiel continued. "Me, I found the Lord to help me create all of this." He heard Giles let out a low rumble again. It was definitely a laugh, and Ezekiel felt a bit offended by his friend's behavior.

"You found a con," Giles countered. "A small group of sheep who were willing to get sucked into it. But then my kind showed up. And I've helped you add a lot more sheep since then."

"I suppose that's one way to look at it. I do have a loyal flock that follows my every word," Ezekiel said. "People who believe in my gospel. Heck, I've been able to convince them that you are protectors sent by God."

"Like I said, you found a good con to pull and enough people who are dumb enough to fall for it."

Ezekiel decided to change the subject. "We have a problem," he said. "Some of my flock were attacked by your minions."

"Not true." Giles snarled. "None of my soldiers would dare to defy me."

"It is true. One of my congregation was killed. The rest of his family had to be rescued by some other humans. Care to tell me what happened?"

Giles growled loudly. "It wasn't my pack."

"Are you telling me it was someone else? Someone that looks like you?"

"Yes."

"Do you know who it is?"

"No."

"Any chance you could find out who it was? Because sooner or later, one of my congregation is going to ask what happened to their missing friend. I need you to guarantee this won't happen again."

"I don't work for you."

"Really? Because the way I see it, what we have here is a partnership," Ezekiel said. "One that continues to work in both of our favors. We help your soldiers with things that they're not able to do with their claw hands. You keep my congregation safe from outsiders. It seems pretty clear cut to me."

"There are others like me," Giles said. "You need to increase your recruiting."

"What?"

"You heard me," Giles growled. "Get more people. I'll take everyone who doesn't want to join your group and turn them into new warriors for me."

"Just get more people," Ezekiel parroted. "You make it sound easy."

"I don't care," Giles continued. "With more pack members, we can cover more area and keep your flock safer."

"I don't like this."

"You don't have to," Giles growled. "Just make it happen. Do you understand me?" He got nose to nose with the preacher and stared him in the eye.

Ezekiel gulped and looked away.

"Good. I'm glad we understand each other," Giles said. He took two steps back and disappeared into the darkened corner of the room.

A moment later, Ezekiel heard a door open and then close. He let out the breath he'd been holding. He made a beeline for the liquor set sitting on the table behind his desk. He shakily poured two fingers in a glass and immediately slammed the drink. Giles appearing had been an absolute boost to his efforts. His congregation numbers had massively swelled in recent days. But he couldn't help but feel like the situation was quickly spiraling out of his control. How much longer would it be until he had no choice but to kneel in submission before his former friend-turned-monster? He shuddered at the thought and quickly poured himself another strong drink. He had to find a way to somehow regain control of the situation.

CHAPTER SEVENTEEN

For all of the perks which supposedly came with being one of the most important people in the world, the job was an absolute emotional meat grinder. President Vickers' sleep lately had been sporadic at best. When she did fall into a deep sleep, her dreams were often filled with people she once knew being attacked and turned into Reapers. She hadn't asked for a colossal shit sandwich to be dropped in her lap. But complaining wasn't going to do a thing to fix the situation. Like any leader worth their name, she was going to have to take charge, find the solution to the Reaper infestation, and lead her country to victory. So she didn't have to like it, but the future of the country she loved was counting on her to stop the Reapers for good.

She had no idea what time it was, but Special-Agent-in-Charge Nash was currently escorting her through one of the below water corridors of the *U.S.S. Eisenhower*. As they approached an intersection, she heard two men talking loudly. She reached out and grabbed Nash's elbow, signaling her to stop.

"You think she knows what she's doing?" a male voice said a bit too loudly. "You know, our new president?"

Vickers saw Nash flinch in response. Once more, she motioned for the Special-Agent-In-Charge to continue standing down. Vickers wanted to hear what else the sailors were saying about her when they thought no one else was listening.

"How could she?" another male voice answered. "She only became president because everybody else got killed. What was she doing before, getting coffee and taking dictation?"

Both voices laughed out loud, and Vickers felt the blood rush to her face. She motioned for Nash to follow her and stepped around the corner. "Oh, shit," one of the men said. He immediately scurried down the corridor in the opposite direction. The remaining man looked like a deer caught in headlights. Vickers estimated this stocky African-American man to be in his mid-twenties. Vickers glanced at the name tag on the front of his uniform. "At ease, Seaman Dobbs," Vickers said.

"I'm sorry, ma'am," he stammered. "Just guys being silly, you know?"

From the sound of his voice, Vickers knew he had been the one who questioned if she knew what she was doing.

"Oh, I've been known to enjoy silly talk," Vickers said coolly. "Care to tell me what you guys thought was so funny?"

"I ... I'm not sure it's a good idea, ma'am."

"Are you refusing to answer the President of the United States?"

"Answer the question, sailor," Nash said. From the tone of her voice, it was obvious she wasn't making a suggestion.

"It's just, it would be rude," Dobbs stammered. He quickly added, "Madam President."

"I see." Vickers smirked. "Seaman Dobbs, I'd like you to come with us."

"Ma'am, I don't think that's a good idea," Special-Agent-In-Charge Nash protested. "He doesn't have the proper security clearances."

"Then I say that we temporarily give it to him," Vickers said. "Lead the way, Nash. Dobbs, you're with me."

"Ma'am, with all due respect, I shouldn't be going with you," Dobbs protested as he trailed two steps behind the President.

"Seaman Dobbs, I won't hear of it. The way I see it, you have two choices."

"Ma'am?"

"The first choice is you can come quietly with us. You'll join us in our meeting, which I promise you will be far more enlightening than any childish gossip in the hall. The second option is Special-Agent-In-Charge Nash will escort you by any means necessary to the brig. Once you arrive there, you'll be held for insubordination until a proper trial can be arranged. Now, Mr. Dobbs, think very, very carefully. You only get one chance to choose. Which option will you take?"

"I-I'll come with you."

"An excellent choice," President Vickers said. "Please follow Agent Nash and me."

They rounded the next corner, and then in fifty yards they came to another intersection and turned right. As they approached the middle of the corridor, there was a doorway on the right. Vickers watched as Special-Agent-In-Charge Nash leaned over, tapped on the door twice, then opened it and gestured for the President to step through. President Vickers stepped through, then motioned for Dobbs to follow her. The seaman stepped tentatively into the room, looking like he was very much out of his element.

"Seaman, I believe you're in the wrong place," Captain Carson Flores said. The solidly-built commanding officer of the *U.S.S. Eisenhower* glared at the low-ranking subordinate. "This is a high-level meeting."

"Captain, I tried telling the President that," Special-Agent-In-Charge Nash said, "but she overruled me."

"This is a matter of national security," Flores said. "This man does not belong in this meeting. Dobbs, you're dismissed."

"No, he's not," Vickers disagreed. "Until further notice, I want you to consider Seaman Dobbs to be the ambassador of the crew."

"What?" Captain Flores demanded.

Vickers glanced at Dobbs, who looked like he wanted to be anywhere but in the current room. That was exactly the response she was looking for. It was time to turn the heat up a little bit more under the immature sailor's backside.

"Apparently, the seaman and his peers are confused as to what we are doing in meetings like this. Some of them might suggest we're having a tea party. Others might think I might be inclined to fetch coffee or take dictation while others offer up pearls of advice." Vickers stared at Dobbs as she spoke, and the man quietly looked at the floor in embarrassment. "So, I'd like him to hear that the leaders of their country on this ship know what the fuck they're doing. I would like Mr. Dobbs, acting in the capacity of crew ambassador, to go back and report that we are indeed taking steps to not only stop the Reaper incursions, but to defeat them as quickly as possible."

Flores shot up out of his seat. "Madam President, with all due respect, if any of my crew has acted inappropriately-"

"Respectfully, I see no reason why Seaman Dobbs can't sit in on this meeting, to a certain point," Vickers interrupted. "Now, once we get into discussing things that require the highest security clearance levels, then the newly-appointed ambassador can return to his normal station or whatever task you decide to give him. But until then, please consider him to be my guest for this meeting."

"This is highly unusual," the captain protested.

"We're living in a highly unusual world these days," Vickers answered. "Captain, do I need to make it an official order, or can we just play nice in the sandbox instead?"

"Fine." Flores glowered. "Seaman Dobbs, you will stand quietly and observe this meeting until you are dismissed by President Vickers or myself. You are not permitted to speak unless prompted to do so. If you so much as fart loudly, you will spend the next six months doing every single unpleasant task Master Chief Heyward or I decide to give you. Do I make myself clear?"

"Crystal clear, Captain," Dobbs said loudly. He backed into a corner of the room and stood at attention.

The phone in the conference room rang, and Vickers saw Flores activate the speakerphone. "Hello?"

"This is General Weindahl speaking. Is the president there?"

"I am, Rasheed," Vickers said, "along with Captain Flores, Special-Agent-In-Charge Nash, and Seaman Dobbs."

"I'm afraid I'm not familiar with the seaman," Weindahl said coolly. "Can anyone explain why he's attending our meeting?"

"He's the guest of the president," the captain said. "At her insistence, he's sitting in on this meeting, at least until we get to the top security clearance details. I'd like the record to reflect it's the president's decision."

"Indeed," Weindahl said. "It's been my experience that our president doesn't always like to follow the standard playbook of doing things."

"General, why don't you get this meeting started?" Vickers said. "It would be good to wrap up this meeting before another crisis shows up on our doorsteps."

"Of course," Weindahl said. "Madam President, we're in the process of finishing the positioning of resources needed for Operation Flashpoint."

"What are our targets?"

"We should be able to hit Philadelphia and Washington, D.C. in the first wave. We can choose to hit New York or Boston as well. Unfortunately, we don't have enough resources to hit all four cities at once."

"Let's go with New York City, since it's the largest infestation of Reapers at this time."

"I concur."

"Are those the only cities we're hitting?"

"No, we have a second wave in the works. It would hit Chicago and Dallas. Any future waves will require resetting resources and moving assets around to set up the attacks."

"I'm afraid you have me at a bit of a loss," Vickers said. "What resources are at a premium to launch these attacks?"

"Pilots," Weindahl said. "Each type of military plane requires specialized training. Among all of the military personnel we've lost, the group we've had the worst losses among is pilots."

"Even more than infantry?" Vickers asked.

"Yes, that's right. It takes the Air Force about one year to put a candidate through their UPT or Undergraduate Pilot Training and costs over one million dollars to do so. We don't just let anybody climb into the cockpit."

"Seeing that a single F-35 costs more than eighty billion dollars, I don't blame you for being picky on who becomes a fighter pilot," Vickers said. "Let's go back to the limited resources. So we're talking about needing to move pilots from one part of the country to another in order to set up additional attacks?"

"The short answer is, it depends," Weindahl said. "In some areas, we lack pilots. In others, it's not enough bombers or fighter planes. In many areas, we're lacking trained personnel to properly maintain the aircraft we do have."

"Which is why we're shuffling pieces around to set up attacks."

"Yes, that's right," Weindahl replied. "Unfortunately for us, when the Reapers attack a base, they kill or transform everyone on the base. We wind up losing some of the personnel that we can least afford to lose."

"Couldn't we use one or two bombers?" Flores asked. "They could move from city to city, dropping bombs on each one along the way."

"Bombers would be more efficient," Weindahl agreed, "except our intel suggests that the Reapers may have some way to communicate with each other. The moment we begin to bomb one city, we fully expect they will begin alerting the rest. The time it would take a bomber to travel from one city to the next would allow them to spread the word among their numbers to hide underground."

"Or leave the city," Vickers interrupted.

"That's right. We don't want to give our enemy any chance to scatter their forces. Operation Flashpoint is predicated on striking the Reapers at multiple places all at once."

"Hit them hard, and hit them fast," Flores murmured. "I like it."

"Indeed," Weindahl said. "The timing of the mission is critical."

"If that's true, wouldn't waiting to do a second wave of attacks also give them a chance to hide?" Vickers asked.

"That's a possibility," Weindahl admitted, "but right now, ma'am, I don't see what other choice we have."

"What do you mean?" Vickers asked.

"We're tracking Reaper pack movements," Weindahl said. "In some areas, we expect the forward operating bases where our planes would need to launch from to be attacked in the next twelve hours."

"So we're racing against the clock," Vickers said. "If we don't launch the planes in time, then we risk not being able to launch them at all."

"We believe the bombings will force the remaining Reapers to pull back their packs and regroup elsewhere," Weindahl said. "Once that happens, we could gain new targets of opportunities to strike."

"Sounds good, but what happens if Operation Flashpoint is not successful?"

"Then we can use alternate methods to attack the other Reaper-infested cities."

"Like nukes," Vickers said.

"Yes, Madam President."

"You know how I feel about detonating nuclear weapons on our own soil, Rasheed."

"I understand, Madam President. We're doing everything we can to avoid that alternative."

"What else do you have for me, Rasheed?"

"I'm afraid that the Reapers continue to spread out in other parts of the country. I have confirmed reports that San Diego, San Francisco, and Seattle have all fallen. Current estimates put their numbers at approximately forty million nationwide. Reapers are now being reported moving over the borders of Mexico and Canada."

Vickers glanced at Dobbs and saw the man look like he was about to faint. "Seaman, are you feeling well?"

"I...I could use some fresh air," the man stammered.

"Fair enough." Vickers smiled. "Mr. Dobbs, unless someone objects, you can step outside and get your needed breather."

"You're dismissed, Seaman," Flores added.

Dobbs threw up a hasty salute and stumbled toward the door. Nash opened it and let the sailor step out in the hallway, closing it behind him.

"Now that the good seaman has departed our meeting," Vickers quipped, "how bad is it in Mexico and Canada?"

"It's still early for them, ma'am," Weindahl said, "but our allies are requesting our help."

"Do we actually have anything to offer right now?"

"I'm afraid not."

"Damn it," Vickers said. "Our hands are completely tied."

"Indeed. We lack the personnel to send troops to bolster the border or help our allies," Weindahl said. "Assuming we see a high kill rate with Operation Flashpoint, perhaps we can suggest they can do the same in their own countries."

"Let's hope so," Vickers said. "In the meantime, tell them what we already know about the Reapers."

"I'm afraid there's not much to tell them that they don't already know."

"Maybe," Vickers said. "It can't hurt to tell to them to move as many of their critical personnel offshore while they can."

"Yes, ma'am."

"And, Rasheed?"

"Ma'am?"

"Two things. First, I want you offshore before Operation Flashpoint begins."

"With all due respect, we're in the middle of a military operation. Moving to another location right now is not feasible."

"No more excuses. Make it happen," Vickers said. "Or do I need to order a Navy SEAL platoon to come and personally escort you out of the Pentagon?"

"That won't be necessary. I'll leave within the hour."

"Excellent. I know you don't want to do it, but it's for your own safety. Rasheed, you might be the important person in our military."

"If you think so, Madam President. And the second thing you wanted to tell me?"

"Right. Make sure you mention to our allies that I'm not talking about their politicians," Vickers said. "Without their key military personnel, scientists, engineers, or doctors, their country's not going to have much of a chance to recover. The last time I checked, a bunch of politicians aren't much help in a firefight or building a town."

The room immediately filled a short round of laughter.

"No, ma'am, they assuredly are not," Weindahl said with a chuckle.

CHAPTER EIGHTEEN

The conversation grew more serious as the men took positions around the kitchen table. It was time to figure out what they might need to leave Rehoboth by boat.

"There's going to be things we might need to protect our group," Foster said. "We might have some of them here or in our packs. If not, then we'll need to scavenge them before we cast off."

"There's not much on my boat right now," Randy said. "Like I said, I had to hustle my family out of Raleigh because things were quickly going to shit there."

"Nobody blames you for that," Foster said. "You did what you had to do to keep your family safe. There's no shame in doing that."

"Foster, you might be able to buy some supplies from Disciple-run stores," Gregory said. "It's a little risky because they might try to sway you to join their ranks, but you're from out of town, so they won't be able to track you down easily."

"Good idea, but let's consider it as Plan B or C. I'd rather we stay away from their parts of town if we can help it," Foster said. "My gut feeling is that's trouble looking for a place to happen."

"I can't say you're wrong," Gregory admitted.

"Once we cast off," Foster said, "we want to avoid having to dock someplace to get more supplies." He felt something digging into the left side of his back. He subconsciously reached back and felt the SWAT satellite phone there and shifted it a few inches forward. His back muscles silently thanked him for the reprieve.

"Why?" Randy asked. "We can just dock quick enough to get fuel or supplies and still avoid trouble. We can travel close to the shoreline, so if we have any problems, we can get to land pretty easily."

"I'm more worried about human hostiles than Reapers along the shorelines," Foster said. "The monsters seem to avoid large bodies of water. I fully expect some groups of people will take advantage of that and use places like a marina as a gang or group base."

"Yeah. We ran into a few assholes as we were leaving Raleigh," Randy said softly. "Saw one guy carjack a pregnant woman. I thought about stopping, but with my family in the car, I-I just-"

"There wasn't much you could have done to help," Foster said softly. "You had to worry about keeping your family safe."

"I guess."

"Do you know how to shoot?"

"I'm rusty," Randy admitted. "It's been years since I fired that shotgun at anything."

"How about you, Gregory?" Foster asked.

"I'm decent with a pistol," Gregory answered. "I got a Glock upstairs. I try to go to the range once or twice a month just to keep in practice. I figure you never know when you might need to use a gun to protect your family."

"That's good to know," Foster said. "Randy, let me check in with the rest of my group. Then you and I can head out to your boat."

"I can hardly wait," Randy quipped. He stared morosely at his coffee cup.

"You can't stay in the house here forever," Gregory pointed out.

"No, I suppose I can't," Randy muttered.

Foster stepped out of the kitchen and had managed to get a few steps into the living room when he saw Walker coming toward him. There was a troubled look on the former Ranger's face, but Foster waited until the man was within earshot to ask what was wrong.

"I decided to assess the place for security," Walker said softly.

"And?"

"There's some real vulnerabilities."

"Okay, let's hear it."

"I'm worried about the upstairs," Walker said. "There's no boarding across any of the windows."

"That's a problem, but we already knew about it," Foster said. "Gregory did say he's been keeping his family hidden in the basement at night. We'll definitely need to address that."

"Agreed," Walker said. "He wasn't kidding when he said there's no scrap wood left. Short of breaking apart the dining room table, we're out of wood to use for fortifying the doors and windows."

"What about other furniture?"

"Most of it is made out of compressed wood or particle board."

"Which is damn near useless to reinforce an opening," Foster said. "Shit, that isn't good at all."

Walker said nothing.

"Breaking up and using furniture is less than ideal, but it's better than nothing," Foster said. "Maybe we can move some of the heavier stuff against the windows and block them for now."

"It would be better than nothing," Walker admitted. "At the very least, it might slow Reapers coming through the window long enough to get everyone out of the house. I think we need to continue keeping everyone in the basement at night and keep the noise to a bare minimum."

"Doesn't sound like there's any other good options right now," Foster said. "We should plan on sending out at least one team to do some scavenging for lumber as soon as possible."

"And nails. There's practically none here."

"You're kidding. There's no nails in the house?"

"I said practically none. There's about a third of a box of penny nails."

"Which are useless for boarding up a door or window," Foster said. "Didn't we have some from our last location?"

"Uh-huh. They got left along with all of our tools at the last house."

"In that case, we should probably add a tool box with some of the basics in each vehicle," Foster said. "That way we have them if we need them."

"Sure. While we're adding stuff, I suggest we keep a bug-out bag in each truck," Walker said. "That's in addition to what we carry into wherever we're staying."

"All good ideas, but that's even more stuff we need to scavenge and find," Foster said. He pinched the bridge of his nose to stave off a looming headache. "I feel like the list of stuff we need to survive just keeps growing longer and longer."

"Blame it on the Reapers," Walker replied. "The days of stopping by the grocery store or Home Depot on your way home from work are now gone."

"Home Depot," Foster said excitedly. "I saw one on the way into town. I bet they'd have everything we need."

"Sure," Sams said. "There's a Lowe's Hardware store, too. I bet you go to either one and you'll find a few hundred Reapers waiting for you in their personal playhouse."

"Derrick raises a good point," Walker said. "Unless all of us are going, we should stick with mom-and-pop stores for scavenging. Otherwise, the odds of succeeding will be extremely low."

"Gregory is our local guide," Foster said. "I'll ask him for some possible locations. Anything else?"

"The front door sucks," Sams said. "I doubt it would hold up to much of a breaching attack."

"That was next on my list," Walker said. "The door is hollow."

Foster swore under his breath. "All the more reason for us to get what we need for Randy's boat and get the hell out of here."

"I couldn't agree more," Walker said. "The problem is we're going to need at least one day, maybe two, to collect everything we need before casting off."

"Fuel might be a problem, too," Foster admitted. "I'm going with Randy to check out the boat and assess the marina. I'm hoping we can fuel up there. Otherwise, we have to worry about hauling gasoline to the boat and refueling it manually."

"Ugh. Even if we can clear out the Reapers at the marina, we don't know if the marina pumps are still operational," Walker said. "I'm really not digging the idea of lugging containers of fuel."

"We don't know where we're casting off to," Sams pointed out. "So how can we know how much fuel we're going to need?"

"Filling the tank is usually a good start," Walker replied. "But I get your point."

"It's probably going to take more than one tank of fuel," Sams said. "And how do we know any other potential destinations won't be far worse than Rehoboth? At least we can walk the beach here."

"You mean, when you're not avoiding Reaper packs and the Disciples looking for new candidates to convert," Foster said. "Don't worry; I'll figure out an alternate place for us to set off toward."

"You might want to figure out it soon," Sams said. "Even with reinforcing this place, I'm not convinced it would hold up to a sizable Reaper attack."

CHAPTER NINETEEN

There was a distinctive knock at the door, and Ezekiel called out to enter without bothering to look up from his desk. The door opened slowly and Joseph stepped in, carefully closing the door behind him.

"You asked to see me?" Joseph asked.

"Yes. I was wondering how our recruitment efforts are going."

"Good. Great," Joseph said. "Never been better."

Ezekiel set his pen down carefully on his desk and said, "Really?"

"Yes, of course."

"When you've known somebody as long as I've known you," Ezekiel said, "You learn their habits and their mannerisms. You learn how to tell when they're telling the truth and when they're not. Joseph, please don't insult my intelligence and lie to me."

"I'm sorry, sir."

"What's really going on?"

"We're actually seeing a decrease in recruitment."

"Why do you suppose that is?"

"Well, it's not due to a lack of effort," Joseph admitted. "The thing is, in the best of times, there's a limited number of people in the Rehoboth Beach area. At this time of year, it's off-peak for the tourists, so there's just a few thousand locals here."

"What about the surrounding areas?"

"We're trying to expand," Joseph said. "The problem is, we don't have as much influence there. Especially since a lot of people have already fled the area to get away from those things."

"Reapers?"

"Yes," Joseph said. "Heaven knows I hate that name."

"I'm afraid for many of them, it's quite fitting," Ezekiel said. "Please continue."

"The thing is, the people who were able to get away have already done so. The ones who decided to stay here either didn't have another place to go, or maybe they're hiding in the hopes that the monsters don't find them."

"Interesting. Have you tried spreading the word on how we have been chosen as God's people? Or how we're able to use the Reapers as our protectors?"

"I have, and some people have stepped forward to ask for more information. But lately, it hasn't been as many as we expected."

"It seems like some people have too many options in front of them."

"I'm not sure I follow, sir."

"Perhaps we need to limit their options."

"What do you mean?"

"God has chosen us as his blessed flock. He has given us these Reapers as our protection against people who may want to try and harm us," Ezekiel said. He stood up and began to pace as he talked. "Then a portion of our congregation has stepped forward and embraced a similar role."

"The Guardians."

"Yes, that's right," Ezekiel continued. "This area is part of God's lands. And since we are God's chosen people, that would in turn make this our lands."

"We've been using that argument more frequently lately. One of our guardians, Walter, has been claiming anything found on our lands belongs to the Disciples."

"I like it," Ezekiel said excitedly. "See that he is rewarded for his quick thinking."

"I will, sir."

"I'm curious, how well is it working?"

"I-It seems to have worked with some of our new recruitments."

"But not all?"

"No, I'm afraid not."

"I see. I have something I want you to do for me, Joseph."

"Of course, sir. What is it?"

"Make it more difficult for anyone to leave this area."

"You mean, like roadblocks?"

"Among other things, of course. In short, make our people spread the word: God has given us the ability to control these monsters. We command these monsters to protect us. Join our group, and you'll be spared."

"We're already telling prospects that," Joseph reminded him. "I'm not sure how much effective the message is with some people."

"Then perhaps I'll arrange for a demonstration or two to help convince them," Ezekiel said with a smile. "But we need to make sure that it's very difficult for anyone to leave without our blessing."

"It won't be easy. There's a lot of the town we don't have control over right now."

"I don't expect it to be," Ezekiel said, "but I'm confident you'll find a way to make it happen. Remember, God has blessed the Disciples of the Divine. He has blessed this place we call home, too. He has given his word that everything in this area is ours."

"As you wish, Ezekiel," Joseph said. He bowed briefly, then turned and left the room. "Will there be anything else, sir?"

"Not at this time. Thank you, Joseph."

Joseph bowed once, then turned and left the room. Ezekiel watched as he opened the door, stepped through, and closed it behind him, returning to his paperwork. By leaving it up to Joseph how to make it happen, he gave him a level of deniability. If any of his congregation somehow found the courage to ask him if he was responsible for preventing them from leaving town, he could look them in the eye, quite convincingly, and tell them no.

CHAPTER TWENTY

Vasquez eased the F-35 Lightning II down until the landing wheels made contact with the tarmac. She heard them chirp and began to throttle her single-engine plane down until it gradually came to a complete stop. She felt a yawn escape her mouth and realized she felt utterly exhausted. After more than twelve hours in the air, it was no wonder why. At least she'd had the hindsight to call base and request additional air support for Fort Devers. Hopefully, someone else from her base would be able to help the military installation while she was offline.

Vasquez pressed the latch, and the F-35's hatch began to open. A moment later, she saw the mobile staircase had arrived and she used it to disembark her plane. She began to walk toward the building where the pilot's quarters would be found. With a little bit of luck, she'd find an open bunk without any trouble. She spotted a soldier trotting in her direction, and her spirits started to sink a little.

The soldier stopped in front of her and threw up a quick salute.

Vasquez returned it half-heartedly. She was dog-tired, and right now the only thing she was thinking about was getting some sleep. She pulled off her helmet, revealing her closely-cropped short hair, and tucked it under her arm so she could hear the private better.

"Captain, you're needed in the pilot briefing room," the soldier said.

"Please tell me you're kidding," Vasquez protested. "I just landed."

"Wish I was, ma'am. Colonel Johnson wants all incoming pilots to report to him immediately."

"Great. Tell him I'll be there shortly."

"I'm sorry, but that's not an option," the soldier answered. "I'm supposed to make sure you report in a timely manner."

"Private, I've been in a plane for the last twelve hours. Right about now, I would kill somebody for a good cup of coffee and a hot meal."

The man shifted his hand to his holstered weapon, and Vasquez quickly blurted, "Relax, Private. I was kidding."

"Captain, I need to escort you to the pilot briefing room."

Vasquez shook her head in disbelief. "Join the Air Force. Travel and get to see the world," she quipped. "The only thing I'm seeing is the inside of my cockpit."

"You don't want to keep the colonel waiting," the soldier answered. "He's not in the best of moods."

"I'll take that under advisement," she said. Vasquez pushed past the soldier and trudged toward the briefing room. She saw the soldier was following her a few steps back. "Don't worry. I'm too damn tired to hop the fence and go AWOL."

"You shouldn't joke about that," the soldier said. "It's been a real problem at some of our bases."

"Private, remind me to invite you to the next party I throw."

"Ma'am?"

"You have a natural gift for making people want to leave." Vasquez turned and continued walking without waiting to see if the soldier had any type of verbal comeback.

Ten minutes later, she trudged into the pilot briefing room and saw there were five other pilots already sitting. Each one of them looked as tired as Vasquez felt.

"Vasquez, you look like shit," Captain Tom "Ace" Sanders whispered as he moved his helmet off the seat next to him and motioned that it was available for Vasquez if she wanted it. "No offense."

"None taken," she whispered back. "It's temporary for me. What's your excuse?"

Sanders chuckled under his breath. He offered a fist to Vasquez, and she gave it a quick bump in return.

"Captain Vasquez, grab a seat," Colonel Johnson said. "I'm about to start the briefing."

"I can hardly wait," Vasquez muttered. She flopped into the seat that Sanders had cleared for her.

"What was that, Captain?" Johnson answered back.

"I said, I'm glad I'm not late," Vasquez lied.

A series of chuckles sounded out. The colonel flashed an angry look at the pilots, and the room immediately went silent.

Vasquez set her helmet carefully on the floor between her feet. She had heard through the grapevine that their helmets cost the military four hundred thousand dollars apiece. She didn't doubt it, but since the helmet was customized for her and vital for controlling her plane, there was no way in hell she was letting it out of her sight anytime soon.

"We have a priority mission," Johnson continued. "We have identified several high-value targets containing high concentrations of hostiles. We aim to take those targets out. This mission, code-named Operation Flashpoint, begins at 0400."

Vasquez looked at her watch, and her eyebrows went up. She had five hours max until she had to be back in the cockpit. Five hours to grab some sleep, and that's if she skipped grabbing a shower. She casually tilted her head and sniffed near her armpit and immediately decided that skipping a shower wasn't an option. Maybe she could grab a fast shower and sleep in her flight suit. She'd look a little rumpled when she woke up, but the shower might help her fall asleep faster. Odds were, nobody would bother to pointing out she wouldn't look neatly pressed under the circumstances. When it came to the schedules they were keeping, everyone on the base was burning both ends of the candle with a blowtorch lately.

"This is a multi-city attack. Weathers and Thompkins, your

target will be New York City. Sanders and Vasquez, you have Philadelphia. Conklin and Feiler will take care of Washington, D.C. We're going to burn these bastards out using napalm bombs. The external hardpoints on the F-35s will allow you to carry this specialized load."

Captain Jack "Stormy" Weathers raised his hand from the back of the room.

"Yes?" the colonel said.

"Why can't they use bombers and drop a bunch of cluster munitions on them instead?" Weathers asked.

Vasquez nodded her head in agreement. The cluster munition was a nasty bomb that released a few hundred grenade-size bomblets and could easily saturate an area.

"Four reasons," the colonel said. He held up four fingers for emphasis. "First, due to the previous Reaper attacks, we lost a number of bases and key personnel. To be honest, we're scrambling a bit lately. The bombers we had were previously deployed elsewhere. They would take too long to return here in time for this mission. Second, our plan is built around executing our attack as fast as possible. That requires using our existing pool of F-35s to hit them fast and get away before they have time to react."

A rumble of approval sounded out in the room. It made sense to Vasquez. Every pilot currently in the room flew an F-35.

The colonel lowered two fingers and continued. "Third, we're trying to preserve as much of the existing buildings and structures as possible," he said. "Clusters will likely blow much of the targeted cities to shit. Then there's the issue with unexploded bomblets."

Vasquez felt her breath catch. Cluster munitions could cover a wide area, but they didn't always explode on impact. Any cluster bomblets which hadn't detonated could act as unintended land mines to kill or maim civilians long after the mission had ended. They would have to use military personnel or bomb squads to locate and remove any undetonated bomblets. Based on past history, it would be a task that could take decades to complete.

"Uh, sir, that's only three reasons," Weathers said. "What's the fourth one?"

"We have plenty of napalm. I can't say the same for our cluster munitions. Any other questions?"

"Sir, what about Fort Devers?" Vasquez asked. "The fort is under attack. If we're getting pulled off air support for this mission, then is another squadron assisting those boys in the meantime?"

"I'm afraid it's too late for that," Johnson said. "The brass at Devers made the call. They feel the base is only hours away from being overrun. We've sent several troop transports and are airlifting as many personnel out as we can."

Vasquez nodded once slightly and looked at her feet. She was really getting tired of hearing about the Reapers continuing to win.

She spotted a hand shoot up in her peripheral vision and scowled. History had taught her if Weathers had a question at this part of a mission briefing, it was something likely to annoy their commanding officer.

"Yes, Stormy?" Johnson asked in a tone of voice that suggested he knew he wasn't going to like the question.

"Sir, you're talking about killing millions of Americans," Weathers protested. "I think—"

"That's enough, Captain," the colonel interrupted. "It's no longer millions of Americans in those cities. It's millions of Reapers. Get it?"

"Yeah, message received," Weathers said glumly.

"If we can wipe out a large portion of them in one coordinated attack, then our odds of beating them becomes significantly better," Johnson said. "This is our way to hit the Reapers hard before they know what the hell is happening."

The colonel paused for dramatic effect and the room went deadly silent.

"We realize there's a small chance some civilians managed to hunker down in the cities and avoid the Reapers. That's why we're planning to do an overhead city broadcast one hour before bombing commences. That should allow any civilians who are still there to evacuate the city."

Vasquez grimaced. An hour wasn't much time for anyone in the city to escape safely. It was even harder if they didn't already have easy access to a vehicle. The reality was Operation Flashpoint wasn't just going to kill Reapers. Any civilians still inside the city limits would perish, too. Vasquez pushed those feelings of dread to the back of her mind and focused on the mission details. A lot of people were going to be counting on them to execute Operation Flashpoint and kick the Reapers in the proverbial teeth.

"Any questions?"

The room stayed silent.

"Good. You got some time before you go wheels up. I suggest you grab some sleep and be ready to rock at 0400. You're dismissed."

"Hey, Vasquez," a familiar voice said. "Aren't you from Philadelphia?"

Vasquez turned and saw it was Weathers. She felt a groan coming up in her throat and immediately suppressed it. Weathers was a great fighter jock, but he was also a regular pain in the ass. "Yeah, Stormy," she replied cautiously. "Grew up in Northeast Philly. Why?"

"You okay with bombing your old hometown?"

"That's the mission. My personal feelings have nothing to do with it."

"Really? You don't have any family still there? Any friends?"

Vasquez saw Ace moving closer. She had a feeling her friend was getting ready to step in. She flashed him a look, letting him know that she had things under control, and he slowed his approach.

"Hey, Stormy, I'd love to keep chatting, but I just got back to base. I need to get some rack time before this mission," she answered. "I'll see you at 0400."

Ace came to a stop next to him. Her friend had at least two inches and twenty pounds on Weathers. From the look on his face, if Weathers said the wrong thing right now, she'd be pulling Ace off of him.

"Yeah, okay. Catch you guys later." Weathers blurted before he fled the room.

Ace waited until the other pilot left the room before saying, "You all right?"

"Yeah, I'm good," Vasquez said.

"If you want to kick his ass, I'd be happy to help."

"I appreciate the offer," she said. "Maybe another time."

"Fair enough," Ace said. "You know I always got your back." He offered a fist bump, and Vasquez tapped his fist with hers lightly.

"I know. See you at 0400, Ace." Vasquez turned and headed toward the pilot's sleeping quarters. With a little bit of luck, she'd be able to find an open shower and then grab some quality sleep before she had to be back in action.

CHAPTER TWENTY-ONE

"Charles, do you have a minute?" Foster asked.

"For you, I have several," he replied.

"I might be pulling on an old scab here, but I'm at a loss on what happened between your daughter and you."

"It's a lot of old history."

"That's true for every family," Foster said. "You're going to need to give me more than that."

"When you look at some families, they have the ideal child. One who always listens to their parents, does what's asked of them. They're respectful and kind," Charles said. "Then there's other families. They have children who want to question and argue everything. They'll want to test every boundary put in front of them and resist every rule they hear. For Helen and me, we had one of each kind."

"Let me guess. Your daughter was the one who wanted to continually test boundaries?"

"Yes, that's right. When we first became parents, we tried to handle them equally but with a firm hand," Charles said. "Within a few years, we realized that wasn't working. I saw far too many times where our daughter would run roughshod over Helen. I felt like I needed to make a conscious choice to become the disciplinarian of the family."

"I'm guessing that Lauren didn't like that."

"Not in the least. She was always resentful. She always felt I was too controlling of her mother. Eventually she started accusing me of trying to control her too."

"Sounds like most teenagers."

"Perhaps. I think it was because her mom would almost never come to her defense in public," Charles said. "What Lauren didn't realize is that Helen preferred to discuss things in private. If she didn't agree with a decision I made, the two of us would talk it out privately, and never in front of the children."

"Makes sense. It helps keep the image of their parents being unified."

"Absolutely. Except our daughter's view was that I was controlling the situation and her mom was too intimidated to speak up."

Foster did a double take. "Really? I can't picture you bullying anyone. No offense, but you're not exactly the most physically imposing man."

Charles laughed. "I never have been, but there's more to parenting than just being bigger than your kids."

"I've never been a parent, so I'll take your word on it."

"The final straw came when Helen and I decided to go out one night for dinner. While we were gone, our daughter decided to have her boyfriend over."

"Oh, boy."

"Oh, boy, indeed. We got home and found them passed out on the living room couch. There was drug paraphernalia everywhere," Charles said. "Well, that was it. I completely lost my temper. I couldn't have her around Gregory if she was doing drugs. So I started screaming at her. She tried telling me the drugs weren't hers. But how could I trust her when she had lied to us so many times in the past? I was sure she was lying to us again. So I told her she was no longer welcome in our house and needed to leave immediately."

"Wow, that's pretty serious."

"I-I didn't feel like I had a choice," Charles admitted. "Gregory was just seventeen then. I had to think of what was best for him. Being around someone who refused to admit she had a problem with drugs? That wasn't a good idea at all."

"I think a number of parents probably would make a similar decision. They'd have to focus on what was best for their remaining children."

"That was also my experience when I was a priest. It's especially true when the troubled child is nearly an adult," Charles said. He paused for a moment before continuing. "It wasn't until years later I found out that she had been telling us the truth. The drugs were not hers. Her boyfriend had brought them with him along with two bottles of wine. It wasn't until she had passed out from drinking that he began to do drugs in our living room."

"Damn, that puts things in a whole different light. How did you ever find that out?"

"Lauren confided in a friend who later told Helen."

"The friend took a bit of a risk, then."

"Yes, she did," Charles said. "She did it because she felt it was wrong for Lauren to be estranged from her family. The problem was, I couldn't betray her friend's confidence."

"Was it Randy?"

"Oh, heavens no," Charles said. "He's been a godsend for my daughter. I couldn't have picked a better man for her if I had tried. I found out years later Lauren dumped the druggie boyfriend right after she was evicted from our home. But she's never forgiven me. She blamed me for ruining her life. Worse, she blamed me for convincing her mother that somehow she was to blame for what happened."

"Well, it was her fault. She invited her boyfriend over when you weren't home. Her guest, her responsibility."

"Most people would probably reach the same logical conclusion," Charles agreed. "Unfortunately, not everybody thinks in such a logical manner. Especially my daughter."

"I think the time has come for the two of you to bury the damn hatchet. If we're going to keep everybody safe, this needs to become water under the bridge."

"I couldn't agree more, but she won't even talk to me."

"At some point, she'll have to. Just be patient."

"I've been waiting for years," Charles said. "I'm willing to wait as long as it takes."

"Let me see what I can do to help make the peace."

"You can try. But to be honest, several others before you have tried and failed. What makes you think you can succeed where others have not?"

"Maybe I'll fail even worse," Foster admitted. "But for the sake of you and the group, I'm willing to make the effort. Let me give it some thought and come up with the best way to do this."

"Of course. Like I said, I'm willing to wait as long as it takes," Charles said. "Despite my daughter's anger toward me, I've never stopped loving her. Asking her to leave our home was the hardest thing I've ever done."

CHAPTER TWENTY-TWO

After the enlightening conversation with Charles, Foster decided he should check in with Walker or Sams and see where they stood with guns and munitions. He came across Sams, sitting in the kitchen, enjoying an apple.

"Any more of those things?" Foster asked.

"Sorry, last one."

"We'll have to look for more on our next scavenging run."

"Good idea," Sams said. "Something on your mind?"

"Two things. I need to find Randy and go look at his boat. Have you seen him?"

"Nope. What's the other thing you're thinking about?"

"What's our current ammo situation?"

"Not as much as we'd like, but hopefully enough to get the job done."

"Meaning?"

"We're getting low on 9mm," Sams said. "Nick's been training Gregory, Randy, Lizzy, and Henry with the Glocks."

"Isn't he worried about attracting attention?" Foster asked. He saw the door to the living room open, and Amanda walked into the room.

"One of the neighbors was an aspiring rock guitarist," Sams said.

"Apparently he soundproofed his basement so the neighbors wouldn't complain. Nick found some ear plugs. Those combined with some studio earphones are good enough to protect their hearing while they do target practice."

"Huh. I wouldn't have thought that would work."

"Me neither," Sams admitted.

"Malcolm, you have a minute?" Amanda asked.

"Sure," Foster replied. "What's up?"

"Not here. Let's take a walk."

"Okay," Foster said as he drew out the word. He turned toward Sams and said, "We're going to go outside to talk."

"Outside?" Sams asked. "Aren't you worried about making too much noise and drawing Reapers?"

"We'll talk quietly," Foster said. "Or maybe we'll hang out in the garage."

"Let's go to the garage," Amanda blurted. "Just to talk, I mean."

"Yeah. Got it," Sams said carefully. "No hanky panky. Just a man and a woman having a, uh, talk. Be careful out there. All right?"

Foster shook his head and began walking toward the back door. He glanced back and saw that Amanda was following closely behind. The two of them stepped out of the house and headed to the garage.

Foster stopped short of the garage's side entrance, turned back, and faced Amanda. He saw her motion toward the door. Foster opened it and stepped in, letting his eyes adjust to the dimmer lighting. He heard the door close a moment later, and the interior got a little bit darker. A flashlight went on, and he turned and saw Amanda was holding it skywards to act as an impromptu lamp.

"What's on your mind?" Foster said.

"Well, it's just that I've been thinking about you know what."

"You're going to have to give me a better clue than that."

"You know, the thing."

"The thing?" Foster asked.

"Yes, *the thing*," Amanda said, putting more emphasis on the last two words.

"Wait. Are you talking about the kiss?"

"Yes, the kissing thing," Amanda stammered.

"Okay. What about it?"

"I think it was a mistake," Amanda blurted. "I mean-"

"Wait, what?"

"I just—I overreacted. You know, it was a spur-of-the-moment thing. I had been trapped. I was scared for my life, and I-I just want to say I'm sorry."

"Uh, you just lost me."

"Well, it's just that I kind of forced myself on you."

Foster chuckled. "I'm quite capable of defending myself if I need to."

"I know that. It's just-"

"It's okay."

"Really?"

"Amanda, it's all right," Foster said. "I get it. With everything going on. We're struggling to stay alive and-"

The walkie-talkie interrupted him in mid-sentence.

"Hey, boy toy," Sams said over the walkie-talkie. "Are you there? Or are you too busy to talk right now?"

Foster shook his head in disbelief. He brought the walkie-talkie up to his mouth and pressed the transmit button. "You realize you're the last person who should be calling me that, right?"

"Of course," Sams answered. "But if you two are done talking, we have something here you're going to want to see."

"Copy that. We're returning to the house in a minute," Foster said. He turned his attention back to the attractive doctor and added, "Sorry about that."

"Not your fault. Derrick can be like a hyper puppy sometimes."

"No argument here."

"You know, you're right," Amanda said. "We do have a lot going on. I guess we'll just say it was a spur-of-the-moment thing, right?"

"Sure."

"Okay, cool."

There was an uncomfortable silence between the two of them as both seemed to run out of ideas of what to say at the same time.

"Was there anything else you want to talk about? If not, I've got to get back and see what Derrick needs."

"No, we're okay."

"Okay, cool. Hey, Amanda?"

"Yes?"

"If you see Randy, can you tell him I'm looking for him? I still need him to show me his boat."

"Of course."

"Thanks. I appreciate it." Foster turned and headed toward the door. He opened it and stepped outside, not waiting to see if Amanda was following him.

Amanda waited a silent count of three before she started to follow Foster. As they walked unknowingly in tandem, she studied his posture. From the way he was holding his shoulders, Amanda could tell that Malcolm was struggling to keep his feelings in check.

If what I did was the right thing, then why do I feel so bad about it? Amanda thought to herself. After that conversation, she felt less clear on where things stood between the two of them. Was he really okay with her decision? Or was he only saying what he thought she wanted to hear? It was a confusing mess, but right now wasn't the time to try and sort it out. Amanda pushed the thought to the back of her mind and continued to follow Foster back to the house.

"Where's the fire?" Foster asked.

"Mudroom," Sams answered. "Nick had a breakthrough. I think you're going to want to see it."

"Great," Foster said. He took three steps toward the mudroom, which was located on the opposite of the ground floor, before stopping. He turned back toward Sams and asked, "Are you coming with?"

"No need." Sams smiled. "I've already seen Nick's invention."

"Gotcha," Foster said. He turned and resumed heading toward the mudroom alone.

Two minutes later, he'd reached his destination. He tapped twice lightly on the closed door before opening it and stepping into the room. As he did, Foster saw Walker was bent over a collapsible card table. The man seemed to be completely absorbed in whatever he was working on. Foster stood there quietly, watching his movements. He couldn't figure out what the man was doing or whether he should stay.

"Staring at a guy while he's working and not saying a thing is kind of rude," Walker said quietly.

"Sorry," Foster answered. "I didn't want to interrupt you if you were doing something critical."

"It's critical, but I don't mind the interruption."

"Fair enough. What are you working on?"

"I've been thinking about your dagger."

Foster's eyebrows shot up.

"Not that one, asshole," Walker said. "I'm a married man."

"That doesn't stop some guys."

"It does with this one." Walker continued. "Your dagger contains a mixture of metals, including silver. I started thinking about what weapon has worked against Reapers. Then I started considering how well the Reaper bullet worked, too. I reached the somewhat amateur conclusion that the monsters are allergic to silver."

"Not allergic," Foster corrected. "Our resident doctor says it sends Reapers into anaphylactic shock and they die."

"And here I thought they were werewolves."

"Yeah, except for the fact they travel in packs, are active at any time of the day or night, and aren't limited by whatever the moon might be doing."

"Don't forget some of them talk and have armor plates covering half of their bodies, too."

"Yeah, that was a pretty crazy thing to discover," Foster said. "Then there's the troop-like behavior. It's like something is telling them where to go and what to attack."

"Somebody at a much higher pay grade or a lot of extra letters after their last name is going to have to figure that stuff out," Walker admitted. "I'm worried about what other abilities they might have that we don't even know about yet."

"Me too, buddy," Foster added.

"Anyway, let's get back to the experiment," Walker said. "I don't have all the right equipment to create new knives or spears. Plus, silver is a pretty soft metal. It can chip or break pretty easily. The ideal weapon composition might be a mix of metals with just enough silver included to trigger a Reaper's fatal reaction. I just don't have the equipment or know-how to create a blended weapon from scratch."

"So, what am I looking at?" Foster asked.

"An experiment. The short explanation is I soldered silver onto a few of our existing knife blades."

"Wait, what?"

"Think of it as a long strip of silver on the knife blade. If it works, it'll kill the Reapers no matter where you stab or slice them. If it doesn't, well then it's still a sharp knife. You still can bury it in their heads."

"I like it," Foster said. "How many knives have you coated?"

"Two, for now," Walker answered. "I figured one for Sams and one for me. No offense, but we have the most training in hand-to-hand combat out of everyone in the group."

"None taken. Like you said, if the solder doesn't work, either one of you can still eliminate the hostile with it."

"I don't have any reason to think it won't, but I'd feel a lot better after we test it."

"How much material you got left?" Foster asked. "Could you do any additional knives?"

"Probably just another knife or two. Why?"

"Maybe somebody else in the group would want an experimental weapon. Definitely better than having no weapon at all."

"Yeah, maybe," Walker said. "I was thinking of asking Gregory if I could give one to his son."

"I think he'd be more open to it than offering his eleven-year-old a Glock."

"Yeah, probably."

"You got a name picked out for your treated knives yet? Maybe Reaper knives? It would go with your Reaper bullets."

"Nah, the bullets were special." Walker grinned. "They killed a Reaper that was hundreds of yards away. This is just a little dip in some melted silver. Until these things prove they're special, they don't get a special name."

CHAPTER TWENTY-THREE

The satellite phone on Foster's left hip suddenly began to ring, and Walker looked at it quizzically.

"Is that who I think it is?"

"You bet," Foster answered. He pressed the button on his phone and then said, "Black?"

"One and the same," SWAT Sergeant Vince Black replied. "I'm checking in to see how you guys are doing. This is a good time to talk?"

"As good as any," Foster answered. "Are you guys still in the city?" He saw Walker motion he was leaving the room. Foster gave a quick nod of acknowledgment and turned his attention back to the phone call.

"Negative," Black answered. "Sixth District fell while we were on a mission."

"How the hell did that happen?"

"Same way lots of other places go under. An overwhelming number of Reapers attacked, and everybody had to bail or stay and die."

"Okay, so where are you guys at now?"

"Offshore. We're on an island."

"Wait, what? An island?"

"If you keep making me repeat myself, this is going to take a long fucking time."

"You got a hot date or something, Sergeant?"

"Not hardly. But I really don't feel like giving you a long-winded, blow-by-blow explanation."

"Then give me the short version instead."

"Fine. We got an offer from the Lieutenant Governor that was too good to turn down," Black said. "We had to rescue his daughter from a building at University of Penn. In return, he provided enough helicopter transport to get everyone from the precinct to Hope Island."

"Never heard of it."

"Me neither until the mission briefing. It's off the coast of Rhode Island."

"How'd the mission go?"

"I lost four men, but we rescued the princess."

"Damn."

"Actually, she's not really a princess, but—"

"Yeah, I get it, Black," Foster said. "I'm sorry you lost some of your men. Anybody I know?"

"Uh-huh. Nico. Hawkins. Diaz. Graves."

"Damn. I liked all of them. I'm sorry, man."

"Thanks," Black said. He paused for an uncomfortable moment before adding, "So where are you at, Foster?"

"Rehoboth Beach."

"Really? With all of this shit going down, you're taking a vacation? That's kind of ballsy."

Foster chuckled. "Actually, Charles has family here. We've connected with them and are planning on getting everyone out of here by boat."

"Do you actually have a boat? Or is this one of your pie-in-the-sky ideas?"

"Yeah, we do. Charles's son-in-law owns one. It's big enough to fit all of us, but I'm not sure where we're going to go," Foster said. "We have to get fuel and other supplies secured first."

"Well, that's kind of why I'm calling you," Black said. "The guy in charge of the military here seems like a decent enough cat."

"This cat got a name?"

"Yeah. Captain Tom Abrahams," Black said. "Anyway, Kimball kept insisting I tell him about some of your findings about the Reapers. So I did, and that's when he got real interested. Now he wants to talk to you."

"What's to talk about? The damn things are deathly vulnerable to silver."

"I know that. You know that," Black said in a low voice. "But they don't know that. You figured it out there in the field, and that's a proven fact. That's some very valuable intel. You take that and anything you've learned about the Reapers since we last talked and share it with Abrahams. Especially if it's anything that could help the military kick more Reaper ass."

"Uh-huh. What's Abrahams willing to offer in return?"

"If the intel you provide is good enough, it should be your golden ticket for bringing your group here. Which I'll point out is currently 100 percent Reaper-free."

"Sounds promising. What's it like there?"

"They're a small island in the middle of the ocean. Got some lodging, everybody's pitching in to work on stuff. Some of the soldiers are still doing scavenging missions. We've been tasked mostly with base security here on the island."

"From SWAT to security guard," Foster quipped. "Sounds like a bit of drop in stature."

"And that's perfectly fine with me. I'm happy to make sure to do my part here."

"This is Vince Black, right? The same guy who used to lead a group of bad-ass SWAT guys that kicked ass and took names every day?"

"I'm still the same guy. Except my mission has changed. Right now, it's to make sure this place stays safe."

"At this rate, Black, they're gonna have you riding a desk in another month."

"I doubt it," Black said. "I've only seen one desk on the island, and that's in Captain Abraham's office. If I'm working from there, then a lot of bad shit has happened, because I'm not part of the military chain of command."

"Good point. I was just busting your balls because I can."

"Uh-huh. Anyways, the good news is they haven't had a single Reaper attack. It looks like those bastards won't cross the ocean."

"Really? You're kidding."

"Have you ever known me to kid?"

"Not about stuff like this."

"Exactly. So let's set up a time where you can talk to Abrahams. Knock the captain's socks off, and maybe you'll be playing cards with my guys before the end of the week."

"Sounds like a plan. When do you want to talk?"

"Let's keep it simple," Black suggested. "How about twenty-four hours from now?"

"Sounds good. I'll make it work on my end."

"Great. I gotta run. Black out."

"Hey, Black?"

"Yeah?"

"Thanks for setting this up. It could be a helluva opportunity for my group."

"Uh-huh. Talk to you tomorrow," Black answered before hanging up.

Foster stepped out of the room and saw Walker was waiting in the hallway.

"What was that about?" Walker asked.

"A possible escape plan," Foster said. He proceeded to fill Walker in on what Black had told him.

"Very interesting," Walker said. "I just wonder what kind of ropes it comes with."

"Don't you mean strings?" Foster asked.

"Nope. If you're dealing with the military, they'd never use something as thin as string." Walker smiled. "There's definitely at least one rope attached to that deal."

CHAPTER TWENTY-FOUR

After the meeting with Flores and Weindahl mercifully ended, President Vickers insisted that she had to have something to eat before tackling any other pressing issues. Special-Agent-In-Charge Nash had calmly led her through a winding series of corridors until they reached the staff entrance of the kitchen. Once inside, Vickers was pleasantly surprised to see the staff had a hot roast beef sandwich and French fries waiting for her. She felt a little guilty eating it while many Americans were likely eating whatever they could find while avoiding the Reapers. But feeling guilty wasn't going to stop them. She needed a solid plan of attack to put down the monsters for good. Now with a solid meal finally in her, she felt reenergized and ready to tackle the challenges, emergencies, and problems waiting for her.

Several hours later, she was in another meeting with General Weindahl. He had finally arrived by helicopter, so the two of them took over the conference room to meet face to face.

"Rasheed, do you need any motion sickness medicine?" Vickers asked. "I can ask someone to get it for you."

"That won't be necessary," Weindahl said. "I've already taken it."

"Excellent. What's our combat effectiveness?"

"Currently holding at 19 percent," Weindahl said. "Once we realized the Reapers were focusing their attacks on our bases, we began moving personnel to more secure locations. Those locations do include some offshore bases."

"That's good. I just wish we'd been able to do that before the attacks began."

"Indeed. Hindsight is always 20/20 and correct."

"Yeah, it is." Vickers sighed. "Where are we with our top-tier operators?"

"Fortunately, those haven't been hit as hard. We had a number of overseas operations in the works when the Reaper outbreak began. As a result, Navy SEALs are operating at 80 percent effectiveness. Rangers, Delta Force, and Special Forces are all reporting in at 70 percent of normal capacity."

"That might be the best news I've heard all day. I want all of them moved to our offshore bases and ships. That way, we can stage future operations for them from far more secure bases."

"It's a sound idea, but I'm not sure that's possible," Weindahl said. "Some of them are still engaged in covert missions and are operating under radio-silent conditions. Others are active in other non-covert tasks that our allies are extremely dependent on."

"Like what?"

"Militia training. Embassy security consulting in certain hot zones, like the Middle East."

"Any Reaper movement in those areas?"

"No, not yet," Weindahl said. "Like I mentioned earlier, there's some reports of early Reaper activity in Canada and Mexico. But so far, we're not hearing any Reaper sightings overseas."

"Well, I suppose that will have to pass as good news for now," Vickers quipped. "Any chance of our allies sending troops to help?"

"We haven't reached out yet," Weindahl admitted. "We've been entirely focused on containing the problem within our own borders."

"Uh-huh," Vickers said slowly. "Rasheed, what aren't you telling me?"

Weindahl sighed. "I'm concerned about asking for outside help," he said carefully. "We had arguably the largest military force in the world prior to the Reaper outbreak. By disclosing our current diminished military strength, it could alert our enemies that we are vulnerable to a new outside attack."

"You think China or Russia would make a move on us?"

"I can't rule it out as a possibility," Weindahl said. "At the very least, I think asking our allies for help would send them into a panic."

"Really?"

"Yes. Even at our current depleted levels, we still have larger military forces than some of our allies. I suspect their immediate reaction would be to refuse aid and focus on protecting their own country instead."

"I still want every special operator not engaged in an active mission moved offshore."

"I'll see what we can do."

"Not good enough," Vickers argued. "I want the orders to move them put into action ten minutes ago. Do you catch my drift?"

"Yes, Madam President."

"Look, I know you hate the idea of running away," Vickers said. "Heaven knows, I hate it, too. But right now, we don't know what the biggest weakness for the Reapers is besides a bullet in the head. Our special operators are our elite fighters. If we can hold them in reserve, then we still have them for future battles."

"I-I will give the order to move them."

"Excellent. Any news on establishing research centers?"

"It's still in the works."

"See if you can get them to pick up their pace. I want to hear they're operational in the next twenty-four hours."

"I'll stress the urgency, Madam President, but I can't guarantee they can have all of the needed equipment and personnel in place that quickly. It's not like we're ordering a pizza, ma'am."

"Rasheed, I want results, not excuses. The sooner those researchers can come up with something that kills these bastards, the better."

"Did you have something specific that I should direct our scientists to pursue first?"

"Right now, I'm not willing to rule out anything that could help us defeat our enemy," Vickers said. "I do think a cure is probably the least desirable option right now. We're dealing with millions of Reapers within our borders. Manufacturing, distributing, and administering a cure nationwide would take months, if not years. And that's not factoring how long it takes the eggheads to come up with something that works."

"A cure does seem like a long-term answer," Weindahl replied. "I'd recommend our researchers working on a weapon. If we can greatly reduce the number of Reapers, then our troops would have much better odds of eliminating the rest."

"I don't disagree," Vickers said. "But like I said, I don't want to rule out anything that can swing this war back in our favor."

"I understand, Madam President."

"Good. Get those research facilities up and running before there's no one else left to save."

CHAPTER TWENTY-FIVE

Foster left the mudroom with his spirits on the upswing. At the risk of getting cocky, he couldn't see any reason why Nick's enhanced knives wouldn't deliver one-strike kills like his dagger consistently did. He glanced at his watch and decided he needed to find Randy and go check out the man's boat before it got too late. As he worked his way through the house, he made it to the dining room before a voice called out to him.

"Malcolm, a word, please," Charles said. He motioned for Foster to follow him into the kitchen.

Foster waited until the two of them had relocated before asking, "What's on your mind, Padre?"

"Former padre." Charles smiled. "It's been many, many years since I wore the cloth."

"Fair enough," Foster said. "What's on your mind?"

"I heard about your upcoming call with the military commander."

Foster should have been surprised that word had traveled through the group so quickly, but he wasn't. When there wasn't much to do besides working to keep everyone alive, it was easy for people to look for far more enjoyable distractions. "What about it?"

Charles cleared his throat and then said, “I think it would be best if you neglect to mention some of our group’s backgrounds.”

“Which ones? The doctor, the nurse, or the former Army Rangers?”

“Take your pick,” Charles said. “You should probably include yourself, too.”

“Why? Because they might get recruited to help?”

“That's one way to look at it,” Charles answered. “The more likely scenario is that they get forced to help.”

“I'm not sure some people would want me to make that decision for them.”

“You’re probably right. But I think you still need to do it.”

“I'm not sure I agree,” Foster said. “Wouldn’t it be better to let each person decide what’s best for them? I don’t want to put them in a spot where they have no choice.”

“It’s not a matter of being nice,” Charles said. “We already think that of you.”

“Okay, then what is it?”

“It’s a matter of the military making the decision for them. It’s not like they’ll bother asking for any opinions.”

“Probably not.”

“Suppose this captain decides to recall Nick,” Charles continued. “What kind of impact is that going to have on his marriage? Or on our group?”

“It wouldn't be the first time they'd been separated by Nick's official duty.”

“No, it probably hasn't,” Charles said. “But when has Nick ever been put into a situation where he's facing such a daunting foe? In case you hadn't noticed, it would appear that our law enforcement and military are not doing well against the Reapers.”

“I don’t know of any group that’s winning against the Reapers. Well, these Disciples of the Divine supposedly are, but that could be a colossal lie to attract new members.”

“You might be right about these so-called protected Disciples. But they’re not why I asked you to talk,” Charles said. “If you volunteer

Nick's background, then you're putting him in a situation where he has no choice but to rejoin the military. Even if it means he's leaving his wife and friends."

"Which is why I'm leaning toward letting each person make their own decision. I can't force people to stay with our group if they don't want to."

"Of course. But the ones like Derrick, who aren't married? If he left, how would that affect our group? What about Lizzy and Amanda? I imagine that people who already have medical training would be in high demand."

"Okay, I get it. You made your point."

"Good. I was worried I was starting to sound like I was beating a dead horse."

Foster let out a low chuckle. "Not far off from it, Padre."

"I'm not saying we need to turn away their help, if it's offered. An island safe from the Reapers sounds wonderful. But right now, there's no need to tell this soldier everything about our group. Not until we have a better idea of who we're dealing with."

The door into the kitchen swung open, and Sams made a beeline to the refrigerator.

"Okay. Fair point," Foster said. "I'll do my best to keep everyone's secret for now."

"Wait, somebody has a secret?" Sams interrupted. He grabbed a bottle of water out of the fridge and closed it behind him. "Come on, man, spill it."

"It's not anything new for you," Foster said, "but it could be for Abrahams." Foster quickly filled Sams in on his future phone meeting with the captain.

"Yeah, it's probably best to keep it 'need to know' for now," Sams said as he used air quotes for extra emphasis. "At least until we have a better idea who we're dealing with. I'm sure Black means well, but he might totally suck at reading people."

"I wouldn't say that," Foster said. "The guy has been a cop for a lot of years. Police officers read people all the time."

"And military commanders are great at making a complete shit mission sound like it's going to be a walk in the park," Sams countered. "I'm just saying you can't go wrong by playing it safe about our group's background."

"Fair enough."

"Anyways, the real reason I sought you out was because I did some research," Sams said. "Henry was able to help me get online here. We used Google Maps to find Hope Island."

"Okay, cool. So what are we looking at?"

"About three hundred ninety miles by road."

"What about by sea?"

"I don't have a fucking clue," Sams admitted. "I know about as much about boating as you know about women."

"I know a good amount about women."

"Says the guy who had a friend with benefits who may or may not have been married the entire time."

"Yeah, let's not go there, okay?"

"Hey, no offense meant, man. It just seemed like a good example, and-"

"Anything else you want to tell me about the island?" Foster interrupted.

"Yeah. It's connected to the mainland by a bridge."

"Huh. Black didn't mention any bridge."

"Like I said, Black might not have the full story."

"I'll be sure to ask Abrahams about the bridge," Foster said. "If I can ever find Randy, maybe he can tell me how far Hope Island is by sea."

"Yeah, can't help you there," Sams said. "I haven't seen the guy all day."

"Me either," Charles said. "But if I see him, I'll let Randy know you're looking for him."

"Thanks, Charles," Foster replied. "And Derrick? I appreciate the heads up about the research, too."

"Sure thing. I'm gonna go find Gregory and see if he has any apples hidden someplace besides the kitchen."

"You've been hitting the apples hard lately."

"Why wouldn't I? I like them," Sams said. "Besides, it's not like I'm gonna find any apple trees growing on this island we could be heading to."

CHAPTER TWENTY-SIX

"I hear you've been looking for my husband," Lauren said. "Care to tell me why?" She put herself directly in front of Foster and put her hands on her hips for emphasis.

Foster stared at the woman in front of him. He had two choices. The first one was to ignore her and continue on his way. He had at least a foot and eighty pounds on her, so it wasn't likely she would be able to physically stop him from going around her. The second one was to be honest with her and tell the truth. A mental lightbulb lit up, and Foster sprang into action.

Foster flashed an award-winning smile. He said in his politest possible voice, "Yes, Lauren, I have. Did Randy tell you that I asked to see your boat?"

"No, he didn't," she answered. "Why did you want to see it?"

"Because we might need it," Foster said. He proceeded to tell her about receiving the call from Black, the reports of Reapers refusing to cross large bodies of water, and the group's possible escape to Hope Island. Foster watched as her face grew stormier and stormier.

"Come with me," Lauren said, the anger in her voice barely restrained. She turned and immediately headed to the basement.

Foster trailed her by three steps and watched as the woman

stomped down the staircase. He hadn't even reached the basement floor before he heard her say, "Randall Lawrence Bridges, when were you planning on telling me that we might have a place to go that these monsters can't reach us?" Foster headed toward the woman's voice, which was coming from behind a six-foot-high metal storage rack. As he rounded the corner, he saw Randy sitting in a lawn chair. There was a beer sitting on the floor next to the chair and a hardcover book in his hands.

"Uh," Randy stammered. He quickly dropped the book he had been reading, and it landed on the floor with a low thump. "I didn't think-"

"That's right, you didn't," Lauren snarled. "How can Malcolm find out what supplies are needed to get all of us, including your wife and daughter, to this Hope Island if you don't take him to our boat?"

"Well, I tried to tell him, but-"

"I don't want to hear it. If you have one ounce of respect for Emily or me, then you will get your lazy ass out of that chair and take Malcolm to the boat right now."

"But, honey-"

"Don't *but honey* me," Lauren said. "If you don't do this one thing, then so help me you're going to be sleeping alone in the garage until hell freezes over."

Randy sprang to his feet, motioned to Foster, and said, "Let's go, man." He took the stairs two at a time without looking to see if Foster was following him.

Foster turned toward Lauren and silently mouthed a quick thank you to her before following Randy upstairs.

Twenty-five minutes later, the two men finally arrived at the marina. It had been a quiet ride there, but as Foster shut off the Suburban's engine, he heard Randy mutter, "Why did you tell my wife I wouldn't show you the boat?"

"I didn't. She asked me why I was looking for you, and I told her the truth," Foster said. "You think I should have lied to her instead?"

"No," Randy said slowly. "That would only make things worse. I swear my wife can spot a fib from a mile away. Come on, let's get this over with already."

Foster saw the man open the passenger door and exit the Suburban without looking. Foster checked his surroundings, then proceeded to follow Randy as the man made his way through the marina gate, heading directly toward his boat. Foster mentally noted the man had completely ignored anything else going on around him. In the best of times, having no situational awareness was a bad habit to have. In the current Reaper-dominated environment, it could get you or other people around you killed. Foster decided to compensate and focused even more on their surroundings. If trouble came their way, Foster was the only one who was armed, and he'd have to handle the threat. He'd offered Randy a Glock before they left the house, but the man had declined, saying he didn't feel comfortable enough with the weapon to begin carrying it. It was yet another red flag about the man's lack of understanding about the world they were trying to survive in lately.

Unlike other marinas Foster had seen before, the boats weren't spread out evenly across the area. Instead, approximately thirty boats were clustered at the end closest to the marina pumps. A dozen Reapers were casually wandering back and forth there. As Foster watched, he saw two men move through the Reapers and begin working their way toward them.

"There she is," Randy said proudly. *"The Lauren."* He pointed in the opposite direction of the marina pumps.

Foster looked at Randy's pride and joy. There were only four other boats tied in the same area. He glanced back toward the marina pump and saw dozens there. There was something definitely strange about this marina. He turned his attention back to Randy, who was still waiting for his answer.

"I'm afraid I don't know much about boats," Foster admitted. "But she looks like a beauty."

"Absolutely. That's a 27-foot Sea Ray Sundancer," Randy said. "Lauren damn near killed me when I bought it. Spent a month sleeping on the couch before she started to forgive me. Once I took her out on this beauty, that put me back in her good graces again."

"Naming the boat after her probably didn't hurt, either."

"Yeah, probably," Randy admitted. "I just wish we could fuel up here at the marina. It would sure make things easier."

Foster looked toward the marina pumps. He pointed at a handmade sign mounted near the pumps. "Any idea what that says?"

"It's kind of small writing," Randy admitted. "Maybe no fuel? There's a bunch of Reapers there."

"Let's ask these guys coming our way," Foster said. "Let me do all of the talking. Do us both a favor, and don't correct me if I decide to stretch the truth at all."

"You got it," Randy said. "You think maybe they're hoarding their fuel? You know, to discourage anyone from grabbing it?"

"You want to fight through those men and their Reaper friends to double-check?"

Foster saw the color rush out of Randy's face. "N-no way," he stammered.

"Then follow my lead, and let me talk us through it instead," Foster said softly. He saw the two men were now within twenty yards of them. One of the men was wearing a holstered weapon, and Foster instinctively let his shooting hand casually drop by his side. He'd try talking to these strangers, but if things went south, he'd be ready to defend Randy and himself.

"Howdy, boys," Foster said. "Nice day, ain't it?"

"It is indeed," the double-jowled middle-aged man said. "How can we help you gentlemen?"

"Just hanging out with my cousin at his boat," Foster said. "How about you?"

"We work here," the younger man blurted out. He appeared to be sweating profusely, and Foster immediately felt his nerves begin to jangle.

"Calvin, where are your manners?" the older man scolded.

"Sorry," the young man said and immediately looked down at his feet.

"You'll need to forgive my coworker. Young folks sometimes forget their place," the man said. "Name's Walter. We work the marina pumps during the day." He offered his hand.

Foster cautiously shook it and noted Walter's handshake was dry and firm. "I'm Malcolm. This is Randy. I hope you don't mind me asking, but aren't you worried about those Reapers near the gas pumps?"

"Not at all." Walter smiled. "They're not a threat to us."

"Huh. That hasn't been my experience with Reapers."

"Why do you keep calling them that?" Calvin asked. "They're the protectors of God's chosen people."

"Well, that's what they call them in other parts of the country," Foster said. "Or at least around Philadelphia they do."

"Is that where you're from?" Walter asked.

"More or less," Foster lied. "We're planning on leaving soon. But first we need to get some fuel for our boat. We're happy to pay for it, if you're willing to sell it to us."

"I'm sorry, the fuel is private property only," Walter said. "This marina is, too."

"Sorry, I didn't know," Randy said softly. "It was night time, and I didn't see anybody else here."

"Yeah, like my cousin said, we meant no harm," Foster continued. "We just need to buy some fuel and supplies, and then we'll leave as soon as we can."

"I'm afraid it's not my decision to make," Walter said. "The marina and the fuel don't belong to me. They belong to the Disciples."

"Disciples of the Divine?" Foster asked. He felt his heart begin to sink.

"Yes. You've heard of us?" Calvin said. "I thought you just got here."

"I met some of your congregation in town," Foster said. He quickly added, "They seemed very nice."

"It pleases my heart to hear you say that," Walter said. "I'm sure Ezekiel would agree."

"Sorry, you lost me," Foster said. "Who's Ezekiel?"

"He's our pastor," Walter replied. "God has given him the ability to guide us through these troubling times. The divine spirit also saw fit to give Ezekiel the ability to control these transformed people."

"That's quite a gift," Foster said. "Would I need to talk to him about buying some fuel?"

"It's not that simple," Walter said. "Resources like fuel are hard to come by because there's no shipments coming in. They are reserved for our congregation only. I'm afraid I cannot make an exception."

"Can't or won't?" Randy demanded. "We just need some fuel, and then we'll be on our way."

"Relax, cousin," Foster warned. "These boys aren't our enemies. We'll just need to find some fuel someplace else."

"That's right," Walter said smoothly. "The truth is, you boys seem like good folks. I'm supposed to tell anyone who isn't that they're trespassing and they need to leave immediately. Seeing as your boat is on our property, well, we'd be within our rights to take it."

"I don't recommend doing that," Foster said. He let his hand drop onto his holstered Glock. "Friend."

"Malcolm, relax," Walter said in a soothing voice. "I didn't say we wanted to do that. You boys seem like good folks. But I do have people I need to answer to."

"Everybody does," Foster said. His hand stayed planted against his Glock, ready to pull it if needed. "What's your point?"

"My point is you'll need to move your boat soon," Walter said. "I can give you a day or two at most. After that, my hands are tied. If you and your boat are still here, then you'll need to surrender to our constables."

"The boat or us?" Randy stammered.

"Why, both." Walter smiled. "We live in a very dangerous world now, friends. Being part of our Disciples is the only way we can guarantee you and your property are kept safe."

Foster saw the color leave Randy's face once more.

"It's a big decision to make," Foster said carefully. "One that I don't think we should rush into. Can you give us a few days to think on it? I'd also like to see how the rest of the town is doing. Make sure it's safe for us to stay here. If you don't mind, maybe we'll attend one of your congregation's ministries, too."

"We would like that," Walter said. "I need to get back to work. Calvin, why don't you give these boys directions to the church?"

"Yes, sir," Calvin mumbled.

"Two days, gentlemen. I will need your answer then," Walter said as he backed away. He made a show of opening hands outward like what he was about to say was out of his control. "Best I can do for you under the circumstances."

"We'll let you know then," Foster answered. "Thanks."

Calvin watched Walter walk away before speaking. "You seem like good people," Calvin said. He lowered his voice to a near whisper. "Get out of town as soon as you can. You don't and you won't ever get to leave until you die. Understand me?"

"Yes. Why are you telling us this?" Foster asked.

"If anybody asks, you didn't hear it from me." Calvin spun on his heels and hurried after his boss.

"Strange guy," Randy muttered.

"Strange people, too," Foster quipped. "Sounds like we have two days tops to get out of town before we have a bunch of trouble that we don't want. Let's do a quick check on the boat and then talk."

CHAPTER TWENTY-SEVEN

The two men made their way onto *The Lauren.* Once on board, Foster began actively checking the immediate surroundings. He wasn't very familiar with boats, but he hoped he could see if anything appeared to be out of place. After getting the full tour, Foster was convinced the boat was exactly as Randy had described it. *The Lauren* was in good operating condition but had almost no supplies remaining on it.

"What do you think?" Randy asked.

"Hold that thought," Foster said in a low voice. "Let's head back to the truck. I'm not sure if those guys come back again, they'll be as polite."

"Okay," Randy said nervously.

The two men walked quietly back to the Suburban.

Randy started to get into the vehicle, but Foster motioned for him to stay put. There was a man about two hundred yards away that appeared to be watching them. Foster decided to keep an eye on the man while Randy and he talked.

"We're going to need some food and water for our trip," Foster said softly.

"Shouldn't need much," Randy said, following Foster's lead on keeping his voice low. "It probably won't take us more than a day to get there."

"Maybe, but I'd feel better if we had two or even three days' worth of food in case we run into a problem."

"I guess, but I'm worried about all of the weight we're adding on the boat."

"You mentioned that before," Foster said. "Is it going to be close?"

"Hard to say. I think if everybody brings the bare minimum, we should be okay."

"With the Disciple guards, I'd say fueling up at the marina is no longer an option."

"What about a surprise attack?" Randy asked. "Walker, Sams, and you are all experienced shooters."

"And?"

"And if you hit them fast, we might be able to fuel up quick and scoot before they realize what happened."

"Take a glance at the fueling area," Foster said. He saw Randy turning his body toward it and quickly added, "Just with your eyes."

"Sorry," Randy muttered. He turned back toward Foster and moved his eyes instead. "Lots of open space between here and there."

"That's right. There's also a dozen Reapers near the pumps too. We don't know if they increase their security at night or not. But that's probably a moot point."

"Why?"

"Because if the Disciples don't see us coming, then the Reapers will probably hear us," Foster said. "Either one can call for reinforcements."

"Ah, hell. It looks like we're going to have to transport fuel here, then."

"Yeah, looks like. How much fuel are we talking?"

"Good question," Randy said. He scratched his chin as he thought aloud. "*The Lauren* has an eighty-four gallon tank in her. How far away is this place we're heading to?"

"Almost four hundred miles by land. No clue what it is by sea."

"Huh. I'd feel better if I could look at a nautical chart and get the exact distance," Randy said. "But let's suppose it's the same distance by sea. My boat has a three hundred horsepower motor. We'll burn thirty gallons of fuel every hour."

"Ouch. You're talking about needing to stop for fuel every couple of hours."

"Afraid so."

"Is there a way that we can extend the amount of fuel that we have?"

"Not really. We don't have a lot of options," Randy said. "We could add canisters of fuel on the boat, but those portable jugs can be pretty dangerous if they're not put someplace securely."

"How fast can your boat go?"

"Well, the boat's capable of going 40 miles per hour. But running at top speed will cause us to burn fuel even quicker."

"Which means even more fuel stops."

"And a rougher ride for anyone who suffers from motion sickness."

"Huh, I hadn't thought of that," Foster said. "I honestly don't know if anyone in our group would be affected."

"That's another reason to not run the boat at full throttle," Randy said. "I think it's better to average a steady twenty knots instead. That's not full speed, but it's still moving at a good clip, and we'll get better fuel efficiency."

"Tell me about the extra fuel tanks."

"Portable fuel canisters. They got ones designed for being on boats. But to be honest, they make a lot of boat owners nervous as hell to have on board. Including me."

"How big of containers are we talking about?"

"Well, they make them in all sizes, but the ones that are probably easiest to find would be six or twelve gallon," Randy said. "I've seen a few twelve-gallon tanks that actually have a set of wheels."

"So you can roll them like a piece of luggage?"

"Yes, that's right."

"So if we're able to add one or two of those twelve-gallon tanks, canisters, then that'll extend how much longer we can travel before we need to stop for gas," Foster said. "It would give us more control about where we stop for more fuel."

"I suppose, but it's-"

"We don't have to open it up full speed," Foster interrupted. "We just need to make consistent progress. We have binoculars, so if we use them to watch the shoreline, we might be able to pick the places to dock where there's no Reaper activity."

"Yeah, but those fuel canisters can be pretty dangerous," Randy said. "If that shit blows up on the boat, then we're all in deep trouble."

"I understand," Foster said. "Let me see if I can raise Nick." He pulled out the walkie-talkie, clicked twice, waited, then clicked it twice more.

A moment later, he heard the same pattern repeated back to him.

"Nick or Sams," Foster said. "Come in, please?"

"Good timing," Walker answered. "We're just getting ready to leave home plate. What's up?"

Foster noticed Walker was using baseball lingo to help disguise where they might be located. He decided he'd do the same. "We struck out on the marina fuel," Foster said. "I'll explain later, but I need to add something to your shopping list."

"Copy that. What are we looking for?"

"Portable fuel canisters," Foster said. "They need to be rated for nautical use."

"You want to take fuel on the boat with us?" Walker said. "Isn't that dangerous?"

"Possibly. But for now we need to use them to fuel the boat."

"You can't get fuel at the marina?"

"Negative," Foster said. "Like I said, I'll fill you in when we're back at the clubhouse."

"Uh-huh," Walker said. "Can't wait to hear it."

"If you can find six or twelve-gallon size ones, that might work best," Foster said. "I think bigger might be cumbersome to move, unless it has wheels."

"I'll see what we can do, but I'm not gonna make any promises."

"Fair enough. Good hunting, boys."

"Likewise," Walker said. "See you later."

"We use those canisters to carry the fuel onto the boat," Randy said, "but we're still going to need eighty-four gallons. That's gonna be a lot of trips back and forth to a gas station."

"We don't have to just get it from the station. We can also drain it from our automobiles," Foster said. "We're not planning on taking them with us. And since we've been driving them, we know the gas in their tanks is still good."

"This actually might work," Randy said. "As long as Murphy's Law doesn't rear its ugly head."

"Then let's hope Mr. Murphy decides to go on vacation this week." Foster smiled.

CHAPTER TWENTY-EIGHT

Foster and Randy finally caught a bit of good luck outside of the marina when they found a deserted truck complete with empty boat hitch. There was a dead man slumped over the steering wheel. The body held a revolver loosely in his right hand. There was a visible bite mark on his left forearm. Despite Randy's reservations about searching the truck, they hit pay dirt in the truck's covered hatchback. Inside there were two empty canisters that Randy claimed were nautical rated. The two men grabbed them and headed back to Gregory's home. About an hour later, Walker and Sams arrived. The former Rangers had brought back a truckload of scavenged supplies, including two brand-new wheelable twelve-gallon nautical fuel tanks.

Foster, Randy, Sams, and Walker had taken turns showering while Gregory and Amanda prepared dinner for the group.

A freshly-showered Foster had come downstairs and found a veritable feast of baked manicotti, broiled steaks, and baked spare ribs spread out on the table.

"Damn, I could learn to eat like this all the time," Foster quipped.

"Don't get too used to it," Amanda replied. "This was the last of the food in Gregory's freezer. Lauren said the boat's freezer wouldn't be big enough to store it. We figured it was better than leaving it behind."

"Gotcha," Foster said. "Can someone pass the mashed potatoes?"

Gregory offered the heaping bowl. As he transferred it into Foster's waiting hands, he said, "I heard there was a problem with the marina."

"Yeah, there was. The fuel and a good portion of the marina is controlled by the Disciples," Foster said. "We had a bit of a run-in with them."

"Is it bad?" Gregory asked.

"Well, I wouldn't call it good," Foster said. "They gave us two days to decide if we're joining or getting out of town."

"Which sounds like we need to be out of there in a day and a half tops," Walker answered.

"My thoughts exactly," Foster said. "Gregory, do you have that location where we can get fuel?"

"Yeah. There's a neighborhood gas station that some of the locals like to use. It's not in Disciple territory."

"Is it close?"

"About a mile away," Gregory said. "It's in a part of town where a good number of people left when things started getting crazy around here."

"That should work," Foster said. "Randy and I'll hit that tomorrow. I could use somebody else to go with us when we get the fuel."

"I could go," Lizzy said, "but I'm not sure how much help I'll be in lifting full fuel canisters."

Foster started to speak and caught Walker giving him the stink eye. It was obvious what the former Ranger thought about his wife joining Foster and Randy on the future scavenging mission. "Uh, let me think about it and get back to you."

"I'd just like to get out of the house," Lizzy said. "You know, do something to help out there, for a change."

"There's a lot of things we need to get done here, too," Sams pointed out. "Staying here to fortify the place, reload ammo, and other critical tasks has been a big help for the entire group."

"Speaking of ammo, I've got some things to work on," Walker said. "I got a new idea on something, which might help."

"Okay, great," Foster said. "Is there anything you need us to do?"

"I think I'm okay for now, but I'll let you know if that changes."

"Nick and I managed to grab a bunch of packaged food. Between what we have here and today's run, we probably have at least two days' worth of food for everybody now," Sams said. "But that still leaves water to worry about. Does the boat have a desalinization unit?"

"Randy?" Lauren asked. "Does the boat have one of those things?"

"Yes, it does." Randy smiled. "I added one about two months ago. Gives us fresh water while we're offshore. It probably wouldn't hurt to grab some additional filters for it if we can."

"Maybe we can do some scavenging tomorrow and find them. How quickly does the machine work?"

"Not very," Randy admitted. "I bought it secondhand. We might have to be a bit skimpy with sharing water during the first leg of the trip while it works."

"Twelve people, including kids, not be able to drink any water for four to eight hours?" Sams thought aloud. "It's doable, but wouldn't be my first choice."

"I agree," Foster said. "Since it's a secondhand unit, we also need to worry about it crapping out during the journey."

Randy protested, "It's not going to-"

"I'm hoping you're right and it works flawlessly," Foster said. "But what if it doesn't?"

"Then we'd have a problem," Walker admitted. "I'd rather plan for the worst and not need it than get caught with our pants around our ankles."

"Nicholas," Lizzy warned.

"Everybody knows what I meant," Walker said. "Clean drinking water is more important than food."

"Then we're going to need a bunch of water," Foster said. "Figure at least two gallons per person. With a dozen of us, we're looking at twenty-five gallons of water for the trip."

"That's about what my boat's water tank will hold," Randy said. "But I'm worried about the amount of weight we're going to put on *The Lauren.* If you add fifty or one hundred pounds of water, the twelve of us, and all of our stuff, we might be sitting low in the water."

"So?" Randall said. "What's the big deal?"

"If there's debris in the water, we'll be more vulnerable to damaging the hull or running aground when we go to dock."

"You worry too much," Randall said. "We'll be fine. Please pass the steak before Sams eats all of them."

"What?" Sams protested. "It's incredible."

"It is quite good," Foster admitted.

"It's not just good," Sams continued. "It's awesome. Amanda, you're gonna make a great wife for some lucky guy someday."

"I'm sure I will," Amanda smirked, "but I didn't make the steak."

"Wait, what?" Sams stammered. "Then who did?"

Gregory raised his hand slowly, and the room erupted in laughter.

"Ah, hell." Sams groaned. "Sorry, man."

"So now that we've gotten the Derrick putting his foot in his mouth part of our program out of the way," Foster grinned, "let's talk about what we need to get done tomorrow."

"What do you need us to do?" Gregory said.

"We need bottled water," Foster said. "Any additional packaged food can't hurt. If we don't use it on the boat, then we can bring it with us onto Hope Island. Gregory, maybe Amanda and you can go look for supplies in one of the places in town that you think are safest. Randall and Lauren, maybe you can get the kids to help you start packing. Focus on just the bare necessities for your families."

A chorus of yeses sounded out briefly. Foster took a deep breath and continued speaking. "Randy and I will go out for fuel. Nick and Sams, maybe you guys can go out and get additional supplies. If you see any additional fuel canisters, that might be good."

"What about me?" Lizzy said. "You gave tasks for everyone but me."

Foster glanced at Walker quickly and saw the man was staring even more intently at him.

"What about staying on guard duty?" Foster suggested. "With most of us out of the house tomorrow, we could really use somebody to stay on their toes in case any Reapers show up."

"We'll see about that," Lizzy said. She turned and stalked out of the room.

"Maybe I should go talk to her," Walker said softly.

"I think that would be best," Foster said. He shot his friend a look that suggested he was at fault for Lizzy being so upset.

"Right." Walker sighed. He turned and walked slowly after his wife.

"Randy, can you make a list of what type of filters you need for the desalinization unit?"

"Sure."

"Great. And if you think of anything else we really need for the boat, please write that down. It will help the rest of us with trying to track those things down."

"Of course," Randy said. "How long you figure it'll take us to do all of these things tomorrow?"

"Good question," Foster said. "I'd like us to head out tomorrow morning and meet back here by lunchtime. If we get everything done in time, then maybe we can take off tomorrow afternoon."

"Sounds like a plan," Sams said. He leaned over and stabbed the last remaining steak and pulled it onto his plate. "I'll take the last steak and first watch tonight."

CHAPTER TWENTY-NINE

It was early morning when Foster found Randy and Lizzy both waiting for him by the back door.

"Malcolm, I'm going," Lizzy said firmly, with her hands on her hips. "It's not up for discussion."

"What about keeping everyone else safe here?" Foster asked.

"Not my problem right now. Why don't you ask my thick-headed, knuckle-dragging husband if he wants to do it?"

"If I was you," Randy cautioned, "I wouldn't do that. It might wind up being harmful to your health."

"I don't see any need to ask Nick. It sounds like Lizzy and her husband reached some type of understanding," Foster said simply. He could only imagine what kind of verbal battle had taken place last night between the Walkers. Especially since Nick and Sams had left earlier than planned to begin their scavenging run. He looked at Randy and Lizzy. Both of them seemed nervous but ready to go. Foster motioned for the two of them to follow him. "Let's roll."

The Reaper sat on the hill approximately five hundred yards away from the humans. He watched as they came and went into a strange structure. A small voice in the back of his head told him it was called a house, but he didn't have any way to know for sure. What he did know is that his master would be pleased he found these people. It looked like several of them could be ideal candidates to join their pack. He'd been watching this structure since his scouting groups had sensed there might be humans in it. He'd sent them back to the den and personally kept watch all night long.

His master had chosen him because he always followed his master's orders. In this case, they were to find humans but not attack them. Even so, he might risk his master's ire and ask him if it would be okay to feed on one of the smaller humans. They probably wouldn't make a very suitable packmate.

He felt a rumbling in his belly. The same small voice told him it meant he was hungry. Which was completely true. He'd happily feed, if given the opportunity.

But he'd seen how his master had punished other packmates who failed to follow their leader's commandments. And avoiding his master's disapproval meant far more to him than a new potential meal. He carefully climbed down from his perch. It was time to return home. He couldn't wait to tell his master what he had seen.

Ten minutes later, Foster pulled the Suburban to a stop at the gas station. He shifted the vehicle into park and shut the engine off, leaving the keys in the ignition.

"I don't understand why we had to bring this big gas guzzler," Lizzy complained.

"Simple," Foster answered. "It has lots of cargo space so we can store more cans of fuel. It's also got a bigger gas tank than the Tucson or Land Cruiser. That means we can roll out of here with the most potential fuel for one trip. We can even drain fuel from this vehicle's gas tank to help with topping off the boat."

"Gonna take more than a topping off," Randy pointed out. "My boat holds eighty-four gallons of fuel."

"I figure we're going to have to make at least two gas station runs," Foster said. "Especially if we take some extra fuel on the boat."

"The place looks quiet," Lizzy said.

"Gotta love gas stations off the beaten path," Randy replied. "Nobody but the locals know they exist. It doesn't get a lot of traffic, but even so we need to keep an eye out for any would-be stragglers."

"How do you want to do this?" Lizzy asked.

"Well, I'm guessing there isn't going to be anybody working at the station for us to pay," Foster said. "We'll try using a credit card to start."

"Do you think they'll still work?" Randy asked.

"Hope so. I'd prefer not to steal the gasoline," Foster said. "Especially if the Disciples show up acting like they're the local law enforcement. No point in giving them an excuse to give us any unwanted trouble." He checked his surroundings and got out of the driver's side door. He closed the door carefully, ensuring the noise was kept to a bare minimum. He watched as Randy and Lizzy climbed out the other side and did the same.

"Lizzy, I want you on the front side of the vehicle. Keep an eye out for any incoming visitors," Foster said. "I'll watch the back side while Randy fills the canisters."

"Gotcha," Lizzy said. She drew a Glock from the holster on her right hip and held it in a ready position. Foster would have felt more comfortable if the woman was using a rifle, but she confessed that she felt far more comfortable with a handgun.

"Good news," Randy said. "It looks like they still have electricity here."

"Awesome," Foster said. He pulled out his wallet, grabbed his American Express card, and offered it to Randy. He'd worry about paying the bill at a later time. That was assuming it would ever arrive in the mail. "Use this," he said.

"Thanks," Randy said as he grabbed the card and swiped it. "Pump is live."

"Great," Foster said. "Do the Suburban's tank first and then the containers."

"Why?" Randy asked. "We need fuel for the boat, not the Suburban."

"If we have to bail fast, we can always drain gas from the Suburban someplace safe and put it into containers for the boat then."

"If you say so."

"According to the owner's manual, the Suburban's tank holds thirty-one gallons of fuel," Foster said. "You got a bigger container here that I might have overlooked?"

"Yeah, yeah," Randy grumbled. "No need to rub it in."

"Here, let me help," Foster said. He hurried over and unscrewed the cap on the first container. He set it on the ground near Randy and lined up the other ones, repeating the process with each fuel canister. He watched as Randy pulled the nozzle out of the fuel pump and inserted it into the side of the Suburban. Foster turned his attention back to watching the surrounding area for any Reapers.

"Pump is working really slow," Randy called out.

"Damn. Any ideas why?"

"Maybe a clogged fuel filter," Randy said. "Other possibility is the station's underground tank might be low. I'm guessing it's been a while since this place had a fuel delivery."

"There's nothing we can do to fix either one of those problems right now."

"Want to go to another gas station?" Randy asked. "It might go faster."

"It could be eyeball deep in Reapers or Disciples, too," Foster answered. "I'm afraid I don't know this area very well. Do you know of any other gas stations nearby?"

"Afraid not. I'm Virginia-born and raised."

"Gotcha," Foster said. "I'm going to go back to keeping an eye out for trouble."

A few minutes later, he heard Randy call out, "Suburban's full. Switching to the canisters now."

"Good," Lizzy said. "The sooner we get done here, the better."

"Anything on your side, Lizzy?" Foster asked. "I got nothing on my end."

"Still quiet," Lizzy answered. "This place just gives me the creeps."

A few minutes later, Randy called out, “Moving on to the second canister.”

“That was quicker than I expected,” Foster said. “Not that I’m complaining.”

“It doesn’t take long to fill a six-gallon canister,” Randy pointed out. “If this thing was pumping anywhere the normal ten gallons per minute speed, we’d be further along than we already are.”

“You know how fast gas is supposed to pump?” Foster said. “I didn’t have the foggiest idea.”

“Not by choice,” Randy admitted. “I got a buddy, Del, who worked at a gas station. At least, I did before all of this stuff happened. He used to like to share gas station trivia after he’d gotten a few beers under his belt. That’s how I knew about the fuel filter stuff.”

“Makes sense,” Foster said. “Do you know if your friend is, you know?”

“Alive? No clue. When the shit hit the fan, I was more worried about getting my family the hell out of Raleigh. But I tend to doubt it. Del rented a room near the gas station in town.”

“Guys, I got something,” Lizzy said excitedly.

“What is it?” Foster asked.

“I see a Reaper.”

“Hold your fire,” Foster said. “We don't want to engage them if we don't need to.” He quickly added, “How far out?”

“Maybe two hundred yards?”

“Keep an eye on them.”

“Oh, hell.”

“What's wrong?” Foster asked.

“They're moving this way.”

Foster swore under his breath. “I knew we should've brought another person,” he said. “Randy, how's it coming with the fuel canisters?”

“Two done, four to go.”

“Coming to you,” Foster said as he moved toward Randy. “I’ll load the full ones. Keep pumping fuel as long as you can.”

“Just make sure none of those things eat my face. ’Cause Lauren will be awfully mad at both of us if they do.”

Foster reached Randy, grabbed the two full containers, and carried them to the back of the Suburban. He placed both of them on the open hatch and slid each one into the back of the vehicle. Foster then worked his way along the driver's side of the vehicle and began to head toward the front where Lizzy was still on overwatch.

"There's four of them now," Lizzy said, her voice noticeably straining with each word.

"Coming up on your left," Foster said. "Don't shoot me." He continued to scan the area in front of him as he moved. As he reached the front of the Suburban, he noticed three more Reapers appear at the edge of the woods. They were about three hundred and fifty yards away.

"Randy, time to wrap it up," Foster said in a low voice. He brought his rifle up into a shooting position.

"Just a little longer," Randy replied. "I got three cans left."

"We're about to have company," Foster said. "I need you to stop pumping fuel and get those cans loaded in the truck."

"Are you serious?" Randy said. "I could use a hand if we're gonna get it done fast."

"You want me to help you with the cans or keep them from eating your face? Because I can't do both at once."

A shot rang out, and Foster saw one of the Reapers get struck in the chest. A fresh wound appeared and Foster watched as it immediately began to close back up. The Reaper began to run toward them.

"Head shots only," Foster said. "Wait until they're closer to engage."

"I know that," Lizzy shouted. "This is not the first time I've fought Reapers."

Foster bit back a snarky comment. Now wasn't the time to argue with Lizzy. They had to work together, or all of them could likely fall to the incoming pack. Foster shifted his aim, acquired the charging Reaper, and fired once. He saw his shot strike the monster in the shoulder. The Reaper staggered back on its heels and then dropped onto all fours and continued to charge toward them. Foster felt a jolt of adrenaline course through his body. He adjusted his aim and fired twice. Foster saw one of the shots score a direct hit to the monster's throat. The Reaper spun like some type of demented top and crashed sideways to the ground.

Foster shifted his aim to the next incoming target. He heard Lizzy firing, too.

"Lizzy, take out the ones that get past the gas station sign," Foster shouted. "I'll use my rifle to pick off the ones farther out."

"I-I'm trying, Malcolm," Lizzy yelled back. "Changing."

"Covering you," Foster said. He fired a double-tap at a Reaper that had managed to get about twenty yards away. He saw the top of the monster's head explode in a crimson fury. The Reaper collapsed harmlessly nearby, but Foster didn't have time to admire his handiwork. He pivoted seamlessly to his left and fired three times, kneecapping a pair of Reapers which had been charging toward his blind side. The flurry of lead hobbled the hostiles long enough for Foster to carefully aim a head shot at each one. The demonic duo were dropped in their tracks, and Foster heard gunfire to his right once more. He wasn't sure how many bullets were left in his current magazine and silently cursed himself for losing track during a firefight.

"Reloading," Foster said. "Cover me."

"Hurry up!" Lizzy shouted back.

Foster pulled the rifle's current magazine and slammed a fresh one in its place. He seamlessly tucked the empty magazine in his vest and brought his weapon back up to play.

Foster spotted a Reaper just outside the gas station sign coming toward them. From its physical build and the tattered three-piece suit it was wearing, he quickly determined this hostile had once been a businessman. The monster suddenly stopped its charge, banged on its chest, and let out a loud roar. Foster sighted on the Reaper's face and immediately shot it between the eyes. He watched the monster's head snap back, and then the creature toppled backward and went limp.

"Dumbass," Foster muttered under his breath.

There was a series of growls and yips from the dead monster's right, and then a dozen more Reapers came charging out of the woods.

"Oh, hell," Foster moaned. Maybe that Reaper hadn't been so stupid after all. The damn thing had managed to call in additional reinforcements before Foster had managed to kill it. He shifted his aim and resumed firing more.

"Randy, what's going on with the fuel?" Foster yelled.

"Still working on it."

"Leave the rest of them. We gotta go."

"I just need a little more time."

"Not happening. We're out of time," Foster said, firing even more rapidly. He heard Lizzy's gunfire joining in. "Get as many of those cans as you can in the truck now."

Foster heard Randy swear out loud and shifted his attention back to firing again. Then he heard the weapon click dry.

"Changing," Foster said as he performed a fast combat swap. He brought his weapon up to fire and saw there were dozens of Reapers now pouring in from different directions.

"Lizzy, fall back and help Randy get the canisters into the vehicle."

"Really? You expect me to lift those things?"

"Would you rather stay here and deal with all of these by yourself?"

"You don't have to be a jerk about it," Lizzy yelled. "I'm moving."

Foster continued shooting. He performed another combat swap and kept shooting. There were dozens of dead Reapers around them now, and he saw nearly as many still emerging from the woods in front of him.

Foster heard a pounding sound on the Suburban behind him, and then Randy shouted, "Move your ass, Yankee." He heard two doors slam behind him and began working his way back toward the driver's side door, firing every step of the way. Foster opened the driver's side door, jumped in, and pulled the door shut right behind him. He heard the locks engage, and then a trio of Reapers slammed into the passenger side of the Suburban. Lizzy screamed in surprise, and Foster felt his heart slam even faster against his chest. He turned the key in the Suburban's ignition, and the engine turned over immediately. He threw the vehicle in drive and stomped on the gas accelerator. The Suburban lurched forward, pushing several Reapers out of the way, and began to slowly build up speed. Foster cut the steering wheel toward the roadway and felt the tires grab the smoother surface with ease.

The Suburban picked up speed, and he glanced in the rearview mirror, seeing the carnage they had managed to escape from unharmed.

"Holy cow," Randy said. "That was close."

"Too close," Foster agreed. "Do we head back or try to find another gas station and collect some more fuel?"

"I say head back," Randy replied. "I don't have the foggiest idea where to find another gas station. Especially one that doesn't have either Reapers or those Disciple wackos hanging around."

"Good point," Foster said. "Return to home base it is."

"Malcolm, I'm sorry I yelled at you," Lizzy said. "I-I guess I just panicked a little, with all of those things rushing toward us."

"Apology accepted." Foster smiled. "Even seasoned cops and military personnel get scared sometimes."

"Do you think we got enough fuel?" Lizzy asked.

"I hope so," Randy said. "If not, it's gonna be a long swim to Hope Island."

CHAPTER THIRTY

After leaving the gas station, the three of them headed back to their makeshift base. As they pulled up behind Gregory's house, Foster noticed Nick and Sams had already returned from their scavenging mission. The rear door opened, and Walker stepped outside to greet them.

"Good timing," Walker said. "We just got back a little while ago."

"How did it go?" Foster asked.

"Struck out on the filters," Walker said. "We did find about six gallons of water."

"That's not going to be enough," Foster said. "Maybe Gregory and Amanda will get lucky and find some more."

"Yeah, maybe," Walker said. "We saw several Reaper packs moving around."

"Any problems with them?" Foster asked.

"Not this time," Walker said. "We were able to avoid them. But I got the sense they're starting to linger around some of the more obvious places to scavenge."

"Like they've been ordered to stand guard?"

"Yeah, exactly. I think I'm going to work on my latest weapon idea some more."

"Good idea," Foster said. "I wish you'd had better luck with those desalinization filters."

"Already ahead of you on that," Walker said. "I asked our local yokel about it."

"What did Gregory say?"

"There's a marine supply store in the middle of town. The problem is it's smack-dab in the middle of Disciple territory."

"Which means we need to be careful if we go there," Foster said. "I think Randy and I could pull it off. Especially if we play it off as being new-in-town visitors."

"Yeah, that could work," Walker replied. "Let me get cracking on the weapon tinkering."

"Would you like some help?" Lizzy asked shyly.

"I would love some," Walker smiled. He placed his arm around his wife's shoulder, and the two of them began walking toward the house.

"Nick, you mind if I store the fuel in the back of the Land Cruiser?" Foster shouted.

"Not at all. It's unlocked," Walker called back. "There's a holster in the back if you need it." The former Ranger steered his wife toward the house and a moment later disappeared inside. Foster turned his attention back to the Suburban and opened the rear hatch.

"Why are we moving the fuel again?" Randy asked.

"Nick struck out on the desalinization filters," Foster answered. "We're going to visit a marine supply store in town. There could be other things we can get there."

"And if the trunk is empty, then we have a place to put it," Randy said as he reached into the back of the Suburban and grabbed a fuel canister. "Makes sense."

Foster opened the back of the Land Cruiser, grabbed the IWB holster, and donned it. The Inside the Waistband device was perfect for concealing his Glock before he went into the marine store. He grabbed a canister from Randy and began helping the man transfer the fuel.

Thirty minutes later, Foster pulled into the parking lot. He was surprised to see it was nearly vacant. He picked an open mid-aisle spot close to the West Marine store and shut off the engine.

"Why didn't you park closer to the door?" Randy asked. "There's plenty of spots there."

"We're both going into the store. You know this boating stuff far better than I do."

"You didn't answer my question."

"If things go bad in the store, I want to make sure nobody blocks us in and we can get out of the lot," Foster said. "Parking by the door cuts off one of our potential exits."

"You think we're gonna have a problem in store?"

"I hope not," Foster said. "But I'd rather prepare for trouble and be wrong than get caught with my pants down."

"Oh man, I knew I shouldn't have come with you," Randy moaned. "You're gonna get us killed."

"Have some faith," Foster said as he slid his Glock into his IWB holster and pushed his jacket back in place. Foster did a quick once-over glance and felt confident that there wasn't any noticeable weapon bulge. He opened the driver's side door and exited the Suburban. He heard the passenger door as well and knew Randy had gotten out of the vehicle, too.

"I feel like I'm going to throw up," Randy complained.

"Relax. We're just going into the store to buy some supplies."

"Yeah, okay."

On the other side of the parking lot, a man was slouching low behind the steering wheel of a beat-up Honda Odyssey. When he'd joined the Disciples, the powers that be decided his birth name of Andrei Jesus Martinez was too long and simply dubbed him Andy. It made him seethe inside, but it was a small slight for the protection being a member of the group provided him. Andy had pulled the watch shift for the lot today. It had been three hours of mind-numbing duty until the dark-colored Suburban pulled in and parked. He brought up a pair of binoculars and saw two men climb out of the SUV. He reached for a walkie-talkie sitting on the passenger seat, brought it up to his mouth, and depressed the transmit button.

"Guardian Central, this is Andy," he said. "What kind of vehicle was added to last night's watch report?" He released the transmit button and waited.

There was a brief pause, and then a voice answered, "A Suburban. Why?"

"I got one that just parked outside West Marine," he said. "Two men just went into the store."

A new voice sounded over the walkie. "Andy, this is Walter. We can be there in ten minutes."

"A-are they dangerous?" Andy stammered. "I'm not armed."

"Probably not," Walter said. "But it can't hurt to be cautious. If they come out of the store before we get there, I just need you to stall them for a few minutes."

"How do you want me to do that?" Andy demanded.

"Use your head," Walter snapped. "Ask them for directions or something. Just keep them from leaving before I get there."

The door's bell sounded out, announcing their arrival as Foster and Randy stepped into the West Marine store. As the two men stepped into the store, Foster was immediately impressed by the size. This place definitely had a number of things that would be good to add to their supplies.

"Can I help you?" a voice said. Foster turned toward it, and then the man immediately blurted out, "Oh, it's you."

"Hi, Calvin," Foster said. "Long time no see."

"What are you doing?" Calvin hissed. "You shouldn't be here."

Foster looked the man over. Calvin was dressed differently than the last time he had seen him. Today the man was wearing a West Marine staff shirt along with a pair of jeans. The Disciple armband was openly on display, wrapped around the man's left bicep.

"We just needed to get some supplies," Foster said. "Then we'll be on our way."

Another man came up. "Are you being helped?"

"Yeah, I got them," Calvin said loudly. "Jonathan, why don't you go on break?"

"Uh, okay. Friends of yours?"

"A couple of candidates. I met them at the last meeting," Calvin said quickly. "Don't worry, they're okay."

"If you say so," Jonathan said. "Since you offered, I'm stepping out for a smoke."

Calvin waited until his coworker was gone and then blurted, "Do you realize how much trouble I can get in, lying for you?"

"We appreciate it," Foster said. "Like I said, we just want to get a few supplies and get out of here."

"Wait, I thought you worked at the marina," Randy said. "What are you doing here?"

"They rotate some of us sometimes based on where they need us. Somebody called out sick at the marina yesterday, so Walter asked me to go there and help."

"Then who covered this store?"

"Just Jonathan. But it's not a big deal," Calvin said. "There aren't too many people coming in here lately. What do you need?"

"Couple of life jackets and some fishing supplies," Foster said. "Maybe a few other things to help restock the boat."

"Water filters, too. If you got them," Randy added.

"I don't think we have any left," Calvin said. He rushed along, grabbing stuff off the shelves. Foster spotted the life jackets stacked on a floor-level shelf. There were only two remaining, and he grabbed them both.

"Wait a minute," Calvin said in an accusatory fashion. "You don't already have life jackets in your boat?"

"They're in bad shape," Foster lied. "I figured we might as well replace them while we have the chance."

"Uh-huh," Calvin said. He began shoving the items into a shopping bag.

"How much we owe you?" Foster said. "Wait, why aren't you ringing that up?"

"You need to get out of here," Calvin said. "No charge today."

"What about the water filters?" Randy asked.

"No time. You need to leave right now," Calvin said nervously. "If anybody asks, you didn't get any of this from me or talk to me."

"Got it," Foster said. "Come on, Randy, let's go. Thanks Calvin."

The man made a dismissive motion and scurried back into the stockroom.

Foster grabbed the shopping bags and headed for the front door with Randy following him a few steps behind.

Foster moved to the Suburban, unlocked the doors, and put the bags into the back seat. He closed the door and reached for the driver's side door.

As he did, a voice called out, "Hi, can you help me?"

"I'm not sure," Foster said carefully. "What do you need?"

A man was peeking around the corner of a Honda Odyssey, and Foster frowned. He didn't remember seeing the vehicle when they entered the store.

"Relax, man. We mean you no harm," Foster said loudly. He slowly dropped his right hand to his waist and let it hang there. If his instincts about this stranger were wrong, then he could easily grab his concealed Glock in a few seconds. "Why don't you step out where we can see, and then we can talk."

A man slowly moved away from the minivan with his hands raised above his head. "Don't shoot," he said.

"Relax," Foster answered. "What's your name?"

"A-Andy," the man said nervously. He unconsciously took the green scarf that was dangling loosely from his neck and tossed it back over his shoulder. A split second later, he realized his mistake of moving unexpectedly and blurted, "Sorry, I just—"

"It's okay," Foster said. "Are you here alone?"

"N-no," Andy stammered. "Well, I mean, my family is nearby. I'm just looking for food for them. Can you help?"

"I'm afraid we don't have any on us," Foster said. "There's a few stores nearby. Have you tried any of them yet?"

"Not yet. I-I saw some strange men with guns near one of them. I was afraid to go there. I-I don't want any trouble."

"I don't blame you," Foster said. "Listen, we have friends nearby. Safe lodging. If you and your family are interested."

"Thanks, but we're okay for now," Andy said. "I-if you don't mind, I'd like to get going now. I've been away too long, and my wife has to be going out of her mind worrying."

"I understand," Foster said. "Stay safe."

"You too," Andy said before darting back to the Odyssey. He climbed in, started the engine, and pulled away.

Foster and Randy watched him drive away in silence.

"Strange man," Randy said softly.

"Yeah. Probably better he didn't want to join us," Foster said. "Come on, let's head back and bring the rest of the group up to speed."

"Sounds good," Randy replied.

Foster began to open the Suburban's driver's side door and stopped in his tracks. He heard an engine race nearby and immediately began scanning his surroundings. As he did, two trucks pulled up in front of their Suburban and screeched to a halt.

"Oh, shit," Randy said. "Trouble."

"Hopefully not," Foster said. "Let me try and handle this."

CHAPTER THIRTY-ONE

Four men immediately piled out of the two vehicles. As they did, Foster recognized one of them.

"Walter, long time, no see." Foster said with an enthusiasm that he didn't feel. He slowly closed the driver's side door to the Suburban.

"Had a report that there was some trouble here," Walter answered back. "I didn't realize it was you boys." He glanced to his left and right before saying, "Stand down, gentlemen."

"Yeah, it's just little old us." Foster smiled.

"You're quite a ways away from the marina," Walter said. "Care to tell me what you boys are doing down here?"

"A little sightseeing. A little shopping," Foster said. "I figured we might as well since this is our first time to Rehoboth Beach."

"You don't say," Walter said as he flashed a big grin. "How are you finding things?"

"Everybody seems to be really nice," Foster said. "Really nice."

"Good, good. I'm glad to hear that," Walter said. He paused for a moment before asking, "What's in the truck?"

"Just some stuff we brought with us."

"You didn't buy anything in the boating store?" Walter asked as he began to walk around the Suburban. Foster watched him and the other three men, who had continued to stay in front.

"No, I didn't see anything we liked," Foster answered. "Turns out most of what was in there was a bit too much for our current budget, I'm afraid. We've been forced to mostly try to barter for supplies."

"That so?" Walter challenged. He pointed toward the back seat and said, "Then how come you got a bag in there that says West Marine?"

"Oh, that?" Foster said. He brought his left hand up and snapped his fingers for emphasis. "We had a bag that tore. One of the store employees was nice enough to give me a replacement bag."

"Really?" Walter said indignantly. He continued walking around the front of the Suburban and joined his men there. "You wouldn't be lying to me now, Malcolm, would you?"

"Oh, Walter, I'm deeply offended you would suggest that," Foster said. "Just what kind of man do you think I am?" He let his hand drop down to his side so it was near his holstered weapon. He began scanning the men in front of him, deciding who he might need to shoot first. One of the men had a hunting rifle slung over his right shoulder. Walter was wearing a holster, which appeared to be holding a Beretta. The other two men were armed with just baseball bats. Foster made an immediate tactical decision. If things took a turn for the worse, then he'd shoot Walter first and then the henchman with the still-slung rifle.

"I guess you're right," Walter said. "Suppose there's nothing wrong with you doing barter. Have you boys made a decision yet?"

Foster decided to play dumb. "Decision?" he asked.

"About joining or leaving the town."

"Still thinking your offer through," Foster said. "It's a very interesting offer."

"You got about another day left to make up your minds," Walter said. "Best do it quickly."

"We will. Hey, can you recommend a good restaurant around here?" Foster said. "I promised old Randy here I'd treat him to some lobster while we're in town."

"Probably nothing in your budget," Walter said with a smile. "There are a few restaurants that are a bit particular in who they serve.

These days, they feel safest with just members of Disciples as their customers. I doubt they'd be willing to barter with anyone, too."

"Well, that's a real crying shame," Foster said. "I'm disappointed to hear that. I suppose we'll just wander around and find someplace else to go. If you boys wouldn't mind moving your trucks, we'll be on our way." Foster locked eyes with Walter to see what the older man would do.

Walter looked back at him in an equally intense glare and then flashed a smile. "Well, of course. Boys, let's let our new friends here be on their way." Walter's henchmen began moving backward to the trucks.

Foster watched two of them climb into the first truck. He heard its transmission shift, and the truck began to pull away. The third cohort climbed behind the steering wheel of the remaining truck. He watched as Walter began walking toward the passenger door.

"I'm gonna need your answer tomorrow, Malcolm," he said in a menacing voice. "Please don't keep me waiting."

"You'll have it," Foster replied. He watched Walter climb into the truck and slam the door shut, and then the vehicle pulled away.

"Holy shit," Randy blurted. "How do you do that?"

"It comes with being a cop," Foster said. "Come on, let's get the hell out of here."

"Werc you really going to buy me a lobster?"

"Sure," Foster said. "Right after I win the damn lottery. Come on, man. We got things to do."

The two men climbed into the Suburban. Foster took one last glance around the parking lot and didn't see any other vehicles.

"I bet that guy Andy was a Disciple," Foster thought aloud.

"The weird guy with the scarf?" Randy asked.

"Yeah. It's a helluva coincidence he bailed less than a minute before Walter's crew showed up. Makes me think maybe he was buying time until they arrived." Foster turned the ignition, and the Suburban's engine roared to life. He shifted it into gear and headed for the nearest exit. If he had any doubt about Walter's threat before, he didn't now. They had less than twenty-four hours to get out of town, and Foster intended to do exactly that.

Calvin heard someone coming through the store's rear entrance and put the month-old *Reader's Digest* back on the manager's desk.

"Jonathan, you took long enough for your break," Calvin said as he turned toward the sound. He saw the men approaching him and his heart dropped. "I swear I didn't do anything," Calvin stammered.

He saw Walter's hand raise back, and then it came at his face in a rush. He felt the man's hand slam into his cheek, and the blow dropped him to one knee.

"I told you what would happen if you meddled," Walter said. "But you wouldn't listen."

"I didn't. I swear I-"

"Take him, boys."

"No, no, please," Calvin pleaded. "Walter, please."

Three men bent over, grabbed Calvin, and began to drag him out from the store. Calvin continued to scream for help that was never going to come.

CHAPTER THIRTY-TWO

There was a long, loud banging sound, and Vasquez bolted up in her bunk with a start. She looked around, trying to get her bearings and figuring out which asshole had set an alarm clock to go off in the middle of the night. It was then that she remembered she had been sleeping in the pilot's quarters. She felt groggy, like she had been woken after a long night of heavy drinking. Except she hadn't had a drop of alcohol in months. Vasquez glanced at her watch and groaned. She had barely gotten three hours of rack time. Somebody was definitely going to pay for waking her up early.

Vasquez rolled out of bed and landed on her feet. She felt wobbly for a moment before her instincts kicked in and she realized it wasn't an alarm clock sounding but the base alarm.

"What the hell's going on?" Weathers yelled.

"Damn if I know," Vasquez said.

"What time is it?"

"About 0300."

"Oh man, that's cruel," Weathers groaned. "I was in the middle of a seriously good dream."

Vasquez heard several other pilots complaining in the background and tuned their voices out. Something had to be wrong for the base alarm to be going off. She immediately ruled out some asshole deciding to do a test of the emergency system. With everything going on with the Reapers, there was no need to test anyone's level of readiness. Everyone was already on their toes and ready for the fight of their lives.

"All pilots report to your planes," the PA system interrupted. "This is not a drill. All pilots report to your planes immediately."

"Dream time is over," Vasquez quipped. "Looks like our mission just got moved up." She quickly pulled on her boots and retrieved her pilot survival kit and helmet before heading for the door. If the shit truly did hit the fan, then everything she needed to survive and protect herself was in her kit. As she was approaching the opening, Ace appeared in the hallway, gesturing wildly.

"Double time, people," Ace yelled. "Base is under attack. They want us to launch now."

"You were already up?" Vasquez asked.

"Couldn't sleep," Ace answered. "I was in the mess when I heard the base alarms go off. Figured the shit had just hit the fan."

"You figured right," Vasquez said. "Good hunting, Ace."

"You too, Vas."

Vasquez picked up her pace and ran toward where her plane should be waiting for her. As she exited the building, she heard gunfire somewhere in front of her. She saw two separate groups of soldiers near the planes. The men were actively firing at Reapers. Vasquez heard a sound to her left and looked long enough to see more Reapers were attempting to climb the base's security fence.

"Keep moving," Ace yelled. "They're buying us time."

More gunfire erupted around them, and Vasquez opened her stride, picking up her speed until she was in a full sprint for her plane.

She was still fifty yards from her plane and could already see the crew chief motioning for them to hurry up.

A moment later, Vasquez was climbing into her F-35. She turned to the chief and yelled, "Stay safe, Chief. It's been a privilege to work with you."

"Yeah, you too," the chief answered. "Now, get out of here, before it's too late."

Vasquez threw a quick salute to the crew chief and began her startup sequence. She saw the plane's canopy begin to close around her, and then a moment later, the plane's engine came to life. She moved the stick and began to taxi toward the nearest runway. As she did, she saw several soldiers try to hold the line and give her time to take off. Her eyes fell on one soldier a moment before a horde of Reapers overran the man. There was a flurry of arms and legs moving, and she felt a pang of sorry for the soldier who had likely lost his life trying to give her a chance to escape.

Vasquez pushed the throttle forward a bit more and the plane immediately gained more speed. She only needed a few more seconds to reach takeoff speed. Out of the corner of her eye, she saw a pair of Reapers leap toward her plane. There was a loud thud as something hit her plane and then a low, grinding noise. Vasquez immediately pulled the control stick back, and the high-performance machine went skyward. The ground quickly disappeared below, and she took her plane up to ten thousand feet.

Ace's voice came through the comms. "Close call, Green Mountain Boys," he said. "This is Green Mountain Boy One. I need everybody to call out and let me know if you're still operational."

"Green Mountain Boy Seven," Vasquez replied. "Ready to kick some Reaper ass."

The rest of her squad sounded out, and Vasquez felt an immediate sense of relief. All of them had somehow managed to escape the base before it was overrun.

"Everybody has their targets," Ace said. "That hasn't changed, but our destination has. Hit your targets and then haul ass to Wright-Patterson Air Force Base."

"Anybody else make it out?" Stormy asked.

"Some," Ace admitted. "They're being flown to Scott Air Force Base."

"Why not Wright-Patterson?" Stormy argued.

"Somebody with more stars on their lapel made that call," Ace said. "Stormy, you are welcome to ask the brass next time you see them."

Vasquez chuckled softly. She could only hope Stormy would be foolish enough to openly question the orders that had come from their higher-ups. She quickly entered the changes to her flight plan, and the computer immediately came back with updated metrics. "Ace, my computer is saying we just added two hundred miles to our flight plan," she said. "Anybody coming up with the same math?"

"Hold on," Ace answered. "Yeah, same here."

"D.C. to Wright-Patterson only adds about eighty miles on our last leg," Conklin sounded out. "Lucky break, I guess."

"What's the big deal, Vas?" Stormy called out. "Two hundred miles farther is no big deal."

"Probably," Vasquez said. "But my fuel is already at 80 percent."

"Really?" Ace asked. "I'm at 94 percent. Anyone else seeing lower than usual fuel?"

"I'm at 89 percent," Conklin answered. "Plenty of juice to go purge the capital of Reapers and still be back to base in time for dinner."

"It'll be fine, Ace," Vasquez insisted. "Don't worry about it."

"Maybe they didn't get to finish topping off some of the planes?" Stormy offered. "You know, with the Reapers showing up to crash the party?"

"Yeah, that's probably it," Vasquez said. "It'll be fine."

"I hope you're right, Vas, but two of my flight squad have less than 90 percent fuel, and we haven't been in the air very long," Ace said. "This might affect how long we can wait to start this mission. Everybody hold position while I call it in. I have a feeling the brass are gonna weigh in on this."

CHAPTER THIRTY-THREE

As Foster stepped into the hallway, he saw Sams waiting for him. The former Ranger was gesturing hurriedly for him to pick up the pace.

"Where's the fire, Army?" Foster quipped.

"Quit dragging your feet," Sams said as he motioned for Foster to walk faster. "Come on, you've got to see this."

As Foster reached Sams, the man turned and headed into the next room. Foster followed him in, and as he did, he saw Walker standing near a table. There was a series of bullets lined up, and Nick was grinning ear to ear.

"You got something," Foster said.

"Damn right he does," Sams said. "This is a fucking game changer."

"I wouldn't say that," Walker said. "Not yet. We haven't tested them."

"Okay. Why don't you tell me what I'm looking at?"

"All right," Walker said slowly. "You know how these things get poisoned from silver, right?"

"Of course."

"Okay. And remember how I made the Reaper bullets?"

"Not really. To be honest, you kind of lost me when you were explaining it, then," Foster confessed. "The only reason why I used them initially was because I had run out of everything else. I'm just glad they worked when I fired them."

"Uh-huh, pearls before swine," Walker said. "I should have known better. These are a much simpler design. I took some hollow-point bullets and packed the tips with silver."

"Huh," Foster said. "Then how do you keep the silver from falling out? You melt it?"

"Nope," Walker said. "There's a thin layer of wax holding the silver in place. When the bullet is fired, its velocity causes the wax to begin to melt. By the time the bullet hits the Reaper, the silver is exposed. That's when the bullet punches the silver into their body."

"Like stabbing them with a silver-tipped bullet?" Foster said.

"Yeah, pretty much," Walker said. "The moment the silver punctures their body, it can begin sending them into anaphylactic shock."

"Wow. That is something," Foster said. "What kind of range do these have?"

"Range?" Sams asked. "Why would it change at all?"

"Let me word my question a little differently," Foster said. "Does the wax coating shorten the bullet's range at all? You know, before the wax is gone and the silver starts breaking or burning up, too?"

"I have no idea," Walker admitted. "That's why we need to test them. I'm also hoping that they'll work as intended."

Foster sighed. "So, we have another weapon that we need to test. What guns did you make them for?"

"The Glocks. I only have hollow points for the nine millimeters."

"I think that's a good starting point," Foster said. "If they work like we think they will, it will give our Glocks one shot, one kill ability against the Reapers. How many bullets did you make?"

"Just what you see there. I didn't have many to work with."

"It looks like about a magazine and a half," Foster said as he eyeballed the table. "That only gives each of us a handful to use."

"Which is enough, until we know for sure they work correctly," Walker said. "I figured one of us will field test it. If the first bullet doesn't take them down immediately, then at least shooting it in the head will. I can't count on anybody else in the group staying that calm when a Reaper's rushing toward them."

"Even law enforcement and military folks might shit their pants in that situation."

"Law enforcement might," Walker quipped. "Rangers would just keep firing until the hostile has been neutralized."

The three men chuckled, and Foster said, "Okay, I asked for that one."

"All right, let's talk about these bullets. The way I see it," Sams said, "If this test works, Nick is going to need a lot more hollow points and silver. If it doesn't, then we're still going to need hollow-point ammo for the Glocks."

"There is no such thing as too much ammunition," Foster and Walker said together.

The three men laughed aloud again.

"Sounds like another scavenging mission," Foster said. "Let me ask Gregory for some suggestions on where we should be looking. I prefer some place that isn't being patrolled by the Disciples."

"If you don't mind, I'd like to go with you," Walker said. "There could be other equipment I could use in creating more silver-enhanced weapons or armor, weapons, or ammunition."

"Do we want to take the enhanced bullets with us or do a small controlled test later?" Sams asked.

"My vote is controlled test later," Walker replied. "We need more hollow-point ammunition, period. I'd rather not take a chance on an untested experimental ammo failing in a serious firefight."

"I agree," Sams answered. "We'll find a few stragglers to test the new ammo on later."

"Sounds good to me," Foster said. "Let's go do some shopping."

CHAPTER THIRTY-FOUR

President Vickers was sitting at a desk in her new living quarters, tackling a growing pile of papers that needed her attention. The quarters wouldn't have been her first choice of location or décor, but like everything else that had come about her presidency, it was something forced onto her by the Reapers' actions. She suspected that she had unknowingly bumped one of the officers of the Eisenhower out of their private space. But so far, no one had fessed up on who the previous occupant had been. Vickers glanced at the office walls. There were several places where the contrast in paint color signaled something else had once hung on the walls. Those spots were now conspicuously bare. *Personal photos or maybe some type of awards? I'm definitely going to have to ask Captain Flores,* Vickers thought as she continued to scan progress reports.

There was a tap on the door, and Vickers said, "Come in, Agent Nash."

The Special-Agent-In-Charge looked in sheepishly and said, "It was the knock, right?"

"You have a very distinctive walk, too," Vickers replied. "What can I do for you?"

Nash held a satellite phone out in front of her. "Priority call from

General Weindahl." She began to walk across the room with the phone extended toward the President.

Vickers stood up, accepted the phone, and then sat back down. She held the sat phone up to the side of her face and said, "General, I'm surprised you aren't talking to me in person. We are on the same ship."

"Indeed. Unfortunately, there's too much going on for me to leave the operations center right now."

"Fair enough. What's going on, Rasheed?"

"Madam President, I regret to inform you that several of our bases have been hit by Reapers."

"How bad are we talking?"

"Four bases. Two of which were forward operating bases for Operation Flashpoint."

"Do we need to delay or scrap the mission?"

"I don't believe so. With both Dover Air Force Base and Burlington Air National Guard Base, we managed to keep casualties to a minimum and get a number of pilots out."

"Well, that's good."

"Not exactly. The problem is the planes."

"What about them?" Vickers asked.

"Fuel. They have a limited time they can stay in the air."

"Can we refuel in the air?"

"I'm being told we can't get a tanker to them before the mission is supposed to start."

"Okay, what about refueling at another base?"

"It's possible, but depending on where they are rerouted to, we might have to delay the start of Operation Flashpoint. It could also mean reassigning targets based on the plane's new locations, too. But there's another concern."

"What's that?"

"As you probably already know, military planes are not quiet machines. Their noise profile would likely draw Reapers."

Vickers scratched her cheek absently. "Let me see if I understand the problem. If we direct the planes to a different base, then landing them or starting them back up will make a lot of noise. Enough noise that it's like ringing a dinner bell for the Reapers."

"Yes, that's right," Weindahl said.

"Do you have a suggestion, General?"

"We've gotten reports on all of the planes' current fuel levels. Based on that information, I believe our best course of action is to move the start of Operation Flashpoint up. If we wipe out a large portion of the Reapers along the East Coast, it should buy the bases enough time to land the planes and shut them down before the Reapers are alerted of their new locations."

"How much sooner are we talking?"

"Four hours."

Vickers felt the breath catch in her chest. "Would we still be able to alert any people in the cities?"

"It might be cutting it close, but we should be able to give an hour's warning or close to it," Weindahl said. "I'm told that all currently airborne planes have enough fuel to complete their mission and still land at one of our bases safely."

"Sounds like the best we can do under the circumstances. Rasheed, let's make it happen."

"As you command, Madam President."

"General?"

"Yes, ma'am."

"Don't hesitate to call me if you have any more problems."

"Of course, Madam President," Weindahl said before disconnecting the call.

Vickers looked up and saw Nash was still standing there. "I need you to pass a message to Captain Flores."

"Did you want me to get him on the phone? Or maybe bring him to your quarters?"

"Not this time. I really need to get through all of these action reports in the next hour." Vickers sighed. "Please tell him Operation Flashpoint is being moved up four hours."

"Yes, Madam President," Nash replied before she hurried out of the room.

A noise sounded out, and Vasquez's helmet flashed an incoming message. She began reading it, and her heart immediately jumped into her throat. Operation Flashpoint had just been moved up. In less than one hour, she'd be bombing Philadelphia. The city where she grew up. The place where her family might somehow still be alive inside. Vasquez made a silent prayer that every human still in Philly made it out before they started dropping their bombs.

"Okay, good news," Ace called out. "We're going to get to hit the Reapers a lot sooner."

"Good hunting, everybody," Vasquez answered in a voice she thought sounded clear and unemotional, even if her own nerves were jangling like crazy. She leaned forward slightly against her seat harness and checked the altimeter before banking her fighter hard and heading southeast toward Philadelphia.

The F-35 took off like a rocket, and she gradually ascended to above the cloud level before leveling her ascent. Once she reached the city outskirts, she would patrol out of sight until it was time to start her bombing run. She was glad to see the brass were still going to make a last-minute effort to warn any people still in the cities before the bombs began dropping. She didn't know how many people it would save. But even if it was only a handful, it was worth the delay.

Vasquez glanced around the cockpit, rechecked her altimeter, and adjusted the air conditioning. Suddenly, a warning began flashing in her HUD. A second warning tone began, and she glanced outside in time to see a piece of metal sailing away from her plane's upper fuselage. A new sensor began sounding a moment before the engine cut out, sending her into a descending 360-degree spiral.

Vasquez keyed the mic. "Mayday, mayday. Green Mountain Boy Seven experiencing mechanical failure outside target location." She fought to pull the plane out of its dive, but the controls weren't responding. As the plane continued to spiral downward, Vasquez noticed her vision was graying and narrow. It was somewhere during the second spiraling turn that she lost consciousness and everything went dark.

CHAPTER THIRTY-FIVE

"We're running out of time," Gregory pointed out. "We have maybe a day left until that guy wants your decision."

"There's still a bunch of supplies we need," Foster replied. "Amanda said we have almost no antibiotics or medical supplies. In a pinch, we could probably find some antibiotics at a pet store."

"But a pharmacy would be a better option," Gregory said. "I'm not sure there's any that aren't already controlled by the Disciples."

"We really could use more hollow-point bullets and silver," Walker said. "I'd feel a lot better if I could make some more enhanced bullets before we ship out."

"Hell, at this point, I'd settle for regular old hollow points," Sams said. "There's no such thing as too much ammo."

"Probably should grab more bottled water," Gregory said. "Amanda and I found a few gallons on our last trip, but right now we only have ten gallons of water to take on the boat."

"Which means we'd be crossing our fingers that Randy's desalinization unit can deliver the rest," Foster said. "He says it will be fine, but I'd feel better if we had more bottled water."

"Sounds like we have four distinct things we need," Charles said. "Water, medical supplies, bullets, and silver. Did I forget anything?"

"Antibiotics?" Sams said.

"I included them in the medical supplies." Charles smiled.

"We might be able to get all of it pretty easily," Gregory said aloud. "There's a small pharmacy not far from here. A family-owned place that I think I've been in maybe twice since I moved here."

"Any reason why?"

"Yes. My health insurance insists we use one of the big chains to get prescriptions filled. It was always easier to just do all of our pharmacy shopping there, too."

"You think this family pharmacy might have been overlooked?" Foster asked.

"Probably," Gregory said excitedly. "There's also a small gun shop near it, too."

"How close are we talking?" Walker asked.

"Maybe a half-mile?" Gregory thought aloud. "I'm guessing here."

"Okay, what if we send out two teams? One team to the pharmacy and the other to the gun shop," Foster said. "We can get most of what we need from two stores."

"Maybe everything we need," Sams said. "If we find anything made out of silver, then Nick has metal he can melt down, too."

"Good point," Foster said. "There's five of us. Nick has requested to hit the gun shop personally so he can look for any other equipment he might need."

"So who goes with Nick, and who goes to the pharmacy?" Gregory asked.

"Actually, I have a preference," Walker replied. "I think Foster and I should take the gun shop. Ammo and other equipment can get heavy quickly, so I'd like to take advantage of Foster's strong back."

"Great, I'm going to be Nick's personal pack mule," Foster muttered.

"Saddle up, Trigger," Sams quipped.

"Don't worry, Derrick, I thought of you, too." Walker smiled. "You'll take Gregory and Charles with you to tackle the pharmacy. With three of you, you'll be able to grab the medical supplies pretty quickly."

"Works for me," Sams said. "Let's take two vehicles so we have plenty of room for supplies."

"Randy isn't going to like it if we come back with too much stuff," Charles pointed out. "Especially if it's too many supplies."

"Does your house have an attic?" Walker asked.

"Yes," Gregory said. "But you can only access it through the master bedroom closet."

"Perfect," Walker said. "We can hide the extra supplies there. Most people won't bother to check the attic when they're scavenging."

"Great point," Foster said. "Let's roll out. Nick, you're with me in the Suburban. Charles and Gregory, you're with Derrick in the Tucson. I'd like all of us to be back here in a few hours. Good luck, everybody."

———

It had taken far more effort than Malice would have liked, but he had managed to sneak his soldiers into town, met up with Achilles, and located Foster. The combined group was currently hiding in a pair of buildings at the opposite end of the block from where his scouts had spotted Foster. It was tight quarters for most of the soldiers, but Malice didn't care. Everyone had quickly learned to stay out of his way.

His scouts had confirmed that Foster, along with a group of other humans, had taken up lodging here. He looked around him. Nearly one hundred fifty other soldiers surrounded him. This meager group of warriors against a dozen young and old humans. Weaklings who could not heal from their own injuries. Mortals who could not run or move as fast as any of his soldiers. Not a single one of them had his special qualities and abilities, either. Even the newly-reborn Achilles had superior skills than those humans.

Malice thought about what Beeks had told him. That he was supposed to report in when he found Foster. But so far, he'd resisted doing so. He'd pulled rank and bullied Achilles into staying silent, too.

This was a golden opportunity. Foster and his friends weren't expecting them. They would strike and avenge his brother's loss. An eye for an eye, a tooth for a tooth. To hell with Beeks. His leader would understand when he returned with Foster's head in his grasp.

A soldier came scurrying up and dropped to one knee.

"What is it?" Malice demanded.

"Sir, Fos-ter and others are leaving."

"What? How many?"

"Fos-ter and four others."

Malice growled in frustration. "I want twenty soldiers to stay here with Achilles and watch that house. The rest will come with me and follow Fos-ter. Spread the word now."

"Yes sir," the soldier replied. He jumped to his feet and ran off to relay his leader's orders.

Twenty minutes later, Foster brought the Suburban to a stop at an intersecting street. He shifted the vehicle into park and began to scan his surroundings. There were streetlights on both sides of the roadways, and they illuminated the area almost completely. He immediately spotted the family pharmacy farther ahead on the left. As he began to scan to his right, he heard Walker begin to speak.

"Gun shop to our right," Walker said. "Looks like Gregory was right about how close the two targets are to each other." Like Foster, he had opted to bring one of the suppressed AR-15 rifles with an attached Eotech Optic scope.

"Great," Foster said. "Let's hope the good luck continues."

The two men got out of the Suburban, and a moment later were joined on the street by Sams, Charles, and Gregory. Foster noticed Sams had brought the third suppressed rifle. Charles had opted to bring the Benelli shotgun and had attached a light on it.

"Quiet night," Foster said softly. "Everybody ready?"

"Yeah," Gregory said nervously. He pulled a Glock and penlight out of his jacket and held both pointing toward the ground.

"Incoming," Walker said. "Eleven and three o'clock."

"So much for an easy stroll through town," Sams quipped. He moved to his right and took a position behind an abandoned car. Charles and Gregory followed his lead.

Foster saw Walker head toward the gun shop and take up position behind a mailbox on the left side of the street. Foster ran to a streetlight opposite his friend and crouched behind the partial cover. He brought his rifle up and glassed the area in front of him. He saw eight Reapers approaching and over a dozen following closely behind. Foster committed to his side of the street, trusting Walker would handle the other half of the firing zone.

Foster heard gunfire behind him, stole a quick glance, and saw Sams, Charles, and Gregory were engaging a smaller incoming pack.

Foster turned his attention back toward his own incoming attackers and sighted on the closest Reaper charging in. He let out a quick exhale to help calm his jangling nerves and pulled the trigger once. His rifle fired, and Foster saw the monster's head snap backward. He didn't wait to see if the shot had put the creature down for good before he was already finding another hostile to target. Foster fired and saw the Reaper drop to all fours a moment before his shot sailed harmlessly past. Foster swore under his breath, adjusted his aim, and unleashed three more shots. This time, the trio of bullets stitched their way up the bounding Reaper's torso, with the last one slamming into the creature's jaw. The Reaper spun awkwardly to the side before crumpling to the ground.

The fight was on, and so far it looked like Foster and his group were winning decisively. Foster said a silent prayer of thanks and went back to shooting.

CHAPTER THIRTY-SIX

A wave of panic rolled over Malice as he looked around him. In a matter of seconds, dozens of his soldiers had been wiped out. How could five humans devastate his group so quickly?

The last time he'd led his troops against Fos-ter, he'd discovered too late that the man had partnered with a bunch of other soldiers with powerful guns. But this time? This time it was five humans, including an old man. Could Fos-ter have become even more powerful since then?

He was about to fail again, and the thought was unbearable. How would he face his master, knowing he'd deliberately ignored orders? A shot whistled past his head and struck a building behind him. He looked around wildly and saw Fos-ter and another man each had some type of rifle in their hands. A chill ran up and down Malice's spine. He had heard the stories about how Foster had killed a red-eyed Alpha named Pak. Malice had never met him personally, but he had heard from others that Pak was almost as powerful as their master. Foster had supposedly killed Pak with a rifle shot from hundreds of yards away. If that was true, then what chance did Malice have when he was only a mere football field away?

A new feeling crept up in Malice's spine, and a voice in the back of his head called it despair. This battle was already lost. To continue to fight it would mean he'd suffer even bigger losses. Maybe even his own life. If he died now, then he would have failed to avenge Nails' death. With a growl, Malice ordered his remaining soldiers to retreat. He turned, dropped to all fours, and bounded away as fast as his limbs could carry him.

The comms went alive, and Foster heard Sams say, "All clear here. You guys all right?"

More gunfire sounded to his left, and he saw two Reapers collapse in a hail of bullets.

"Changing," Walker called out.

"Covering," Foster answered. He sighted on the nearest Reaper and fired twice. The first shot missed the moving target, but the second struck the Reaper in the head. A crimson shower exited the back of the monster's head, and the creature collapsed soundlessly. Foster scanned the immediate area and didn't see any more hostiles.

"Hold on, Sams," Foster answered.

"Got a red cape," Walker called out.

"Where?" Foster yelled back.

"Retail strip."

Foster scoped the area ahead. He saw the gun shop was located in the middle of a small two-story retail strip mall. The Reapers appeared to be retreating behind the long set of buildings.

"Foster, give me a sit-rep," Sams said over the comms.

"We're okay," Foster said. "Reapers have retreated toward the gun shop. You?"

"Reapers are down," Sams answered. "There was one that managed to get away. We're moving to the pharmacy while the coast is clear and before any Reaper reinforcements might show up."

"Copy that," Foster said. "Nick and I are proceeding to the gun shop. We'll call you if we need help."

"Good hunting, Foster," Sams replied. "Sams out."

The two men moved in a leapfrog pattern, working their way toward the retail strip of stores. As they reached the stores, Foster stopped at the corner of the closest one and hugged the wall. A moment later, Walker took an overwatch position behind him.

"Clear the whole strip?" Foster asked.

Walker shook his head. "Take too long. They're probably long gone."

"Copy that," Foster said. "I suggest we do a quick peek in the front window of each one to make sure there's nothing waiting to ambush us."

"Yeah, okay."

Five minutes later, the men had finished their visual check. Nothing seemed out of place in any of the stores, and they were back to the front door of the gunsmith shop. Foster hugged the left side of the door frame and Walker the right.

Foster grabbed the door handle with his left hand and tested it. The door began to open easily, and he quickly closed it. He glanced at Walker and signaled he wanted his friend to enter the building first. Walker nodded once and brought his rifle up to a ready position. Foster held up three fingers and began to lower them one at a time. When the last finger dropped, he opened the door and Walker stepped into the breach, doing a quick circle sweep. Foster stepped around the door, following his friend into the store. He saw Walker begin to move to his right, and Foster went left, scanning for any potential hostiles.

"Clear," Walker whispered. "Checking the back room."

"Copy," Foster answered softly. "I'm right behind you."

The two men moved as one through the doorway and then spread out in the backroom.

"Clear," Foster said.

"Over here," Walker called out. "Got stairs going up."

"We should clear the second floor before we start collecting anything," Foster said.

"You want to take lead, or should I?" Walker said.

"Rock, paper, scissors?"

"Screw that," Walker said. "You take point."

Foster chuckled softly. He brought his rifle up into a ready position. Foster slowly worked his way up the stairs, with Walker following several steps behind. It was a short metal staircase with the wall seemingly on all sides. As they approached the second-floor landing, Foster noticed the door was ajar on the next floor. He gestured and threw his fist up.

There was definitely some kind of movement above, and the two men immediately froze in place. The door slammed open as a trio of Reapers came charging through. Foster dropped to a half-squat to give Walker a clear shooting lane. Foster aimed up at the doorway and fired toward the closest Reaper. His first shot struck the monster in the shoulder. Foster instinctively adjusted his aim and began firing rapidly, stitching his shots until he struck the creature in the nose. The monster had barely fallen when a second Reaper immediately filled the gap and Foster was forced to quickly shift his focus to the new hostile.

Foster immediately fired twice, hitting the still-standing Reaper in the face. A bloody macabre splashed against the door, and the creature began to collapse. Out of the corner of his eye, Foster saw a third Reaper ricochet off the dying Reaper and a nearby wall. The monster's momentum allowed it to soar over his shoulder, and a split second later, there was a loud crash behind him. Foster spun around in time to see the Reaper and Walker tumbling down the stairs together, a blur of human and monster limbs flailing.

"Nick," he shouted as he rushed toward the tangled grouping.

Foster took the stairs two at a time, and when he reached the bottom, he saw Walker had managed to maneuver onto his back and was holding the Reaper into his guard. The move was preventing the creature from reaching Walker's neck or face. Foster watched as Walker swung his feet up and over the monster's shoulders and back. A moment later, the former Ranger executed a perfect triangle choke. The monster fought to break out of the submission hold, and Walker immediately shifted the hold into an armbar. The hold was sunk in deep, and Foster knew from experience there was no getting out of it without tapping. The Reaper continued to futilely struggle. Walker executed the hold fully, and a split second later, Foster saw the monster's elbow hyperextend with a loud pop. The Reaper howled in pain and reared back, trying to pull out of the still-locked-in hold. Walker seized the advantage, pulled out his combat knife, and slammed it into the monster's side. The creature's body went stiff and then it began convulsing wildly before it suddenly went still.

Foster hurried toward Nick, who was pinned under the dead weight of the Reaper. He stole a quick glance toward the top of the staircase to make sure there weren't any additional Reapers coming toward them. The coast was clear, so he turned his attention back to his friend.

"Nick, are you hurt?"

"Just my pride," Walker said. "Can't believe the bastard managed to take me down."

"Well, in all fairness, he did bounce off a wall to get to you," Foster said.

"True. I'm lucky I didn't get hurt."

"Lucky still beats dead," Foster said as he leaned over, grabbed the back of the shirt of the dead Reaper, and timed it with Walker's efforts to slide the body off to the side. It was a formerly athletic-looking man, wearing a Nike sweatsuit and a tank top that showed that even before being transformed, he had been someone who was fairly athletic and muscular. He checked the Reaper for a pulse and found none. "Enhanced knife?" Foster asked.

"Uh-huh. Looks like the prototype works after all."

"That's great news," Foster said. "Let's finish clearing the upstairs."

"Yeah, about that. I'm taking the lead this time," Walker said. "You can play catch with any Reapers that manage to get by me."

CHAPTER THIRTY-SEVEN

Haas watched as the young minion staggered sideways toward him. He was hidden in the shadows, and the creature hadn't seen him yet. He reached out mentally to probe the transformed human. It was definitely not one of his. The bond connecting the creature to its master seemed different. Unfamiliar. It wasn't one of Giles's soldiers, either. Each of their bonds was like a personal signature that linked a minion's mind to their own.

But this Reaper didn't belong to either one of them. From the looks of the partially-missing jaw and the unnatural tilt of its head, he wasn't sure it was going to live much longer. Even with its regeneration abilities, Haas thought its injuries were likely too grave to recover from. He felt an overwhelming sense of curiosity spring forward. If there was another like Giles or him in this area, he needed to know who it was. Especially if they were going to avoid a future battle with this unknown Alpha. If this other Alpha had a large amount of troops, then he and Giles could be in trouble.

Haas involuntarily shuddered. It was a not-so-subtle reminder. Hiding out in this area meant they lacked a large pool of humans to turn into their own personal army.

"You're hurt," Haas thought as he reached out mentally to the

injured soldier. He saw the creature stiffen, and it let out a low, pained growl.

Haas had stepped out of the shadows into plain view. He deliberately made a calming motion with his hands.

"Easy," Haas thought in the best soothing voice he could transmit. *"What happened?"*

The creature let out several small yelps, then collapsed onto the ground.

Haas carefully worked his way over. The creature's face had taken on a pale coloring, and it was struggling to stay on its feet.

"Let me help you," Haas said aloud. "I can take the pain away."

Haas wasn't sure what he was doing, so he just let his instincts dictate his movements. He placed his hand on an injured soldier's forehead, reaching into its mind to gain what information that he could. As he reached into the injured creature's mind, he saw a series of flashbacks to when this former human had been transformed into its current state.

"What are you doing?" a new voice demanded. Haas immediately yanked his hand back like he'd touched a hot stove.

That voice. He knew that voice. Haas felt a wave of fear sweep over him, and he fought to keep the feeling from overwhelming him. If his gut feeling was right, then he had no choice but to find out what this soldier was doing in this area.

He reached back into the creature's mind far more aggressively this time. Haas felt the downed soldier's body stiffen and ignored it. His need to know more far outweighed any concern he had for this Reaper's mental well-being.

Haas began to push through its memories. He saw this creature and its packmates receive the order to go find someone. He heard the name repeated again and again. *Fos-ter. Fos-ter.*

Haas saw the battle that they had been in. How this young creature had been shot more than once. There was a bullet lodged in its neck, and its jaw was missing. None of its injuries were healing. But why?

Even before he had been transformed, he hadn't ever gotten any medical training, and he felt the lack of understanding as he tried probing the minion's injuries. He probed deeper into the soldier's neck with his claws. He could feel the bullet. It was definitely lodged in between two pieces of bone in its neck. An old memory surfaced and told him the word he was looking for. The bullet was stuck between two vertebrae. It had to be why the soldier's body wasn't healing the injury.

Then another memory surfaced. One that told him that removing the bullet with his unskilled fingers might paralyze the poor soldier permanently.

As he was probing the soldier's neck, he heard the same voice again.

"I asked what you're doing. Answer me." Then a moment later, the voice said, "*Haas? Is that you?*"

Haas felt a wave of terror wash over him. He'd definitely raised the attention of this soldier's master. Horatio Beeks was probably the last person he'd ever thought he'd cross paths with again. He wanted to run away and hide. But first he needed to do something to cover his tracks so they couldn't find him.

The creature let out a low series of moans.

"Yes, that's right," Haas said aloud. "I did promise I would help with the pain." He stared into the soldier's eyes as he reached over with both hands, grabbed the creature's damaged head, and yanked it forcefully to the side. There was a loud snap and crunching of bones. He kept pulling its head sideways until he felt the spinal cord sever. Haas didn't let go until there was no longer any sign of life in the minion's eyes. He carefully lowered its body and head to the ground. Haas reached over and closed its eyelids. The soldier's body was still. It was finally at peace, but Haas felt anything but calm right now. He looked around to see if anyone else had seen what he had done. The coast was still clear, and he started to head back the way he'd come.

The information he'd discovered was quite troubling. He needed to find a way to share it with Giles without panicking his friend. That wouldn't be an easy thing to do. Giles was not a fighter by any stretch of the imagination. Even so, the chances of survival for them and their own small group of soldiers hung in the balance. If they were going to survive, Haas and Giles were going to have to make some very important decisions in the near future.

CHAPTER THIRTY-EIGHT

Malice paced nervously back and forth. The recent battle with Foster and his friends had wiped out most of the troops with him. Just as bad, the humans had split up and were hunting them. Malice and a handful of his soldiers had taken refuge on the upper floor of some nearby buildings. He had ordered all of them to stay silent. Now was the hard part: waiting until Foster and his gang left the area, thinking they had won. There was no way to twist the facts in his head. He'd gone against Fos-ter and lost badly again.

Malice felt a wave of anger surging forward. Every ounce of his being wanted to scream out in frustration, but he clenched his teeth instead. He mashed his teeth until there was a loud crack and something shifted inside his mouth. He opened his mouth, reached in, and removed a broken tooth. He tossed the fractured tooth across the room. He ran his tongue around in his mouth and felt the remaining part of his teeth was already growing and repairing itself.

"Malice, where are you?" Beeks called out in his head.

Malice startled in place. "*Somewhere hidden,*" he answered. "*Why?*"

"One of your soldiers was accessed by another Alpha. Care to explain?"

Malice's mind began to race. If he told the truth, then his chances of continuing to lead his own soldiers would likely be over. There had to be some way to twist the facts in his favor. "*I have several scouts in the area,*" Malice lied. "*Perhaps one of them ran into trouble before they could alert me?*"

"*What kind of trouble?*"

"*Nothing I can't handle,*" Malice said. At that moment, an idea popped into his head. It was a little risky, but it could be the way out of this mess. He had to steer this conversation carefully and make Beeks think sending reinforcements was his own idea. Malice took a calming breath and then added, "*Master, I have found him.*"

"*Found who?*"

"*Fos-ter. I am awaiting your orders, sir.*"

"*How many are with him?*" *Beeks* said.

"*Not many. Maybe five or six.*"

"*Hmm. You should be able to take them. But still, with what happened before, we can't be too careful.*"

Every ounce of Malice's spirit wanted to speak up. To tell his master that he could still handle things here on his own. But he swallowed his pride and forced himself to stay silent.

"*Instruct your troops to stay where they are,*" *Beeks* commanded. "*I'm sending more family to help you.*"

"*Yes, my Lord. We will not fail you.*"

"*See that you don't,*" *Beeks* snarled. And then his voice was gone.

Malice turned toward the soldiers in the room.

"*Our master is sending reinforcements,*" he mentally commanded. "*Stay hidden, and be quiet until they arrive.*"

A series of whisper-like grunts answered him in reply.

For the first time in hours, Malice smiled. His master was sending more soldiers there. And once they arrived, he would lead hundreds, maybe even thousands of loyal soldiers into battle to finally kill Fos-ter.

The two men were back on the gun shop's second floor. While the store below was only one floor of the strip mall, the second floor appeared to run the length of the entire center, with multiple closed doors. Foster and Walker had begun the slow process of opening each door they came across and clearing the space behind it. They were about halfway across the space when Foster saw Walker's fist shoot up.

"What is it?" Foster whispered. Walker pointed toward the floor. There were several footprints in the dust that had accumulated. Each one had a distinctive shape, like a large animal had been through there. "Recent or old?"

Walker shrugged his shoulders. "Your guess is as good as mine."

"Right," Foster said. "Best to take it slow."

The two men worked their way carefully forward. Walker's fist shot up once more, and Foster froze in place. He watched as Walker pointed out a chunk of fur stuck on a door frame. Walker gestured where he wanted Foster to move. Foster responded with a quick thumbs up, then moved to the left side of the door frame. He hugged the frame with his body, bringing his rifle up to a ready position. He looked up and saw Walker mirror him on the opposite side. Walker held up three fingers and slowly counted down.

At zero, Foster reached out, grabbed the door handle, and opened it. Walker immediately stepped through and hooked to his left, and Foster followed right behind him.

As Foster cleared the doorway, he spotted seven Reapers in the large room. There was one near a closed door at the back of the room which caught his eye. The creature was wearing some type of red cape. One of the Reapers let out a roar, and Foster immediately sprang into action, firing a double-tap into the nearest Reaper. He heard gunfire to his right and instinctively knew that Walker had joined the fight.

CHAPTER THIRTY-NINE

With a practiced motion, Foster unleashed a barrage of lead at the closest Reaper. There was an immediate avalanche of gore that exited the back of the monster's head, and it dropped dead in a heap. Out of the corner of his eye, he saw a new movement. He turned toward it, bringing his weapon around as he looked for the next hostile to shoot. He saw a red cape moving through the now-open door at the opposite side of the room. Foster unleashed a burst of bullets, hoping to stop the fleeing monster.

"Clear," Walker said.

"I'm going after him," Foster said.

"Wait, what?" Walker yelled.

"That's a red eye. We take him out, we kill all of his troops instantly."

"Damn it, Malcolm," Walker said. "Hold on a minute," he said.

Foster charged ahead. He lowered his shoulder, smashing it into the door that was starting to close. He immediately realized he was back in the hallway. Foster moved forward, scanning for the red-eyed Reaper. He came to the first doorway to the left, hugged the frame, listened, and then stepped into the room. Foster did a circle sweep and cleared the room. As he stepped out of the room, he saw Walker approaching.

"I told you to wait," Walker scolded. "I had to make sure all of those hostiles were definitely dead before we left the room."

"Sorry."

"Uh-huh. Let's clear these together," Walker said. "No crazy hero shit, Foster." He moved to the left side of the doorframe.

Foster went to the opposite side and brought his rifle up into a shooting position. Walker began to count from three to zero, dropping a finger with each number. He had reached one when the wall suddenly collapsed onto him with a loud bang.

"Nick," Foster yelled.

The hallway was filled with dust and dirt, and he struggled to see what was happening around him. As the dust started to clear, he saw part of the wall was lying across Nick's chest. The former Ranger was unconscious and lightly bleeding from a small cut on his forehead.

There was a sudden flash of movement, and something knocked Foster to the ground. He scrambled to get back on his feet as a red cape went flying past him into a new office space. The area was nearly bare except for a single desk positioned in the corner. There were no other doors out of the space. Foster fired at the trapped Reaper, the bullets striking the monster in the back and the shoulder. The creature snarled and spun, facing its attacker.

Foster moved into the office, bringing his rifle up once more to fire. He pulled the trigger, and the weapon clicked dry. He instinctively reached for another magazine and discovered he had fired his last one.

"You," the Reaper said. "I've been looking for you."

"Well, you found me," Foster said.

"You killed my brother."

"Yeah? You're gonna have to give me more than that. I've killed a lot of you assholes."

The Reaper growled loudly.

"Okay, fine. We'll do this the hard way. What should I call you?"

"I am Malice. Prepare to die."

"I don't think so," Foster said. He let the rifle drop and immediately reached for his holstered Glock. As he brought the weapon up to fire, the Reaper leapt into action. Foster managed to clear the holster before the Reaper's shoulder slammed into him, knocking him awkwardly onto the floor. As his elbow slammed into the unforgiving floor, a wave of pins and needles sensation flooded through his arm. He felt his fingers spasm open, and the Glock fell out of his hand.

Foster quickly scrambled back, narrowly missing catching a strike aimed at his face. Malice's claws hit the carpeting beside him and a flurry of fibers went up in the air. Foster crabbed sideways, moving to create some space between him and the red-eyed Reaper. He managed to get back onto his feet and shifted into a crouch, waiting for the Reaper's next attack.

"I'm going to kill you," Malice said.

"Keep talking, fur ball," Foster said.

Malice roared and charged toward Foster once more. Foster waited until the last moment, then pivoted to the side. As Malice charged past him, Foster added an additional push, shoving the monster into the desk. The monster's head and shoulders slammed into the furniture, and it crumpled like it was made out of toothpicks. The Reaper staggered to its feet and shook his head. Malice turned towards Foster and let out a roar.

This time, Foster shifted into a fighting stance. He needed to create some space and catch his breath while he could. The more that he could get this monster to chase after him, the quicker it would tire.

Foster studied the red-eyed Reaper in front of him. Malice was even larger than he remembered. The creature easily had fifty pounds and four inches on Foster. Going to the ground with this creature would likely be a fatal mistake. Foster decided then and there he'd try and fight from a distance until he saw a chance to use the silver dagger to end the fight for good.

Malice stalked toward him, and Foster threw a quick jab, striking the Reaper in the nose. He saw the creature's head snap back. He fired a second jab, and this time, there was a loud crunch as its nose gave way. The creature let out a yelp of pain and took a step back. Foster watched in amazement as the monster's nose slowly shifted back into place, and it grinned at him, showing blood on the front of its teeth.

"My turn," Malice said. He threw an overhead strike toward Foster's head. Foster spun to the side, feeling the rush of air go past his left ear. He quickly fired a counter punch, striking the monster in the short ribs. Malice grunted and immediately turned and grabbed Foster with his massive hands.

Foster felt the Reaper's power, and his adrenaline spiked. He really didn't want to go to the ground with this monster. Foster blocked the takedown attempt and immediately brought a knee up, slamming Malice in the groin. He drew his knee back once more and slammed it into the Reaper's groin again. This time, Foster felt the monster's body weight go up in the air, and the monster yelped in pain. Malice's body instinctively doubled over, and his hands immediately released. The monster staggered back a few steps, stood up slowly, and growled, "Not nice."

"Shut up and fight," Foster said. He drew the dagger and shifted into a fighting stance. Malice grinned and raised his hand, showing his claws. Foster felt the bile rush up the back of his throat from his stomach and swallowed hard, pushing it back down. *He needed to create an opening, but how?*

Foster jabbed with the dagger, and Malice quickly retreated. He moved to close the distance, jabbing with the dagger again. Once again, Malice moved easily away. Foster swung the dagger in an arc, and Malice easily sidestepped and swung his own counterstrike with the claws. Foster felt them slice the front of his vest and yelled in surprise. He quickly retreated, grabbing his side, checking for injury. The flak jacket had protected him from the worst of the damage, but he could feel a slight tenderness on the skin. He didn't have time to check if he had been hurt badly. But it was blatantly obvious: what he was doing wasn't working.

Foster holstered the dagger, switching tactics once more. He put his hands up in a boxing stance.

Malice let out a noise that sounded like laughter.

Foster grinned. "Your brother thought he could fight me too. You should have heard him crying like a baby while I was kicking his ass."

Malice roared and charged toward Foster. Foster sidestepped and snapped a punch, striking the Reaper in the ear as it went past. The monster roared in pain and staggered sideways. Foster danced backward, staying light on his feet. He glanced at his surroundings and saw that he was close to cornering himself, and quickly moved sideways to avoid getting boxed in. Malice charged him once more, and Foster stepped to the opposite side this time, firing another jab, hitting the monster in the temple. The blow staggered Malice slightly, and he crashed into the desk again, obliterating what was left of it.

Malice wobbled to his feet, and as his legs straightened, Foster fired a side kick into the side of the monster's knee. He felt the leg crumble sideways, and the Reaper immediately howled in pain. Malice dropped to one knee, clutching his injured joint. As he did, Foster pulled the silver dagger and swung it around, slamming it home into the back of Malice's shoulder. The monster immediately stiffened in pain. Foster yanked the dagger loose and slammed it into the side of the Reaper's neck. The creature let out a small whimper and crumpled to the ground.

"I'm sorry, brother," Malice said. "I-I...failed...you."

Foster watched the life in the Reaper's eyes fade out, and then Malice was gone.

CHAPTER FORTY

She had only lost consciousness for a few seconds, and Vasquez came to with a start. Her instincts immediately took over. The controls were still sluggish, but somehow she managed to get the F-35 out of its cork-spin. Vasquez glanced at her altimeter and swore under her breath. She was already too close to the ground to pull the fighter up in time. There was only one option left, and Vasquez didn't hesitate.

"Green Mountain Boy Seven, bailout! Bailout!" she yelled over the comms before activating the ejection seat system. The canopy jettisoned a moment before the seat rail system sent her seat skywards at more than 12 Gs. The sudden velocity slammed her body against her harness, and she felt an immediate pain as her left collarbone broke from the high-speed impact. Vasquez bit back a yell. The ejection seat served her immediate need to get clear of the failing plane as quickly as possible. She couldn't do anything about any injuries she might have until she landed. Several small rockets propelled her seat even higher, and then she heard a small charge go off a moment before her parachute deployed. She felt her ejection seat move away from her body, and then she was drifting back toward land.

Vasquez glanced at her surroundings. She was over what looked like a forested area. There was a lake in the near distance. One side of the lake had a noticeable clearing which could make a safe place to land. She grasped the parachute's controls and began to steer toward it.

There was a loud explosion, and she glanced toward it. Her plane had crashed into the forest. A large cloud of fire and smoke billowed up from the wreckage.

A gust of wind kicked up, and her parachute suddenly shifted sideways. Vasquez tried to adjust her descent, but her left arm didn't seem to be working correctly. The ground came rushing toward her and she tucked her feet, bent her knees, and got ready for what was going to be a hard landing. The side of her right foot touched down first and then the outside of her right thigh, dissipating some of the impact. She felt the rest of her body slam into the ground and yelped in pain. A moment later, the parachute fluttered to the ground behind her, and she reached up with her right hand and triggered its release. Vasquez pulled herself up onto her feet, took a tentative step, and her right leg went out from under her. She landed in a heap on the ground.

She took a moment to assess her body. Everything felt battered or bruised. If she didn't know better, she'd think she went fifteen rounds with a heavyweight boxer only to find out afterward the fight was declared a draw. She began to gently check her body, starting with the areas bothering her the most. Her right ankle was definitely badly sprained, maybe even broken. She slowly climbed back onto her feet and put some weight on her leg gingerly. It hurt like hell, but this time the ankle didn't give out on her. That was a good sign. The odds were in her favor that she probably hadn't broken her ankle. If she had landed on her feet, then the impact would have definitely snapped her ankle or leg. Vasquez continued to check herself for injuries. A quick palpation of her left collarbone brought a stabbing pain rushing through her limb that was enough to take her breath away. *Broken, definitely broken. Not good*, she thought to herself.

Vasquez hobbled to a nearby cluster of trees and sat down gingerly against the base of the largest one. She was miles away from the nearest base, with a gimpy ankle and a busted collarbone. She'd done everything by the book. Now she just needed to wait until the military sent someone to rescue her. She pulled out her survival kit and laid it in her lap. She opened it carefully, extracted the two pieces of her disassembled GAU-5/A rifle, and quickly assembled it. Vasquez inserted a magazine into the rifle. There were three other full magazines in her kit, giving her one hundred twenty rounds of ammunition if she needed it.

For decades, pilots carried a handgun in their survival kits. But a recent change in Air Force regs provided a weapon with superior range and firepower. The modified M-16 had a ten-inch barrel that could hit a target up to six hundred fifty yards away. Of course, that's what the military manuals said. With a broken collarbone, Vasquez wasn't sure how accurate she could fire the rifle. She hadn't ever tried firing it one-handed and wasn't about to try it right now, either. Seeing how her luck had been lately, she'd probably wind up accidentally shooting herself instead of an intended target.

Vasquez laid the rifle across her lap. It was quiet in the woods, and she hoped it would stay that way. But in the event that she was discovered by any Reapers, then she was ready to protect herself as best as she was able. She just hoped the cavalry would show up before then. A wave of sheer exhaustion came over her. She was working on almost no sleep. She was banged up and injured with at least one broken bone.

"Come on Angel, focus," she said softly. She felt tired. So tired, and yet she had to try to stay awake. Her eyelids fluttered as her head slowly tipped downward. Her breathing grew slower, and then everything went black as Vasquez's body shut down and she lost consciousness.

A small voice sounded in Beeks's head, and he mentally cringed. He really needed more red-eyed commanders so he didn't have to handle every single question or request that came from one of his minions. There was a time when he didn't mind. It helped him feel even more in power. But now with tens of millions of soldiers, it had grown into a massive constant management headache.

"Yes, what is it now?" he snarled.

"My Lord, we have spotted a very strange-looking human," a minion spoke.

"Strange in what way?" Beeks said. He sat up in his throne a bit straighter. This might be something completely new and different than the usual boring requests he got, and Horatio absolutely welcomed the change of pace. "*Show me*," he commanded.

An image appeared in front of him, and Beeks leaned forward to study it closer. It was a smaller-than-usual person about one hundred yards away from his soldier. Beeks squinted to make out more details on the human. It might be a female. The human was wearing a special uniform and helmet. A pilot. The clothing seemed to suggest a military one. Very interesting. He studied the image a little closer. The helmet was open, and its chest was slowly moving. It appeared to be asleep or unconscious.

"Listen to me now. That is a very special human. A pilot."

"A pil-ot?"

"Don't worry about it," Beeks sent telepathically. "*I want them brought to me alive. Tell your packmates that if the human dies, then all of you will die."*

"Yes, my Lord. I understand. We will bring you the human alive," the soldier answered.

Beeks settled back in his throne. Things had definitely become a little more interesting. He couldn't wait to find out why a military pilot was alone in the woods.

CHAPTER FORTY-ONE

After watching his friend complete his fourth lap of the room, Giles felt the need to speak up. "Something on your mind?" he asked.

"There's a new player in the game," Haas grumbled. "It's got me worried."

"Friend or foe?"

"Maybe a little bit of both."

"I see," Giles said carefully. "This new player is like us."

"Yes. He was there with us when we transformed."

"Wait," Giles said. "Are you talking about Horatio Beeks?"

"I'm afraid so. He's put together his own group of soldiers," Haas answered. "An extremely large number of them to the north and west of us."

"That's not hard to do," Giles said. "We've been very picky about who we've added."

"What do we have between us?"

"Maybe two thousand warriors. Why?"

"I accessed the mind of one of his dying soldiers."

"Why the hell would you do that?" Giles demanded. "Now he knows we exist. Or at least you do."

"It was dying. I wanted to see how it had gotten injured so badly. I thought I should find out who had hurt it and keep our group safe from their attacks."

"Well, that makes sense to me," Giles said. "But Beeks has never been a rational man. I'm guessing he didn't like you messing with his soldier."

Haas chuckled. "He's always been a bit unpredictable," he said. "Better to keep Beeks in front of you than let your guard down and have him stab you in the back."

"What did his soldier's mind reveal?"

"There's a group of humans that Beeks really wants to capture. Their leader is a man. Someone they call Fos-ter."

"That name doesn't make sense. Maybe they meant Foster?"

"I'm not sure. My guess is that most of Beeks's soldiers can't pronounce it normally. Probably ours wouldn't be able to, either. Beeks has managed to amass a massive army with millions of soldiers."

"M-millions?"

"Yes," Haas said simply. "Beeks has been busy trying to conquer as much of the area as possible. But this Foster man and his group has caused Beeks a lot of trouble. Beeks is angry about it and has tasked a group of his minions to find the man. They found him here, but most of them got killed trying to capture this Fos-ter."

"Beeks will freak out when he finds out."

"I'm quite sure he will," Haas said softly. "He'll send far more soldiers. And when he does, it will be extremely difficult for us to avoid drawing his attention."

"How long do we have?"

"I'm not sure," Haas admitted. "Our scouts have reported seeing Beeks's minions exploring our boundaries. It's only a matter of time until we cross paths with him."

"Will he ignore us?"

Haas laughed bitterly. "Not a chance in hell," he said. "Horatio Beeks thrives on conflict and violence. The more of it he can get, the happier he is."

"What about reaching out to him for an alliance?" Giles asked. "He lets us keep our area while he continues to expand elsewhere."

"What do we have to offer? Do you really think our numbers are enough to sway someone like Beeks? Even if we include your old friend's cult."

"He doesn't like people calling it a cult," Giles interrupted. "Even if it probably is."

"Our numbers are growing, but it's tiny compared to what Beeks has."

"Do we know he really has so many soldiers?"

"I held his minion's mind. Tore its memories out of its dying brain. It was in no position to lie to me."

"If Beeks has millions of followers, he could wipe us out in no time at all."

"Yes. If he attacked, we would likely perish."

"Let's say we can reach a peace treaty with Beeks," Giles said carefully. "Can we trust him to hold up his end of the deal?"

"Of course," Haas said. "I've known him for years."

"I disagree. What's the old saying? 'Never trust a con?'"

"If that was true, then I shouldn't trust you, either."

"I'm different. So are you," Giles argued. "We've become friends, too. Or, at least, trusted allies."

"We need a way to gain Beeks's trust."

"Easier said than done."

"This group of humans that has been giving him a hard time."

"The one led by this man Foster?"

"Yes, that's right," Haas said. "What if we were to assist in capturing him? We grab this guy and then hand them over to Beeks."

"It might work. At the very least, it would show him that our intentions are good."

"Right. A peace offering that also eliminates a problem for him. I like it."

"It's worth exploring," Giles said. "At least until this group sees our soldiers and starts shooting. From what you've told me, we could lose a lot of our fighters."

"Probably," Haas said. "If we lose too many, then we'd be even weaker to prevent Beeks from just overpowering us and taking over."

Giles began to laugh. His laughter grew louder and louder until Haas finally had enough.

"What's so funny?" Haas demanded.

"I just thought of a way we can handle this problem," Giles said. "Let me tell you how."

Giles began to lay out his idea, and Haas began to smile.

"I like it," Haas said. "How long would you need to make it happen?"

"Not very long at all," Giles said. "This Foster character doesn't know it yet, but his luck is about to run out."

CHAPTER FORTY-TWO

Beeks felt an agonizing pain, like something was being torn apart in his mind. He clutched his head, let out a roar of pain, and began immediately searching for his children, sensing where the disturbance had happened. As he did, he traced the mental threads, finding those which were still intact, and ones that were broken. There was one connection which seemingly had been torn from the roots. As he traced it, he realized it led to Malice.

"Malice, are you there? Answer me," he commanded, but there was nothing. A wave of panic rushed over him, and he reached out to Achilles. Perhaps his other red-eyed Alpha would tell him what had happened to Malice. "*Achilles, answer me*," Beeks commanded.

"Yes, my Lord."

"What has happened to Malice?"

"Sir, I-I'm not at liberty to say."

"Achilles," Beeks said with a tone of voice that suggested he was close to losing his temper.

"My Lord, it's just that Malice swore me to secrecy."

"Tell me what happened," Beeks snarled. He applied a small mental pinch to his soldier's mind and felt Achilles startle in response.

"Yes, my Lord. Malice had seen the one they call Fos-ter leaving a house. He took all his troops, and most of my soldiers too, to pursue the human."

"Wait, what? I spoke to Malice not long ago. He said they had found Foster. I thought it was a bit strange he didn't mind me sending reinforcements."

"I'm afraid I can only imagine what happened."

"What do you mean?"

"My troops who went with him? They are no more," Achilles said. *"I sensed their deaths."*

"How many soldiers do you have with you?"

"Just a handful, my Lord. Enough to watch the home where some of Foster's friends are still hiding."

Beeks began to think wildly. Should he commit more troops going into this town in hopes of catching Foster again? With Malice likely dead, he felt completely exposed. Especially with no red-eyed warriors to protect him against any strong threats. Then there was Haas. He had felt him access the mind of one of his soldiers. What did Haas learn about Beeks's family? What would Haas do next?

A plan began to form in Beeks's mind.

"My Lord, are you still there?" Achilles asked.

"Quiet. I'm thinking," he said. A moment later, he said, *"There are two things I would like you to do."*

"Yes, my Lord?"

"The first is you will return posthaste to our den. You are needed here."

"Yes, my Lord."

"The second thing is I have a special mission. You must pick your bravest soldier to do it."

"As you command, my Lord."

"Excellent." Beeks proceeded to explain what he wanted Achilles's soldiers to do.

"I vow we will not fail you, my Lord."

"See that you don't," Beeks said. *"That is all."*

Beeks broke the connection and then quickly established one with the pack leader that was headed toward Rehoboth Beach. A quick command, and those soldiers were routed back to his den where they could best serve to keep him safe.

After dispatching Malice, Foster had turned his attention to Nick. The two of them had to work together in order to move the rubble off his trapped friend. Once the debris was moved and he saw Walker wobble to his feet, Foster was immediately concerned about his friend's condition. One close look into Walker's eyes, and Foster was pretty sure the man had suffered a concussion. If the recent tumble down the staircase hadn't made the former Ranger woozy, then a wall landing on him probably did. Foster managed to get the former Ranger back to the Suburban without crossing paths with any hostiles. Foster called Sams and gave him a quick report on what had happened. Both men agreed it was crucial to get Nick back to Gregory's house, where Amanda could do a check-up before letting Nick join the fight once more.

Once back at the house, Amanda gave Nick a thorough examination. When she had finished, the group's resident doctor announced that Nick had a slight concussion. She then suggested he take the remainder of the night off and rest. Foster figured the man had to be feeling pretty lousy, because Walker didn't complain or argue with Amanda's diagnosis.

With Nick resting downstairs and Lizzy staying nearby in case he took a turn for the worse, Foster had some time to kill before he was due to talk with Lieutenant Abrahams. He tried to do a three-week-old crossword puzzle, but he couldn't concentrate on it. There was too much crap to worry about handling and not enough time to do it.

Foster glanced at his watch. Just ten more minutes until his meeting. He knew two things for sure. The first was his group really needed a safe place to go. From what Black had told him, Hope Island was definitely it. The second thing was he was completely unsure how the conversation with the Army commander was going to go. The talk with Charles had only created more uncertainty in his mind. On one hand, everyone needed to come together to stop the Reaper invasion. On the other, losing any of his group's key people might lead to great harm or even death for the remaining members.

The satellite phone began to ring.

"Foster," a voice said.

"Black, is that you?" Foster asked.

"One and the same," SWAT Sergeant Vince Black answered. "How are things on your end?"

"Secure for now," Foster said.

"Where are you these days?" Black asked. "On second thought, don't tell me."

"Why?"

"Plausible deniability. If your talk with the lieutenant goes badly, then he can't send my team and me to drag your sorry asses here."

"Is that a possibility?"

"Never say never," Black said. "A member of my team might have been playing cards with several off-duty soldiers. Over the course of several hours of poker and far too many glasses of whiskey, one of the soldier boys might have let it slip that their commander is thinking about conscripting any able-bodied shooters they can find."

"Oh, hell. It's one thing to voluntarily join the military. It's another to be forced to do it."

"My thoughts exactly," Black said. "I'm sure you don't want to lose anyone from your team right now."

"That would be correct."

"Look, I can't tell you what to say," Black said carefully. "As much as it pains me to say this, maybe the less you share about your group, the better."

"Do you think I should cancel the meeting, then?"

"Absolutely not. If it's true about these Reapers being deathly allergic to silver, then you need to tell as many people as possible about it. Alerting the military could be a big help to them."

"You think the lieutenant will take me seriously?"

"I'd like to think so."

"What did you tell him about me?"

"Just that you tucked tail and bolted from the city. And that you're a serious pain in the ass to deal with."

"Black," Foster warned.

"I'm kidding," Black answered. "I told him you evacuated the mayor and a bunch of civilians out of the city. And that you discovered the Reapers' major weakness. He got excited when I told him and wanted to speak with you."

"I don't think I've ever heard you this relaxed before."

"Being able to sleep without worrying about something eating your face helps a lot."

"No Reapers there?"

"Nope. We've seen some on the mainland shorelines, but that's as close as they have been able to get to us. Looks like the rumors that they won't cross large bodies of water are true. I've read an action report that there's a bunch of military and civilians holed up in the old prison on Alcatraz Island, too."

"That's encouraging. Maybe establishing a bunch of offshore operating bases will be the best way to fight back."

"Yeah, maybe. Listen, the lieutenant just showed up. I'm going to turn the phone over to him. Stay frosty, Foster."

"Thanks, Black. You too, man."

There was a fumbling sound over the sat phone, and then a new voice sounded out.

"Malcolm Foster?" a man's voice asked.

"Speaking," Foster answered.

"This is Lieutenant Abrahams," he continued. "Where are you reporting from, soldier?"

"I'm not a soldier," Foster said. "And for right now, my location is secure and not to be disclosed."

"Really? And why is that?"

"Because I don't know you from the man on the moon," Foster said. "For right now, it's the best option to keep the civilians with me safe."

"You do realize that I have several different tracking measures at my disposal to locate you if I really wanted to?"

"Yup. I figure you'll probably do so before we even end this call," Foster said. He paused before saying, "That's why I'm taking the battery out of this phone and leaving this location as soon as we're done talking."

"Okay, hold on. I think maybe we're getting off on the wrong foot here."

"I'd say so."

"Right. Let's start over, shall we? I'm Lieutenant Tom Abrahams. 3rd Battalion, 75th Ranger Regiment."

"You're a long way from Fort Benning, Lieutenant."

"Yes, we are. Of course, Rangers are always ready to deploy anywhere in the world within eighteen hours. We're currently calling Hope Island our Forward Operating Base. What's your story, Foster?"

"I was an active Philadelphia police officer until the Reaper invasion began. I led a group of civilians out of the city, including the mayor."

"I see. Is the mayor still with you?"

"Unfortunately not. We were attacked outside the city, and Mayor Watkins didn't make it," Foster said. "I miss him. Watkins was the only politician I ever met where you shook his hand and didn't feel like you needed to wash it off afterward."

Abrahams chuckled. "They do tend to be a slimy group at times," he said. "Sergeant Black tells me you have some information which might be of interest to us."

"I do. What are you prepared to trade?"

"It depends on how good your intel is. It could be anything from some additional supplies to entry into our secure location."

"Our information is on how to kill the Reapers instantly. I'm not talking about shooting them in the head. And yes, it's been confirmed."

"Then I'd say your information, if proven to be credible, would warrant something closer to entry to Hope Island."

"How did you wind up stationed outside Rhode Island? Because from where I'm standing, asking a bunch of Special Operations and elite light infantry soldiers to babysit a bunch of civilians is like driving a Porsche and never taking it out of first gear. There's a whole of power being wasted."

"You're not the first person to wonder that. Let's just say it's a long story. I'll give you the short version," Abrahams replied. "As soon as the Reaper invasion began, your lieutenant governor used his political connections to have my platoon deployed to secure this location. Black and his men showed up shortly thereafter with a bunch of other civilians, including the lieutenant governor's daughter."

"Interesting story indeed," Foster said. "But isn't there a bridge connecting Hope Island to the mainland?"

"Was. We detonated multiple explosives and eliminated it. Nothing is going to cross there and get onto our location," Abrahams said. "Even so, we take our base security very seriously. Between my men and Sergeant Black's, we have round-the-clock security patrols."

"Sounds promising, but I have to be honest. Even with a platoon of Rangers, you have to be stretched pretty thin there."

"You'd be surprised what forty highly-motivated ass-kickers can accomplish."

Foster chuckled. "I don't doubt it," he said. "My concern is you might decide to start conscripting civilians to bolster your numbers."

"I can't rule it out as a future possibility," Abrahams said slowly. "But until I'm ordered otherwise, I am considering it as a last resort only. I'd love to have more volunteers like Sergeant Black and his SWAT team. I'd prefer not to force anyone to join my command."

"Fair enough."

"Tell me about your group."

"It's composed of about a dozen men, women, and children."

"Care to tell me any skill sets they may have to offer?"

"Not at this time."

"Come on, Foster," Abrahams said. "Are we back to talking in circles again?"

"I think it's prudent if we both limit technical details right now. Especially when it comes to unit strength and skills."

"You're a little on the paranoid side, aren't you?"

"If you knew what we've been through, you'd wonder why we weren't even more."

"That bad, huh?"

Foster said nothing.

"Okay, I'll take your word on it. Black talks highly of you and your group. Do you have a way to reach our location?"

"Yes."

"Okay, here's what I'm willing to propose," Abrahams said. "You bring your group here. They will be quarantined until we're sure everyone is infection-free. You and I will talk in person. If your information checks out, then we will welcome your group to our location. But if your information is bullshit, then you will be escorted back to your boat and you will be sent on your way. No do-overs, no second chances. You don't waste my time, and I won't waste yours."

"Deal," Foster said. "We have two confirmed methods for killing Reapers. We're planning on testing another one in the near future. If that works as well as we think, then we will have three distinct breakthroughs to share."

"Besides shooting them in the head?"

"Yes, that's right."

"Then it sounds like we have a deal, Officer Foster," Abrahams said. "What's your estimated time of arrival?"

"Soon. There's a few things I'd like us to wrap up here first, including that additional testing. I'll call Black on his sat phone once we have a more accurate timetable."

"Excellent. Stay safe, Foster. I look forward to meeting you in person."

"You too, Lieutenant."

CHAPTER FORTY-THREE

"Yes, what is it?" Ezekiel said impatiently.

"We have some new candidates," Joseph said with a practiced calmness.

"And?"

"And they have some reservations about joining. They want to meet you first."

"What did you tell them?"

"That you're an extremely busy man," Joseph said. "You have a lot of congregation members to worry about."

"But they still want to see me."

"Yes."

"Tell them I can meet them in about an hour," Ezekiel answered. "I have some other things to attend to first. Tell them I will send word for them at my first opportunity."

"What would you like me to do with them in the meantime?"

"Let them enjoy a meal and some wine in our community dining area. Perhaps some food in their stomachs will help ease some of their concerns."

"Yes, Ezekiel."

"Anything else?"

"Not at this time."

"Then please leave me. I need a few minutes to take care of some other things."

Ezekiel waited until his follower left the room. He silently counted to fifteen before getting up from his desk. He moved cautiously to the window. He opened the shutters and carefully clipped a Harley Davidson bandana to a thumbscrew inserted in the top of the window frame. The metal bolt had been carefully positioned to not be in plain sight. He closed the shutters once more. Now all he needed to do was wait for Giles to respond to his signal.

Eighty minutes later, Ezekiel was satisfied everything was in place to receive the new candidates. He ordered Joseph to bring the people to his office and waited patiently for them to arrive.

There was a knock at the door, and Ezekiel said with a practiced voice, "Please come in."

He watched as Joseph steered six people into the room. There were two men, two women, and a pair of young children.

"Welcome," Ezekiel said with his voice that he thought made him sound warm and welcoming. "Perhaps we should talk with the children out of the room."

"No way," a man spoke up. "We're not letting our kids out of our sight."

"David," one of the women warned.

"What?" David countered. "For all we know, they'll use our kids like hostages and force us to do what they want."

"I assure you, your children are perfectly safe," Ezekiel said. "No one in my congregation would ever hurt a child."

"Well, that's good to know," David grumbled. "But if it's the same to you, we'd rather keep our children with us while you give us your sales pitch."

Ezekiel studied the man. It was obvious this man was going to be the one who gave him the most trouble. There was often one in every group of candidates, and Ezekiel knew how to handle these types of troublemakers. He clasped his hands in front of himself and said, "Joseph tells me you're considering joining our community."

"We are," a woman said. "But we have some questions, Ezekiel."

"I'm afraid you have me at a disadvantage," Ezekiel said smoothly. "Joseph hasn't told me any of your names."

"I'm Sarah," the woman said. "This is my sister Theresa. Her husband Jacob. Their children, Eva and Taylor. You've already met my boyfriend David."

"I'm pleased to meet all of you."

"I heard you have some type of power over these monsters," David interrupted. "Is that for real?"

"Our community has been blessed by our Lord and Savior in many ways," Ezekiel pitched. "We have a bounty of food and drink. We have a safe place to live and gather. And we have been blessed with a connection to these tortured souls you hear about killing others."

"Tortured souls, huh?" David said skeptically. "You're talking about Reapers, right?"

"I think *tortured souls* is a more fitting description."

"You can guarantee our safety?" Theresa asked.

"Absolutely," Joseph said. "There has never been a single case of anyone in our community being injured, let alone killed by these tortured souls."

"Uh-huh. It sounds too good to true," David said skeptically. "I'm going to need some proof."

"I had a feeling you were going to say that," Ezekiel said. "Joseph, if you would, please."

Joseph nodded once, walked over to the bookcase, and got a small cedar box. He placed it gently on the center of the desk and opened the lid. A small ornamental bell sat in a velvet cushion instead. Joseph stepped away from the desk, moved to another door, and opened it. An alleyway outside became visible.

Ezekiel picked up the bell and held it carefully for everyone to see. "I had a vision one day. Our Lord and Savior came to me in a dream. He told me this would allow me to call the tortured souls if we ever needed their protection. I quickly discovered that they will also follow my word like it was our Savior's own commandments."

He rang the bell twice, paused, and then rang it twice more. There was a loud growl, and then the sound of pounding feet began to grow louder. A Reaper appeared in the doorway and began moving slowly into the room. Several people immediately shrieked in horror.

"It's okay," Ezekiel said with a practiced motion. He turned toward the creature in the doorway and said, "I command you to stop."

The Reaper froze in its tracks.

"That's amazing," Jacob said. "It's a true blessing."

"Oh please, that's probably not even a real Reaper," David protested. "I bet it's some guy in a costume."

Ezekiel turned toward the man. "David, I sense you are not a believer. I believe there is much sin clouding your soul," he said. Ezekiel let his right hand drop loosely by his side. "This sin is affecting your judgment. You must repent your ways before it's too late."

"This is a bunch of bullshit," David said.

"David, please," Sarah pleaded.

"You know, I thought it was too good to be true," David continued. "You kept begging me to give it a chance. Well, now that I've seen this with my own eyes, I've never been more convinced. This whole thing is a scam, Sarah. We should go, right now."

"David, you must repent before it's too late," Ezekiel said, raising his voice with each word. He tapped his right leg twice. "Forgo your evil ways, before it's too late."

"You don't get to tell me-"

A loud roar sounded out, and the Reaper sprang into action. The creature slammed into David, knocking the startled man to the floor. The monster quickly overpowered the man, latched onto his neck, and bit down.

The man screamed out in pain, and an immediate arterial spray shot out of his neck. His legs went limp.

"It's not too late for the rest of you," Ezekiel shouted. "Kneel before me now. Repent your old ways and pledge your souls to our community. We will use our Savior's graces to welcome you into our flock and keep you safe from the evils lurking outside our walls."

The remaining survivors immediately dropped to their knees and began shouting their newfound alliance.

CHAPTER FORTY-FOUR

"Tortured soul," Ezekiel shouted. "By the power granted to me by our divine Savior, I command you to leave the premises."

The Reaper looked up at the preacher and flashed a brief annoyed look before bolting from the room. Joseph, on cue, closed the door behind the fleeing monster, leaving the remaining humans alone with the newly-dead David.

"I wish David had been able to cast aside his demons, but it wasn't to be," Ezekiel said. "I need a few minutes alone to cleanse this room and to help David's soul ascend. Please follow Joseph into the chapel, where we will finish your initiation."

Joseph opened the door leading to the chapel. There was a smattering of voices, and then the group moved as one to follow him.

Ezekiel waited until they had disappeared out of sight to close the door. He silently counted to five and then opened the door to the outdoors. Ezekiel was surprised to see there was nothing in sight. That wasn't what was supposed to happen. He frowned and closed the door firmly.

As he walked back toward his desk, there was a loud click.

"Who is it?" Ezekiel said as a hint of fear crept into his voice.

The noise was coming from a third door. It was an exit that he'd deliberately had installed and hidden from view in his room. He'd learned a long time ago it was always a good idea to have more than one way to escape a room. Especially if your audience unexpectedly shifted from friendly to hostile.

Ezekiel slid the curtain aside, revealing the standard-size door. He picked up a nearby candlestick and hefted it in his hand. The base had a good weight to it and could serve as a decent weapon, if needed.

"Hello?" he called carefully. He waited until a mental count of three, then turned the knob and opened the door.

A Reaper was standing there, waiting impatiently for him.

"You're not supposed to be here yet," Ezekiel scolded. "What if somebody else sees you?"

The monster's hand shot out and grabbed the preacher by the top of the head.

Ezekiel immediately felt a shot of pain and dropped to his knees, clutching the monster's wrist.

"You should show me a lot more respect than that," Giles warned. He applied a bit more pressure to the preacher's head and was rewarded by a louder groan.

"I'm sorry," Ezekiel said between gritted teeth. "You surprised me. That's all."

"It's so easy for you to forget your roots. Where you came from," Giles said. He released his hold on the man's skull, and Ezekiel collapsed into a ball on the floor. "Do you not remember?"

"Of course I do," Ezekiel answered. "It's been mutually beneficial."

Giles chuckled. "You mean you get most of the humans as new members, and I get the occasional rabble-rouser," he said. "At least you could have given me someone who didn't smell so awful."

"If it's any consolation, all of them were badly in need of a proper bath."

"You've managed to create a nice little group for yourself here. And it's grown by leaps and bounds because of my help," Giles said. "It would be a shame to lose it."

"Why would I lose it?"

Giles's hand shot out once more. He grabbed Ezekiel by the back of the neck and yanked him up onto his feet. He pulled the man's face close until they were nearly nose to nose. Ezekiel let out a small whimper of fear.

"What do you want?" the preacher stammered.

"I have something I need done," Giles answered. "I would like your flock to handle it for me."

"W-what?"

"There is a man who has become very important to me. I want you to find this man and bring him to me alive. He is currently with another group nearby. Do I make myself clear?"

"Yes. But you said he's with another group," Ezekiel said. "What would you like us to do with them?"

"You can do whatever you like with them," Giles said. "They are of no concern or use to me. But bring me this Foster man alive."

"We won't fail you."

"You better not," Giles said. "Or our next conversation won't be nearly as pleasant."

CHAPTER FORTY-FIVE

"Wait, I thought you were leaving on your own," Lauren said. "Are you serious about taking him with us on our boat?" she said, pointing at Charles.

Foster felt his jaw drop. They were hours away from leaving, and Lauren waited until now to raise her objections? It was petty and completely ridiculous. "I'm completely serious. He has a name," Foster said. "It's Charles. And in case you forgot, he's your father."

"I know that, I'm not stupid," Lauren answered. "As far as I'm concerned, that man gave up his right to call himself my father years ago."

"You know what? This is bullshit," Foster said. "We don't have time for this. Take a fucking look outside. Take a good look at what's going on out there. We need to be working together, not against each other. I don't care what happened in the past. I don't care whose feelings got hurt, who's to blame, and who wasn't. This needs to end now. We need to work together as a group. If you can't get on the same fucking page as the rest of us, then maybe you need to go on your own way."

"Oh, I'm sure he would like that," Lauren shouted. "Wouldn't he? In case you hadn't noticed, that's our boat, not yours."

"Lauren, please," Charles said. "Please don't do this. If not for me, then for your brother and your mom."

"Mom isn't here. And what would you know about what Mom would want?"

"Because she used to talk to me about everything," Charles said in a deliberate calming tone. "She told me what happened. How the drugs weren't yours."

Lauren did a double take. "Wait, what?"

"That's right. We kept waiting for a time when you were going to be willing to talk to me. But you were so angry all the time," Charles said. "It never seemed to be the right time for us to really talk about what happened. I couldn't ever find the right moment to apologize. What happened that night was the hardest decision I've ever had to make in my life."

"I don't believe you."

"Why would I lie?" Charles said. "You are my daughter, my pride and joy."

"Really? It seemed like every time I turned around, you were always riding my ass about something."

"Because I saw how much potential you had. I knew you were on the cusp of greatness. You know, you could have done anything. You had the top grades in your classes. You were smart, beautiful, even funny. All the best parts of your mom and even me all rolled into one," Charles said. "And yet you wouldn't listen to us. You were constantly fighting us every step of the way. When we came home that night and we saw the drugs and liquor bottles, I felt like you left me no choice. I had to do what was right to protect your brother, and I hated every minute of it."

Lauren sat down, looking stunned. "I don't know what to say."

"Sorry is probably a good start," Foster said. "It sounds like you weren't very fair to your dad."

"What the hell would you know about being a parent?" Lauren shot back.

"Not much," Foster admitted, "but I'm a cop. I understand the importance of protecting those who need me to do so. I understand the importance of steering bad influences away from the innocent.

The way I see it, sometimes being a parent requires a little bit of both of those things."

"I'm sorry," Charles said. "Can you forgive me?"

"I don't know," Lauren said softly. She was visibly struggling to keep her emotions in check. "This is a lot to take in right now."

"You know, your dad might have a point," Randy said. "Maybe it's best if you just sleep on it for now. And, you know, maybe just try not to yell at him so much?"

"You'd like that, wouldn't you?" Lauren said. "I'd be a lot easier to be around then."

"Well, it hasn't been easy sometimes," Randy admitted. "I've seen you get so angry every time you see him. Might be a nice change of pace to see y'all getting along. Plus, what the good officer said kind of makes sense. With those things out there, we really do need to work together to stay alive."

A tear started forming in Lauren's eyes. "You had no idea how much you hurt me."

"I know, and I'm sorry," Charles said. He slowly walked over, opened his arms, and his daughter stepped into them. He wrapped his arms around her and held her in a long embrace as Lauren sobbed against his shoulder. "I'm sorry, dear," Charles said softly. "Can you ever forgive me?"

"I'm sorry too, Daddy," she said.

Foster quietly retreated to the kitchen to let Charles and his daughter continue to talk.

As he entered the room, he saw Derrick eating a bowl of instant oatmeal.

"How's Nick?" Sams asked between bites.

"Resting," Foster answered. "Under spousal guard."

"Huh. I can't believe Nick got concussed. He's probably got the hardest head of any guy I've ever met."

"In all fairness, a red-eyed Reaper did slam a wall into him."

"How was the wall afterward?"

"In pieces," Foster said. "Why?"

"Sounds like a draw to me. The wall was in pieces, and the guy with a skull made out of Adamantium just got a headache."

"Adam what?"

"Adamantium. You know, the stuff Wolverine's skeleton and claws are made out of."

Foster gave Sams a fishy-eyed look.

"You know, *X-Men*. Tell me you at least watched one of the movies."

"Can we get back to reality, please?" Foster said. "I did a quick ammo count, and we have less than one hundred hollow points, and most of them were turned into enhanced bullets. I told Abrahams we had another possible Reaper killing method we were going to test."

"Why the hell did you tell him that? In case you hadn't noticed, we're down one shooter while Nick is on forced bed rest."

"Leverage. Three new ways to kill Reapers fast sounds a helluva lot more interesting than two. I wanted to guarantee all of us are allowed onto a military-controlled remote island."

"Three does sound better," Sams said. "But when, pray tell, are we going to do a test? It's nighttime, and we need to get to the marina first thing in the morning before your big deadline."

"Our big deadline."

"Tomato, toh-mato."

"What if we go out tonight?"

"Uh, in case you hadn't noticed, it's nighttime. The Reapers are tough to deal with during the day. At night, they're a lot harder to see coming your way."

"We need ammo."

"You already said that."

"So let's go get some. Maybe shoot a Reaper with one of the test bullets on the way back?"

"Like a drive-by shooting?"

"If we have to," Foster said. "To be honest, I haven't done much shooting out of a moving vehicle."

"Yeah, me neither. The problem is, you guys already hit the gun shop. There wasn't much ammo left there. I didn't see any other places near us that might still have ammunition."

"Not near us," Foster said excitedly. "But there's one in Disciple territory. I bet at this time of night it's closed."

"Wait, what?"

"Ready to do a nighttime op? We get in, grab what we need, and get out. Easy peasy."

"Do I really have a choice?"

Foster said nothing.

"Aww, hell. Walker picked a lousy time to get hurt."

"You're welcome to go ask Lizzy if Nick can go instead."

"Now you're just being a dick," Sams complained. "Tell me about this place before I change my damn mind."

CHAPTER FORTY-SIX

"I got a bad feeling about this," Sams said.

"You always say that," Foster said. "It doesn't change the fact that we need these supplies. Look, the Disciples are tucked in their beds at home. They don't even have the store security systems on because they don't think anybody would break into one of their stores at night. The Reapers are busy wandering around the parts of town not controlled by the Disciples. Like I said, we grab the stuff we need and then get out."

"Yeah, maybe. Even so, this place gives me the creeps. I mean, because there's spots where it's pitch black. There could be things hiding where we can't see, waiting to jump us."

"Wait, are you scared?"

"What? Never," Sams protested. "I'm an Army Ranger. We don't do scared."

"Then nut up, Army," Foster quipped. "The sooner we get this done, the sooner we get to go rejoin the rest of the group."

"Uh-huh. I knew you were going to say that."

The men worked their way toward the back of the sporting goods store where they were likely to find hunting supplies. For this mission, both men had opted to go with SWAT wireless comm units and their suppressed AR-15 rifles. Each man had removed the Eotech M914

Optic sight from their rifles and were using them as a helmet-mounted monocular instead. They would be relying heavily on them to see in the nearly dark store but would still have the option to use whatever tools or weapons were needed.

"Hold up," Foster said.

"What's wrong?"

"There's some nice backpacks over here," Foster said.

"We both have a backpack already."

"Right. And if we can fill one or two more with additional supplies, then that's even more gear for the group."

"I thought we were worried about too much weight on the boat."

"Randy is worried about extra weight," Foster pointed out. "I say we grab whatever we think we might need and worry about what to pack for the boat later. Like Nick said, we can store any extra supplies in the attic."

"I'm not sure I like tying up our hands with extra baggage. It could make it harder to defend ourselves."

"One bag extra each, Derrick. We can toss it over one shoulder or tie them to our current packs."

"Fine," Sams muttered. "But I don't think we're going to need them."

Foster grabbed two suitable backpacks. He offered one to Sams who reluctantly took it. Foster attached the new backpack to the side of his current one. It dangled awkwardly against his side, but at least he was still able to keep both hands on his rifle.

"I'll take point," Foster said over the comms.

"Copy that," Sams answered.

Foster risked a quick glance back and saw his friend was following a few steps behind, actively scanning for any potential threats which might attack them. This store was located in the heart of Disciple territory, so Foster was more worried about running into a hostile shooter than a Reaper. But so far, the place was dead quiet.

Foster worked his way through aisles of clothes until he reached an aisle end cap with an assorted collection of baseball equipment. He actively scanned left to right. As he did, he spotted something and immediately raised his fist up in the air. Foster slowly re-scanned the area and saw there were three Reapers feasting on a body. There was a bloody trail leading off in the distance, and Foster couldn't help but wonder if the monsters had dragged someone in here to feed on.

"Contact," he whispered over the comms. "Three Reapers. Silent three count."

Sams clicked twice on the comms, acknowledging the message.

Foster motioned to where he wanted Sams to go, and there was another double-click in his ear. He used his peripheral vision to watch the former Ranger begin working his way to the right side of the aisle's entrance. Foster moved to the left side, held up his rifle in a ready position, and mentally counted to three. When he hit zero, he pivoted into the aisle and fired once, striking a startled Reaper between the eyes. He shifted his aim, firing a second time, hitting the nearby Reaper. A series of gunfire erupted next to him, and he saw the third Reaper drop.

A roar sounded behind them, and Foster pivoted to look. Four more Reapers were charging toward them, and he shifted his aim, firing to engage. He unleashed a trio of bullets, striking the lead Reaper in the legs, cutting it down. Foster shifted his aim and fired a double-tap, striking the Reaper in the nose and the forehead, dropping it. He didn't have time to admire his skilled shooting, because the remaining Reapers were now thirty feet away. Foster shifted his aim and fired once more. This time, the bullet flew true, striking the closest Reaper in the jaw. Foster saw the monster stagger sideways and slam into another Reaper. The two monsters fell to the floor in a tangle of flailing limbs. Foster took advantage of it, aiming, firing a double-tap at the tangled duo.

He shifted his aim. The last Reaper remaining was now only fifteen yards away. He unleashed a barrage of bullets, stitching his trail up the monster's body until the last bullet slammed into the creature's eye. The Reaper did a deathly pirouette, collapsing onto the ground, facing away from him. He heard more gunfire behind him and glanced to see Sams had another half-dozen that he was engaged with. There was a roar to Foster's left, and he swung that way.

"Incoming," Foster said. "Twelve o'clock."

"A little busy here," Sams said. "Give me a minute."

"I'll take care of it," Foster said. He turned and fired. He saw two of the monsters drop. The aisle was suddenly clear, and Foster took a step to his right, moving to assist Sams. Foster fired twice more, striking one of the monsters in the shoulder and the neck. The monster staggered and dropped to one knee, where Foster then shot it again, striking it between the eyes. He saw the monster's head snap back, and its momentum caused it to strike another creature in the face. The still-living monster was rocked back onto its heels. The Reaper stopped moving and wiped its paw to try and clear its eyes. Foster fired twice, striking the monster in the chest and then the jaw. The monster fell backward, tripping another monster coming toward them. Foster unloaded his rifle, cutting the remaining two monsters down.

There was a roar behind him, and Foster spun around. He saw another Reaper bearing down on him a split second before it slammed into his chest, knocking him to the ground. Foster lost his grip on his rifle and felt it begin to drop. He felt the weapon's sling go taut, keeping the weapon from getting too far away. Foster brought his hands and legs up, hooked them around the monster, and pulled it into his guard. He shifted his left hand around the monster's neck and sank his grip in. The monster immediately began trying to pull away and he resisted the motion. Foster didn't want to give the Reaper a chance to pull back and lunge for his face. Even so, the monster managed to swing a handful of claws at his side. Foster felt the claws graze his ribs through the fabric of his body armor.

Foster reached down, drew his dagger out of its holster, and brought it up in a half-arc, slamming it into the back of the Reaper's neck. He heard the monster scream and stiffen in his grasp. As he went to pull the dagger away, he felt its blade stick in the monster's neck. He pushed the dead Reaper onto its back, dropped into a half-kneeling position, and began trying to free the embedded dagger. Foster heard a roar and turned his head toward the noise in time to see another Reaper approaching. He barely had to brace himself before the new hostile's shoulder slammed into him and knocked him backward. The body on the floor altered his fall slightly, and Foster felt his right arm bang into a nearby metal aisle shelf. There was an immediate clattering noise, and Foster felt several objects strike him. He winced in pain as each one of these items landed on his body. The Reaper yelped in pain and backpedaled away from the falling metal objects.

Bats. I'm getting hit by fucking bats, Foster thought. He reached out, grabbed one of the aluminum bats, and began to pull it up and across his body. Foster saw movement in his peripheral and instinctively brought the bat up to block a likely attacker. He saw the Reaper dive toward him, its mouth open and ready to chomp down on his neck or face. The monster's momentum carried it into the bat, and Foster saw the aluminum weapon slam into the monster's face. The Reaper howled in pain and flopped backward, clutching its jaw.

Suddenly he saw a boot slam down on the Reaper's neck. A moment later, a Glock appeared and fired once into the monster's chest. The creature howled in pain and began to convulse. Its body spasmed uncontrollably several times and then went still.

Foster's eyes followed the Glock returning back to Sams's holster. "Nice shot. Thanks."

"You're welcome," Sams answered.

"Enhanced bullet?"

"Yup. Worked like a charm. Guess what I'm asking for Christmas?"

"Yeah, me too."

Foster slowly stood up, grabbed his rifle, and brought it back up. He began to sweep the area for any additional hostiles. "Clear," Foster said, panting heavily.

"You okay?"

"Yeah, just a little scratch," Foster answered.

"Good thing Reaper claws can't turn somebody."

"I guess. If it's all the same to you, I'd rather not get hurt."

"Uh-huh. Dude, you really need to hit the gym," Sams says. "You're way too out of breath for such a short workout."

"I'll keep that in mind," Foster replied. He bent over the dead Reaper where his dagger had gotten stuck in its flesh. He put one hand around the weapon's handle, placed a foot on the side of the Reaper's neck, and pulled hard. There was a loud squelch as the dagger pulled free. Foster wiped the blade clean on the dead Reaper's clothing.

"Uh, gross," Sams commented.

Foster studied the dead Reaper. The monster had once been a man. The creature was wearing a tattered pair of blue jeans and a collared shirt. Foster's eyes fell on the shirt, and he immediately swore out loud.

"What's wrong?"

"Remember the guy who warned Randy and me to get out of town?"

"Yeah," Sams replied. "What about him?"

"That's him," Foster said as he pointed to the dead Reaper. "Those bastards turned Calvin into a Reaper."

CHAPTER FORTY-SEVEN

The nighttime mission had been a moderate success. The two men had managed to collect ten boxes of 9mm hollow-point bullets, three multi-tools, two containers of hockey stick wax, and a pair of combat knives. The extra backpacks had come in handy for collecting all of the bottles of water sitting in a point-of-purchase refrigerator next to the cash registers. He wasn't sure if the wax would be the right type for the enhanced bullets, but Foster figured it was best to let Nick make that decision. With a little bit of luck, the former Ranger would be able to use it.

The return trip to the house went smoothly. Two hours after they got back, Walker was up and moving about the living room.

"Does your wife know you're up?" Foster asked.

"She's asleep," Walker said softly. "Best to let her. And before you ask, I'm fine."

"Uh-huh," Sams said. "It's your ass if Lizzy wakes up and finds you missing."

"We brought you back some bullets and wax," Foster said. "I wasn't sure if hockey stick wax would work or not."

"No clue," Walker said as he carefully peeked out a window. "I guess I'll find out when I try it."

"Still quiet out there?" Foster asked.

"No," Walker said. "We've got a problem."

"Only one?" Sams replied. "Things must be improving. About time we caught a break."

"I'm not kidding," Walker said. "We've got uninvited company."

"How many?"

"Six that I can see," Walker said without moving from his window.

"There could be more out there," Foster pointed out. "Everybody, keep the noise down."

"I'm on it," Sams said. He hustled to the other side of the ground floor and glanced out one of the windows.

A moment later, Foster heard the former Ranger swear under his breath. "How bad?" Foster asked. He saw Lauren, Randall, and Randy quietly enter the room from the basement.

"Ten maybe, twelve."

"Thoughts, guys?" Foster asked.

"Time to split," Sams said. "We should get out of here while we can."

"But we're not ready," Randy protested. "We've only got three quarters of the fuel for the boat."

"Keep your voice down," Lauren hissed.

"Your wife has a point," Sams quipped. "It doesn't help our cause to advertise there are humans in here."

"We can forget about fuel if those things get in here and kill everybody," Walker pointed out. He glanced over at Randy and saw the man's face had lost nearly all of its color. "Just being honest," Walker added.

"W-we have guns," Randy said. "Couldn't we make a stand here?"

"Maybe," Foster said. "But there's too many doors and windows for us to adequately cover all of them."

"Don't forget the shitty doors," Sams added.

"Right, the doors won't hold back much of a breaching attempt because they're hollow," Foster said. "As soon as we start shooting, it's going to draw even more Reapers our way."

"Right now they're just snooping around the neighborhood," Walker said softly. "If we move quietly, we might be able to get everybody into the vehicles and get on the road before the Reapers notice."

"Or if we sit tight, they might ignore us completely," Lauren pointed out. "There has to be easier prey for them to hunt than a bunch of folks hiding in a boarded-up house."

"My vote is we stay here and fight if we have to," Randy said. "What do you think, Dad?"

"I think we should listen to the former soldiers," Randall said. "These guys have managed to help their group survive more than one Reaper attack."

"If we stay here, then we have to hope they don't notice us and just move on," Foster said. "Because if we have to start shooting, it's going to be like ringing a damn dinner bell. We'll have hundreds more of those things on our doorstep before we know it."

"Ah, hell," Randy said. "Not much of a choice, huh?"

"Good news," Walker said. "Looks like they're leaving."

"That is good," Foster said. "Derrick, any changes on your end?"

"Same thing. It's like they lost interest."

"I don't like it," Foster said. "We saw them do a similar probe at Uncle Ray's place before they attacked."

"Good point," Sams said. "Lay low or bug out?"

"Time to go," Foster said. "We don't have much time left on the Disciple deadline, too. I say we take only what we can carry in one trip to the vehicles. Nick, any suggestions on handling exfil?"

"Sams and I will stay on lookout," Walker said. "You get everybody else to line their bags in the hallway leading to the back door. Like you said, take only what you can carry. Figure we'll only get one trip to the vehicles before one of those things notices the activity."

"That works," Foster said. "We can always come back for anything left behind later. But right now, we need to make sure we're clear of the imminent threat."

"Exactly," Walker said. "Keys for the vehicles are under the driver's side mat."

"Except for the Suburban," Foster added.

"Where'd you put the keys for the Suburban?" Walker asked.

"Driver's side sun visor."

"Gotcha," Walker said. "Exfil plan should be to get everybody into the Suburban and the Tucson. Leave the Land Cruiser for Derrick and me. We'll bring up the rear and cover everybody's exit to the SUVs."

"That might work," Foster said, "but who's going to cover for you guys as you try and make your way out of the house to the Land Cruiser?"

"Deputy Donuts does have a point," Sams said. "Maybe we should try and leave as one group. It might be faster that way."

"Yeah, maybe," Walker said. "We might have to play it a bit by ear."

"Sounds like the makings of a plan. Let's get everyone else up quietly and get everything ready to roll out."

CHAPTER FORTY-EIGHT

"Shit," Walker muttered.

"What's wrong?" Foster asked.

"Reapers are back," Walker said. "Three of them. About a block away, but they're slowly working their way toward us. Right now they seem to be more interested in something by that mailbox."

"Maybe roadkill?" Sams suggested.

"Your guess is as good as anyone else's," Foster replied. "For all we know, they could be checking out somebody's week-old trash."

"Right now, they're just snooping around the neighborhood," Walker said softly. "Keep the noise down. Maybe they'll pass."

"Not likely," Sams said from the far side of the living room. "I've got a dozen that just showed up. Shit, they're coming this way."

"What do you think?" Foster said. "Any chance they'll pass by like they did last time?"

"Wishful thinking," Sams said. "Five more just showed up. I really don't like the looks of this."

"Do we need to evac?" Foster asked.

"Can't hurt to get everybody ready just in case," Sams answered.

"Copy that," Foster said. "You heard Derrick. Get ready quietly, and assemble by the back door."

He watched as the rest of the group immediately went into action, collecting their things. Two minutes later, the civilians had all gathered near the back door.

“Nick, we're ready to evac if needed,” Foster said.

“Hold for now,” Walker answered. “Right now, they’re just gathering outside. Until they make a move, I can’t say for sure they’re going to stage an assault.”

“Okay, we’ll wait, then,” Foster said. He turned toward the rest of the group waiting by the rear door and added, “Hang tight, everybody. Let’s hope they go away and we don’t have to leave right now.” Foster looked over the civilians. Everyone looked ready, but most of them looked like they were scared shitless. He shared their fear, but now wasn't the right time to let his true feelings show.

“Here we go. Incoming,” Walker said.

“Multiple contacts,” Sams yelled. Foster saw Sams pull his rifle up and begin firing.

“Foster, I need you,” Walker said. “I got two dozen more that just showed up.”

“On it,” Foster said, rushing to the open embrasure between Walker and Sams. He looked through the opening, and his heart dropped in his chest. There were dozens of Reapers flooding into the neighborhood, and all of them appeared to be heading toward their location. Foster focused on the closest target and fired once. He saw the monster's head snap back. Gunfire increased around him. He saw a swarm of Reapers come charging toward them. He was firing as fast as he could.

“Reloading,” he heard Walker shout.

“Changing,” Sams said. There was a loud bang against the front door, and the structure vibrated from something impacting it. There was another bang, and the wood vibrated once more. The impacts started coming faster and faster.

“I can't see the front door,” Foster said. “Anybody got a shot at the Reapers trying to breach there?”

“Negative,” Sams said. “Totally wrong angle for me. Got my hands full here.”

“Dammit. More of them showing up,” Sams said. “Lizzy, Nick, anybody?”

“Negative on the front door,” Walker said. “Maybe someone can hit them from upstairs.”

The front door began to buckle.

“No time. Front door is about to be breached,” Foster said. “We need to get the hell out of here.”

“That settles it. Time to leave, everyone,” Walker yelled. “Foster, fall back and lead them out. Sams and I will cover your exfil.”

“I'm on it,” Foster said. “I'll take the Suburban. Lizzy and Amanda, with me. Gregory, Emily, and Henry, you're with Charles in the Tucson. Lauren, Randall, and Randy. You're in the Land Cruiser with Nick and Sams.”

“You’re not separating me from my kid,” Lauren protested.

“We don’t have time for this,” Foster answered. “We’re all heading to the same place. Move your ass, or stay here and die. Your choice.”

“Lauren, it’s just a short drive,” Randy pleaded. “We need to get out of here before it’s too late.”

There was a loud crash as the inside panel of the front door gave way. A new hole appeared, and a Reaper head popped through it. Foster fired once and struck the Reaper in the head. It went limp in the opening, buying them a few precious seconds of time.

“Foster, get those people out of here,” Sams yelled. The door began to buckle, and Foster saw the former Ranger fire twice through it.

Foster began to backpedal, and as he did, he saw the rest of the front door literally disintegrate in front of them as six Reapers slammed into it and stumbled into the new opening. He picked one of the Reapers and fired once, striking the creature in the nose and dropping it immediately. He heard gunfire to his right and knew Sams was actively firing his weapon. Foster saw another monster's head snap sideways, and it crumpled to the ground, and then the third one disappeared in a cloud of bloody mist.

“Move, move, move,” Sams shouted, hustling sideways, aiming and firing at the now-open breach in the front of the building.

“Nick, fall back!” Foster yelled. “Breach! We got to go!” He took a deep breath, exhaled, slid the bar away from the rear door, pushed the rear door open, stepped out, and brought his rifle up into a ready position, actively scanning for any targets.

As he moved toward the Suburban, which was the front most vehicle, he saw a Reaper sniffing near the right front tire. Foster's movement caused the Reaper to look up. It let out a low growl, and Foster immediately fired, striking the monster between the eyes. The bullet caused the Reaper's head to snap back, and it fell onto its back, dead. A series of other growls and roars sounded out throughout the neighborhood.

"They know we're here," Foster said. "Get in the vehicles now."

He immediately rushed to the Suburban, opened the driver's side door, and took up a shooting position, continuing to seek any incoming hostiles. Foster saw two Reapers come tearing around the corner. One saw him and dropped to all fours right as Foster fired. He realized his mistake that he was shooting at them over the hood of the Suburban. He couldn't risk hitting the engine block with his shots. He took a step forward to give himself a clearer shooting lane. He heard the side doors of the Suburban open and Amanda yell, "Malcolm, let's go!"

Foster unleashed a barrage of bullets, stitching them across the pair of Reapers still charging toward him. He saw the bullet strike home, and the monsters' bodies staggered. The hostiles were temporarily delayed, and Foster immediately retreated to the driver's side seat of the Suburban and climbed in. He pulled the door shut with a loud bang and immediately engaged the door locks. Another monster came flying up, smashed into the side of the Suburban, and bounced off it. The creature growled, stood up, and charged again.

Foster lifted the visor, and the keys dropped into his expecting hand. He hurried to put the key in the ignition. He heard a vehicle start up behind him, glanced in the rear mirror, and saw that Charles had managed to get his family into their vehicle. The elderly man flashed the headlights, signaling he was ready to go. He glanced up, saw that Sams and Walker were still firing, and that more Reapers were coming from the rear. At least a dozen were now bearing down on the two men as they worked their way toward the Land Cruiser. He saw both men work in tandem, opening their doors and jumping in the Land Cruiser in time, pulling the doors shut.

Foster stuck the key in the Suburban's ignition, turned it, and the vehicle roared to life. He threw it in gear and stomped on the accelerator. The armored vehicle lurched forward, slamming a Reaper that was in front of it, knocking it out of the way. Foster watched as the creature's body pinballed off the front of the vehicle, spinning, and landing off to the side. The monster appeared to be dazed, picked itself up slowly, and began chasing after their vehicles.

Foster swerved on through the driveway, over the sidewalk, and onto the roadway, with a loud bang as the tail end of the Suburban hit. He winced at the sound, knowing that he had likely scraped the underside of the vehicle. He swung the wheel hard to the left and began driving toward the marina. A quick glance in his rearview mirror showed that everybody else had managed to make it out alive.

Lizzy let out a loud whoop of appreciation. "Yeah! We did it!"

Amanda started laughing. "You get excited about the smallest of things," she said.

"Try it sometime. You might like it." Lizzy laughed.

"Next stop, marina," Foster said. "Then we blow this pop stand and head to Hope Island."

CHAPTER FORTY-NINE

The lone Reaper looked carefully up the street. It felt somewhat nervous being alone from its packmates, but then it wasn't here to hunt. The monster found an intersection and began to carefully sniff the air. There were others in the area like him, but they were not part of his pack. He reached out to his master to confirm that this was indeed the scent he was looking for.

The Reaper couldn't feel his master's answer fill his mind, and it made him nervous. Of course, his master was very busy and was known to not always answer questions from foot soldiers like him. It was probably best if he did exactly what his pack leader had told him. He turned his attention back to the area around him, stood as tall as he could, and let out a loud roar. He beat his chest twice, paused for a moment, and then roared once more.

Another Reaper emerged from the shadows, and the two monsters studied each other carefully. They looked similar but somehow different because they were not packmates.

Three more creatures stepped out of the shadows, and the Reaper felt a small spike of a feeling he wasn't familiar with. A small voice somewhere in his mind said it was called fear. A louder voice spoke and said he had nothing to be afraid of. He wasn't here to fight. He was here for a completely different purpose.

The Reaper slowly knelt, lifted his hands up, and placed them on his head like his pack leader had told him to do. He lowered his eyes to stare at a spot in front of him on the ground and waited for the other warriors to approach.

He felt their eyes on him, and then he began to speak in a series of growls and yips. He felt several hands grab his arms and lift him up. He didn't resist. It was very important that he didn't. He was here on a special mission. If he followed his master's orders exactly, then it would bring much honor to his packmates and him.

Haas paced nervously, waiting for his soldiers to return.

"You're sure it's not one of ours?" Giles asked.

"Positive. My warriors would know the difference."

There was a loud bang as a door was pushed open into this space. It was the ideal entranceway for their warriors because it lacked an actual doorknob. Haas still remembered the look of dismay on Giles's face when he realized that their minions couldn't figure out how to operate a doorknob. He'd finally gotten tired of having to open and close the door for their soldiers and just tore the knob out in a fit of rage. It might have been a bit childish on his friend's part, but at least they no longer had to worry about some idiotic minion slamming repeatedly against the door until one of them opened it. Haas pushed the memory to the back of his mind and put a far more serious look on his face.

"Bring him here," Haas ordered.

His soldiers half-carried, half-dragged the captured soldier forward. They released their captive, and he collapsed in a heap in front of Haas.

The soldier immediately shifted onto his knees, staring at the floor, keeping his hands on top of his head.

His actions were quite curious to Haas, and he couldn't help but growl, "Who are you?"

The soldier answered in a soft yelp, closely followed by a short growl.

"Messenger, huh?" Haas said. "Interesting."

"Who do you think sent him?" Giles thought aloud.

The messenger began to answer.

"Hold still," Haas interrupted. He reached out with his hand and grabbed the creature's forehead. He felt the submitting messenger stiffen in pain, but he wisely did not fight back. Haas was glad he wouldn't have to torture this lowly creature in order to get the information he wanted.

Haas began to search through the messenger's thoughts. As he did, a new voice sounded out in his head.

"Ah, excellent. I see you got my messenger. Can I just say that for once, I'm glad you didn't kill the messenger?" Beeks said.

"Bad joke," Haas answered.

"You have to give me some credit, Dwayne. How often have you known me to make jokes?"

"You seem to be in an unusually good mood," Haas admitted.

"I am. It has come to my attention that my good friend also managed to survive that clusterfuck known as Bergstrom Biogenics," Beeks sent. *"So tell me. Is your pocket protector geek with you, too?"*

Haas looked over at Giles and mentally said, *"No, he's not."*

"Dwayne, tsk, tsk. I have a very strong feeling you're being less than truthful."

Haas remained silent.

"But that's okay. You can just as easily pass the word on."

"And what word is that?"

"Oh, it's simple. I would like to talk about an alliance with you and your nerd friend."

"Why would you be interested in that?"

"Oh, that's easy," Beeks sent. *"I've got millions of soldiers and most of the country under my control. You don't. But I couldn't care less about that. I think two old friends could definitely reach a compromise that we both are happy with."*

"When and where?"

"Ah, excellent. I will be in touch. Let me set up a location just for the meet."

"I can't wait," Haas said.

"I'm looking forward to it, too," Beeks answered. *"I'll be in touch. In the meantime, please take care of my messenger. Otherwise we could have an unwanted delay until a new one arrives."*

"Don't worry, Beeks. Your messenger is safe for now. This better not be some kind of game."

"Of course not, Haas. That's not how good friends treat each other, right?"

"Right."

"Excellent. I'll be in touch," Beeks said.

A moment later, Haas felt his former jailhouse friend's presence leave. The messenger collapsed on the floor in front of him, too exhausted to care about the breach in etiquette.

Haas decided to ignore the transgression. He turned to his soldiers and said, "Find lodging for our guest. Do not hurt him, but do not let him leave or mingle with the others, either."

A series of affirmative growls sounded out, and his warriors sprang into action. Haas waited until his minions had removed the messenger from the room before he turned his attention to Giles and said, "We need to talk."

CHAPTER FIFTY

There was a loud snapping noise near her, and Vasquez came to with a start. She saw a group of Reapers creeping toward her, and her adrenaline immediately skyrocketed. She brought her GAU-5/A rifle up to her right shoulder and began firing as fast as she could pull the trigger. She saw several monsters get hit by the barrage of bullets. She kept firing until the weapon clicked dry. Vasquez instinctively reached for another magazine with her left hand, and an immediate jolt of pain stopped her movement. Vasquez gritted her teeth and fought through the pain to grab the needed magazine. The pain was nearly unbearable, but she somehow managed to drop the spent magazine and slide a new one in its place. Vasquez brought her head up and looked. The Reapers were even closer. Worse, they had seemed to have grown in numbers. She brought the rifle up once more and screamed, "Come on, you bastards." If she was going to die, then she was going to take as many of these things with her as possible.

Beeks watched as his minions tried to sneak up on the unconscious human. They had managed to get halfway there when Beeks heard a loud snap and knew one of his soldiers had managed to step on a fallen branch.

"You idiots. Capture the pilot now," Beeks commanded.

Beeks saw the pilot startle and bring a rifle up and begin shooting. He felt the bullets striking his children. He felt one and then another get shot in the head and die.

"I want them alive," Beeks snarled.

One of his minions was close enough now that he could make out the pilot's face through their eyes. It was definitely a woman. She was different. A fighter with the spirit of a warrior, and Beeks couldn't help but want her. The feeling surprised him. It wasn't lust. It was respect. She was someone that somehow was being brave in the face of danger. That was someone who would make an excellent fighter in his army. Perhaps even a red-eyed Alpha once she had accepted the inevitable and surrendered to her eventual transformation.

Beeks saw the woman struggling to load the rifle. There was something wrong with one of her arms.

"What are you waiting for? Grab the woman," Beeks ordered. *"But do not kill her, or you will all die."*

Beeks saw the woman bring the weapon up and begin firing again. He heard the woman scream something, but he wasn't sure what she was saying.

Several more of his warriors were hit by the flying bullets. Beeks felt another minion's life force disappear and lost his cool.

"Get her! Now, or I will kill all of you where you stand," Beeks mentally screamed.

He saw four minions slam into the woman from her left side. Beeks heard the woman scream out in pain and grab momentarily toward her left shoulder before using her right hand to attempt to push off her attackers. Six more Reapers piled onto her, and yet the pilot continued to battle in a losing attempt to get free.

Beeks watched his soldiers slowly overpower the woman, pinning her arms and legs to the ground. An idea popped into his head, and he decided to act on it.

Beeks reached out and took control of one of the Reapers. He compelled his soldier to move toward her exposed neck and sink its teeth into the tender flesh. The woman screamed in pain, but Beeks ignored her. He needed information, and this pilot had it.

Beeks drew from his life force and channeled some energy through his conduit.

"What are you doing here?" Beeks asked mentally. He reached out and touched the woman's mind. She was definitely a fighter. She continued to mentally struggle against his powers. Even so, she was no match for his telepathic abilities.

"I asked you a question. What are you doing here?" Beeks asked again.

The pilot continued to struggle against his control. Beeks felt her body and mind continue to weaken.

"Why are you here?" Beeks insisted. He felt the pilot's body go limp. He continued to hold the bite, forcing more energy and life force into the woman's body. He felt a new sensation. One where the woman's mind and body could not hold any additional energy. He commanded his conduit to release its hold on the pilot's neck. As the minion slowly withdrew, the pilot came to and Beeks was staring into a new pair of yellow eyes.

"Let her up," Beeks commanded. *"Welcome, my child."*

He watched through another soldier's eyes as she lifted her head and slowly stared off into nowhere.

"What an interesting person you are," Beeks mentally sent. *"You intrigue me. I am your master. Tell me why you are here."*

He felt part of her mind begin to fight against him. Beeks was surprised this pilot was somehow able to try and resist his suggestions. But with her recent injuries and transformation, she had no chance to stop him. Beeks reached into her mind and bulldozed over her resistance.

"Angel. I like your name. Perhaps I'll let you keep it," Beeks said. *"Oh. You're a pilot. A special mission. Tell me what you were supposed to do."*

He felt some resistance spring forward again, and he immediately overpowered it.

"I don't want to hurt you, but I will," Beeks warned her. He gave her a mental pinch and felt her startle in surprise. *"Tell me what I want to know. Now."* Beeks mentally grasped her mind and slowly began to squeeze her pain center until he felt her resistance collapse. And once

it did, her resistance dropped completely and Beeks began to read her thoughts. Within seconds, he knew everything she did.

Beeks released the pressure from the newly-transformed soldier and felt her collapse in exhaustion.

He reached out to the pack leader once more. *"Bring her back to our den. Take care she arrives here safely and alive,"* Beeks commanded.

"Yes, my Lord," the minion answered.

Beeks withdrew from the pack leader's mind. His senses slowly returned to his present location. As he became aware of his surroundings once more, he began to frown. The humans had been up to something very naughty. Something maybe even dangerous to his flock. He needed to do something to protect his family, but what? He had to come up with a plan, and fast. The pilot's mind had suggested there was very little time left. Beeks stood up from his throne, took three striding steps, and then his knees suddenly buckled. A wave of exhaustion swept over him. Reaching long distance to interrogate the pilot had taken far more out of him than he had realized. He turned to return to his throne, took one staggering step, and crashed onto the floor unconscious.

CHAPTER FIFTY-ONE

"Charles, you got a minute?" Amanda asked.

"Of course," Charles said with a smile. "I have as many minutes as you need."

"I need to ask you something," Amanda said slowly, "but I'm not sure how."

"A direct approach would probably be fine."

"Do you regret ever marrying Helen?"

"What? Oh heavens, no," Charles exclaimed. "Why would I?"

"Well, it's just she's not here now, and she was killed by the Reapers at the hospital and—"

"Yes, I miss Helen. I miss her more than I could ever say. She was the love of my life. I can't tell you how many times I wish she hadn't sacrificed herself in order to buy our freedom. But I understand why she did what she did."

"Really?"

"Of course. The truth of the matter is, Helen was very sick with the cancer. The doctor told us the odds weren't good and even with treatment, she would't beat the disease."

"But wasn't she responding to the chemotherapy?"

"It depends on who you ask. I thought she was getting better, but even before she made her final decision, she wasn't nearly as optimistic. The thing is, I managed to have many years with the most wonderful person I've ever known. We raised two wonderful children who are now adults."

"Even your daughter?"

"Especially her," Charles said with a smile. "She's just as spirited as an adult as she was when she was little."

"Wow. It couldn't have been easy."

"Sometimes it wasn't. But I'm thankful for all of the time and experiences we had together. I would have loved to have more time with Helen, but I wouldn't trade what I did have for anything else in the world."

"You really mean that, don't you?"

"Of course. There are only two certainties in life. One day we will be born. And someday in the future, we will die. Everything else in between is to be determined. All we can do is plan for the worst and hope for the best. I'm not sure if I answered your question."

"No, you did," Amanda said. "Thank you."

"Anytime," Charles said with a smile.

"It's a trap," Giles argued. "And you're going to lead us right into it."

"It might be," Haas admitted. "But nobody said we had to blindly step right into it."

"Well, how do you figure he's going to want to meet?"

"He'll send another messenger."

"And let me guess. As soon as he does, you'll want to drop everything and go meet this guy."

"We'll meet him at a time that works for all of us."

"Uh-huh. We couldn't trust him when all of us were doing hard time. We sure as hell can't trust him now."

"Except we've got leverage now," Haas said. "We know where this Foster guy is. Beeks has been hot to find this guy for days. We offer up Foster, and in return he lets us stay in our little area here untouched."

"And we just let him have everything else?"

"He's not an unreasonable man," Haas said. "Horatio will definitely take us up on that deal."

"I don't know."

"What's to know? If he doesn't just take the deal, then he doesn't get Foster. You think he's going to want to be embarrassed in front of his minions? Trust me, he won't."

"There's only two of us."

"So? There's only one of him."

"We've seen what yellow-eyed Reapers can do."

"You and I are stronger than them."

"Yeah, but he's got numbers. A lot more of them than we do."

"You worry too much," Haas said.

"Somebody has to. Especially when you go off on a tangent like this."

"You're not my mother," Haas growled.

"I never said I was," Giles pointed out. "I've got a bad feeling about this, Dwayne."

"You and your bad feelings. I'm telling you, it will be fine. We'll meet him someplace neutral, and we'll talk."

"Just talk, huh?"

"If it makes you feel any better, I'll insist he guarantee our safety. If we don't like how things are going, then we just walk away and he won't ever find out where this Foster human is."

"Yeah, I guess that could work."

"Good. I'm glad we agree," Haas said. "I'll set it up. Don't worry. Everything's going to be fine."

CHAPTER FIFTY-TWO

Beeks came to with a start, and an immediate wave of panic coursed over him. The humans were going to bomb their own cities. He might only have a few moments remaining to warn his children before it was too late. The problem was he didn't know which places they were planning on targeting. The pilot only knew of a few places. That made sense, because one fighter pilot couldn't bomb every possible city in the United States. Could there be other targets throughout the country? He couldn't be sure, and that was a big problem. Beeks staggered to his throne and sat down heavily.

Beeks grimaced at the thought of what he needed to do next. He wasn't fully recovered yet from his long-range interrogation, and now it was going to require another large amount of his mental energy to contact all of his family at once. He'd never had a reason before now to reach out to millions of minions at once. Would this be enough to kill him?

Beeks shifted his position on the throne. It was important that he was sitting down someplace away from most of his troops. If his hunch was right, this mass transmission would wipe out his energy reserves again. He needed to be someplace where he wouldn't be visibly weak in front of his soldiers.

He glanced at the doorway. No one had followed him into his throne room, and his guards remained facing outward at the entranceway.

Perfect, Beeks thought. He closed his eyes and reached out telepathically to his extended family.

"Hear me, children," Beeks thought. *"The humans are about to drop fire from the sky. They are going to try and hurt all of us."* He heard a series of growls and yips, seemingly an equal mix of anger and fear.

"Look around you," Beeks continued. *"Find shelter someplace below ground. Do not be caught out in the open. It will be very dangerous for you to be outdoors when the bombs begin falling. Take your brothers and sisters with you. Go deep underground. I will help and reach out to you after these bombings have ended. Be safe, my children."*

Beeks felt several replies pop up in his mind. The number began to increase, and he quickly decided to turn them off and avoid the likely chaotic noise it would create in his mind. Beeks slumped back in his throne. He noticed he was completely drenched in sweat. Just as bad, his efforts had left him feeling extremely weak. He glanced toward the doorway. His guards had moved back to their standard positions and were still standing with their backs to him. Good. No one had seen him in his weakened state. He didn't have to worry about a potential rebellion for now.

He was tired. So very tired. Maybe he would close his eyes and rest. Just for a few minutes. A quick little nap. Beeks closed his eyes and immediately fell into a deep sleep.

The tension in the room was nearly unbearable as President Vickers scanned the rest of the room. Captain Flores had cleared the room of all nonessential personnel, and now she was glad only a select handful could see how nervous she was.

General Weindahl politely cleared his throat. "Madam President," he said. "We're almost ready to begin Operation Flashpoint."

"How are we seeing this?" the president asked.

"We have drones providing live stream footage."

"Are they in danger of getting spotted by the Reapers?" Vickers asked.

"Negative, ma'am," Weindahl said. "They're maintaining an aerial patrol out at approximately 10,000 feet on the outskirts of the city."

"Is that high enough to avoid being affected by the bombing?"

"We believe so."

"Where are the monsters?"

"The majority of them are still inside the city limits. There's been no intel to suggest otherwise."

"Even so, I'd like you to move one of the drones to capture footage of any creatures trying to flee the bombings."

"I'm not sure that's a good idea, ma'am," Weindahl said. "We may miss the event, or it could put the drone in harm's way. Also, the lower the altitude, the more risk we would be taking of being spotted by the Reapers. As these things have demonstrated, we can't assume they're stupid."

"No, we cannot." Vickers sighed. "Can you at least turn one of the drones to a different view? I want visual confirmation that these bastards are dying from this bombing."

"Make it so," Weindahl ordered.

"One moment, Madam President," the technician answered. There was a series of clacking noises as she typed on the keyboard. A moment later, one of the video streams changed to a wide-angle view.

"Take a look," Flores said. "Upper right corner of the feed. There appear to be several monsters."

Reapers. Why don't you call them what everybody else does? Vickers thought to herself. These things were hardly something that would jump out of a closet in the middle of the night and terrorize young children.

"Can you zoom in after the detonation?" Vickers asked.

"Of course."

"Madam President, it's probably best if you stand back here with me and watch this," Flores suggested.

The president flashed a fishy-eyed look at the captain, who immediately began to verbally backpedal.

"What I mean, ma'am, is you can see all the displays from this spot in the room better."

President Vickers chose to say nothing and took her time walking over to the spot the captain had indicated next to him.

There was a bright flash, and a loud roar came through the speakers. Vickers glanced at the screens and saw huge billowing clouds of flame and smoke.

"Where is that?" Vickers asked.

"Philadelphia. Ma'am, we're getting ready to start the New York bombings. Boston won't be hit for another two minutes."

"I'm surprised you don't have the timing down better," she quipped.

"Under normal circumstances, we would," Weindahl said. "Unfortunately, we're working with bare-bones equipment, and some of our personnel are a bit green with these types of operations."

"They won't be, after today," Vickers said as she continued to watch the screens. A moment later, the images started to become clearer as the dust began to settle.

Vickers squinted as she tried to focus her eyes on the video feed in the upper right corner of the display.

"There's something moving there," she said. "Can you zoom in on it?"

"Yes, Madam President," the technician said. "One minute."

The camera display changed as the drone shifted position and began to zoom in. As the image began to get sharper in focus, Vickers saw two lone Reapers staggering in the aftermath. One was still on fire, and Vickers watched as it dropped to the ground. The creature began to instinctively roll back and forth in an attempt to extinguish the flames. She looked at the second Reaper. It appeared to be struggling to stay on its feet. There were pieces of fur and flesh missing from its torso and leg. The Reaper took two more steps and then collapsed.

"You see that?" Captain Flores yelled. "It worked. It actually worked."

A cheer began to go across the room. Operation Flashpoint had landed the first strike, and it had dealt a serious blow to the Reaper armies.

CHAPTER FIFTY-THREE

Beeks awoke with a start and looked around, unsure of how long he'd been unconscious. He remembered being in his throne, and now he was coming to on the floor again.

I overdid it with transforming the pilot and contacting all of my troops, he thought.

Beeks struggled to his throne and sat down. As he did, his arms started to feel like someone was poking him with a small needle. The sensation spread to his torso, then his legs. A moment later he was hit with a deluge of pain as thousands of his children screamed out in agony.

"It burns, Master, it burns. Make it stop," a voice screamed in his head.

"Get underground now," he mentally shouted again. Some of his minions moved to escape the bombings, and he felt their pain start to diminish. But too many of them didn't, and he felt their pain and their agony like it was his own.

Vickers quietly continued to watch the displays. As she did, one of the Reapers slowly began to rise. It appeared to have once been a middle-aged man. There were visibly graphic wounds all across its body. She could see a number of places where the creature's body hair had been burned off.

As she watched the live feed, the Reaper's wounds began to heal. The skin began to smooth out, and new hair began to form where it had previously been lost.

A feeling of panic swept over Vickers as she watched the Reaper slowly stand upright and reach toward the sky. The creature let out a loud roar and slammed its fist against its chest. A second roar sounded out nearby. Then a third.

Vickers's eyes focused on the other downed Reaper. The creature had managed to snuff out the flames that had been consuming its body. Now it was back on its feet again. The burns were quickly closing up, and the Reaper let out a roar which echoed throughout the conference room.

"Cancel the other bombings," Vickers said quietly.

"But ma'am, they still have a chance of succeeding," Weindahl protested. "We have to give it a try."

"We did," Vickers countered. "We need to face the facts. Operation Flashpoint has failed."

"Madam President, I understand what you're saying, but there's still a chance the bombings can eliminate a significant number of Reapers," Flores pleaded. "We need to try."

"I just watched two Reapers that were burned badly heal their injuries and continue acting like nothing was wrong. Scrub the rest of the mission. That's an order."

"Yes, Madam President," Weindahl sighed. He picked up the phone and said, "Mission aborted. Operation Flashpoint is aborted. All planes are to head to their designated operating bases immediately."

Vickers waited until the general hung up the phone before saying, "This just got a lot more complicated."

"I'm not sure I understand."

"We just learned the Reapers can't be killed by fire. That just limited our options even more."

Every nerve in his body felt like it was on fire. Beeks looked at his arms, but there was nothing physically wrong with them. Another wave of agony swept over him, and Beeks screamed out, feeling pain that wasn't his. His children, he was feeling their pain, and it was overwhelming to feel all of them at once. His hands grabbed the arms of his throne, clutching them as he tried to fight being overwhelmed by the pain.

Then, as quickly as it started, it was over. Beeks reached out slowly and checked on each of his children to see who was injured and who was still alive. As his soldiers reported in, Beeks felt his spirits rise. The humans' bold plan had failed. Now it was time for retribution. He couldn't wait to make them pay for what they had done.

CHAPTER FIFTY-FOUR

The three vehicles came to a stop in the marina parking lot. Foster and the rest of his group stepped outside and gathered near the entrance. A pair of chain-link fence doors were closed. There was a chain threaded through the handles with a padlock clipped in place.

"We made it," Lizzy said. "We finally made it."

"Yeah, but we need to keep moving," Walker said. "We're sitting ducks right now."

"Nick, you want to take overwatch?" Foster asked. "I'll help Gregory and Sams with the gates."

Walker nodded once. He brought his rifle up and began scanning the surrounding areas for any potential threats.

"What do you want the rest of us to do?" Charles asked.

"Good question," Foster said. "If the rest of you wouldn't mind grabbing the rest of the gear from the vehicles, then we should be able to load up the boat a lot faster."

Gregory motioned quickly. "Sams, hand me the bolt cutters," he said.

Sams carefully set down his backpack and unzipped it. He pulled out the small pair of bolt cutters and passed them over to Gregory. "Good thing you had these in your basement."

Foster watched as Gregory sized up the lock, opened the handles of the bolt cutters, and placed the cutting edge around the loop of the keylock. Gregory pushed the handles together, breaking the lock with a loud snap. The man pulled the lock off and instinctively tossed it aside. It clattered loudly against the ground. Gregory began to pull the looped chain out. As he did go, a loud howl sounded, and he dropped the chain in surprise.

"That sounded close," Foster said.

"Too close," Sams replied. He brought his gun up.

"Everybody move through the fence," Foster said. "Keep your eyes peeled for any incoming Reapers. Randy, how soon can you have the boat ready to go?"

"Not long. I need a few minutes to get the boat prepped and ready to launch," Randy said. "I could use some help carrying these fuel canisters."

"Is what we're carrying onto the boat going to be enough fuel?" Walker asked.

"Not even close," Foster said.

"What about draining fuel out of the vehicles?" Sams asked. "If we dump this fuel into the boat, then we can refill the containers from our vehicles."

"As long as we don't draw any unwanted attention, it's still a viable option. But we need to get our current fuel canisters onto the boat as quickly as possible."

"I'll help," Lauren said. "I can get my father-in-law situated onto the boat, too."

"Sounds great," Foster said. "The rest of us will make sure we secure this location."

"What about our families?" Gregory asked.

"Good question," Foster answered. "When Randy is ready to launch, he'll start the boat. Once we hear that, we'll send your families, Amanda, and Lizzy to the boat. Walker, Sams, and I will work our way to you and make sure no hostiles get to the boat while we're still docked."

"Sounds like a decent plan," Randy said. "Come on, Dad, let's get this shit on the road."

"You mean on the water," Randall corrected. "You worry about carrying that fuel. I'll be fine getting to the boat."

"But your leg-" Randy said.

"Ain't broken," Randall interrupted. "The day I can't walk on my own is when I'll tell you to take me behind the shed and shoot me. Now, get a move on, you're holding everybody up."

Foster watched as Randy grabbed two fuel cans and begin walking toward his boat. Lauren followed suit, and her father-in-law followed a few steps behind.

"Incoming," Sams called out. "Two o'clock."

"Damn it, I knew it was too good to be true," Walker grumbled. He moved to the opposite side of the walkway.

"Scrap refilling the canisters," Foster called out. "We need to get the boat ready for launch, pronto." He rushed over, picked up the loose chain, and began looping it back in place. Once it was secured, he pulled out a pair of zip ties and used them to bind the ends of the chain together. It wouldn't be as secure as the previous metal lock had been, but it might buy them a few more minutes to make their escape.

Foster looked at the three Reapers bounding toward them. He brought his rifle up and began to sight on the incoming hostiles.

"Wait until they're close to fire," Sams said. "We just need to buy time until the boat is ready to go."

"Copy that," Walker answered. "Head shots only. Conserve your ammo, people."

"Charles," Randy called from the edge of the boat. "Why don't you come with us now?"

"Soon," Charles answered. "I need to help them keep these things from getting to the boat."

Randy nodded once, then stepped onto the boat and disappeared from sight. A moment later, Lauren stepped onto the boat, set her fuel barrels down, and then turned to help her father-in-law climb aboard.

Foster turned his attention toward the incoming Reapers. It had been less than a minute, but there were now more than a dozen of the creatures heading toward them. He sighted on the closest one and began shooting.

Suddenly, a loud noise sounded out behind him, and Foster felt the ground rush up toward his face. He managed to turn his head at the last minute and avoided slamming his nose and teeth into the macadam. He felt an immediate ringing in his ears. Remembering where he was, Foster forced himself up onto a knee and brought his rifle back into a shooting position, carefully aiming between spaces in the chain-link fencing. The Reapers were still coming toward his group, and Foster sighted on the nearest pair and opened fire. He walked the shots up across their charging bodies, watching the trail of bullets move from their torso up into their necks and faces. The Reapers' bodies staggered from the onslaught until the last couple of bullets delivered the fatal blows.

Foster saw the other monsters begin to drop as the rest of his group joined the fight. He risked a glance over his shoulder, and his blood immediately went cold.

The boat was gone. In its place, there was nothing but flames and pieces of wood falling out of the sky.

"Mom!" Emily screamed out. The teenager rushed toward the still-burning debris.

"Emily, stop," Gregory yelled. He rushed after his niece, with his son following a few steps later.

Foster looked at Charles and saw the man looked completely shell-shocked. In an instant, he had lost several family members, including his daughter.

"Multiple contacts," Sams yelled. "How soon on the boat?"

"Boat is gone," Foster shouted back. "We're going to need a different exit plan." He looked at their parked vehicles. There was no way all of them could reach them before the Reapers did. Foster glanced over at the civilians still near him. "Lizzy, Charles, and Amanda. I need you to keep the rest of the group together and behind us. Check and see if anyone is injured from the explosion."

"I will," Amanda replied. Foster saw Charles move numbly after her.

"Incoming at ten, eleven, and one o'clock," Walker shouted. "Lizzy, I need your help now."

Foster watched as Nick's wife rushed to her husband's side and began firing next to him. He looked at the battle unfolding in front of him. There were hundreds of Reapers charging toward them. As he scanned the area, he did a double take. He looked again and saw there were a dozen armed humans, flanked by Reapers, coming toward them.

"Are you seeing what I'm seeing?" Foster said aloud.

"Turncoats," Walker shouted back. "Are you kidding me?"

CHAPTER FIFTY-FIVE

The meeting request finally came. And when it did, it was the already-captured Reaper simply parroting a new message. Haas should have figured something like that would happen.

Haas and Giles had agreed to the meeting and followed their guest back to Beeks's den. Their former inmate had managed to secure a location that was only a few hours away from their own.

As Haas warily scanned his surroundings, he couldn't help but be a little impressed. He and Giles were being led through a wide corridor. There was one of Beeks's soldiers in front of them and a seemingly endless amount of other ones on the sides of the hallway. As they approached, the minions silently flattened against the walls, creating additional space for them to pass. Giles glanced behind him and saw Beeks's family members shifting back in place after they passed. They weren't actually soldiers in the traditional sense of the word, but he couldn't think of a better word to describe the overwhelming number of minions they were passing.

Haas felt a wave of anxiety come rushing forward. There were so many yellow-eyes around them. Probably thousands of them, and none of them were under his control. Could they get out of there if they had to? If they were fighting any of them individually, it would have been no match. He was completely confident they could manhandle the lesser beings. But two of them against perhaps thousands of Beeks's yellow-eyed minions? He hated to admit it even to himself. If this meeting went badly, then their chances of survival were not good. They were very much at the mercy of Beeks keeping his word of safe passage.

Haas turned his attention to the doorway they were quickly approaching. He noticed there were a pair of guards stationed in front of it. Each one was as big as himself, and he couldn't help but be impressed. The massive duo wordlessly slid sideways, creating an opening for them to pass unabated into the next room.

As Haas stepped through the doorway, he studied his surroundings. It had the look and feel of a huge medieval throne room, complete with decorative draping. His eyes moved from one side of the large room to the other and then shifted back to the middle, where a huge stone throne was situated. Haas didn't have the foggiest idea where they could have found such a large and gaudy seat, but it didn't matter. It was right there in front of him.

He glanced over his shoulder and was pleased to see that Giles was still following him closely. He wouldn't need to worry about his friend lagging behind or getting separated from him.

Haas turned his attention back to the area in front of him. As his eyes adjusted to the lighting, he saw it was Beeks sitting on the throne.

The pack leader flashed a big ear-to-ear grin. "Welcome to my humble abode," he said.

"If this is humble, I'd like to see what braggadocio would look like," Giles muttered softly.

Haas glanced over his shoulder and flashed his friend a knowing look. There was no need to start their attempted treaty talks by antagonizing Horatio Beeks.

"It's a bit much for my taste," Haas admitted.

"Maybe," Beeks replied. "But it serves our needs quite well. I'm surprised that you have lived this long."

"I could say the same for you," Haas answered. "I suspect none of us have many friends remaining anymore."

Beeks chuckled. "Quite true, indeed. You're here to discuss a treaty."

"Yes."

Beeks made a sweeping motion with his hand. "As you can see, I'm doing well on my own."

Haas looked to his left and right. There were dozens of yellow-eyes in the room. "Do all of them need to be here?"

"I don't have a problem with it," Beeks said. "This is a historical meeting between your family and mine."

"I guess," Haas muttered. "Just tell them to stay out of our way."

"Of course," Beeks said smoothly. "So tell me what you have to offer that might interest me?"

Haas looked over to Giles. His friend stepped up and began to speak.

"Greetings, Horatio," Giles began.

"Please, call me Beeks."

"My apologies. I had forgotten you are not fond of your given name," Giles said.

Beeks let out a low growl.

"But that's not important," Giles said quickly. "What is important is that we have contained the man and the group you have been seeking."

Beeks immediately stiffened in his seat. "I'm afraid I don't know what you're talking about."

"Really?" Giles challenged. "I was under the impression you've been trying to capture this Fos-ter character for a while now."

A series of growls sounded out from the room. Several of the yellow-eyes began to pace.

"Control yourselves," Beeks snarled. The room immediately went still. "That's very interesting. You are right. I have been looking for this pesky human. He's managed to elude us more than once. And yet you and your small group of followers have managed to capture him. How do I know you're telling me the truth?"

"Simple," Giles said. "I have used my allies and my pack to accomplish what you have failed to do."

A low growl came out of Beeks's throat. "Speak carefully," he snarled. "You are dangerously close to feeling the full extent of my ire. If there have been failings, it has been members of my pack and not my own."

"Point taken," Giles said. "I meant no disrespect."

"What do you seek in return for Foster and his group of pitiful humans?"

"We would like to have a place for our family to live unopposed and on our own."

"And the rest of the country?"

"It would be yours to do with as you wish," Giles said simply. "This is our peace offering and what we hope will be the beginning of a positive alliance."

"An alliance. How interesting," Beeks said as he slowly rose from his throne. "I think we've gotten off on the wrong foot in the past. May I call you Giles?"

Haas saw his friend nod once and watched as Beeks approached them.

"I think what you're offering is fair," Beeks said. He put his arm loosely around Giles's shoulder and began to walk the two of them across the room. The yellow-eyed minions in the room shifted their positions, creating an easy pathway for the two of them to walk through. "I could see me agreeing to those terms quite nicely."

"I'm glad to hear that," Giles stammered.

Beeks came to a complete stop. "There's just one problem with your offer."

"What's that?" Giles asked.

"I don't need you to capture Foster," Beeks said. His hand went up, and his claws suddenly appeared, fully extended, a moment before he slammed them into the back of Giles's neck.

"No!" Haas roared. As he stepped forward to intervene, dozens of yellow-eyes slammed into him, knocking him to the ground. Haas fought like a demon possessed, pushing and slashing each limb he could access. Even more of Beeks's soldiers poured into the space between Haas and his wounded friend.

Haas surged against the mass of attackers and managed to get back onto one knee before the new sea of transformed humans slammed him back onto the floor. He felt the side of his head smash against the hard throne room floor, and several sets of hands immediately pinned it there. A wave of desperation came over him. Giles was in trouble, and he had to help his friend. Haas let out a roar and fought to break free from his captors. But as he struggled to free himself, he saw Giles was now lying motionless on the floor. He saw Beeks's foot rise up in the air and smash down on his helpless friend's head.

CHAPTER FIFTY-SIX

Foster watched in amazement as the Reapers seemed to halt as one and form a semicircle around the humans in the middle.

"Just when you think you've seen it all," Sams muttered under his breath, "these things pull a new trick out of thin air."

One of the humans stepped forward, and Foster recognized him immediately. Walter brought a bullhorn up to his face, and a moment later a loud squeak sounded from the device.

The noise ended, and the man began to talk. "Hello, Malcolm," he said smoothly.

"I need Nick and you to come up with an escape plan while I stall them," Foster said softly over the group comms. A pair of double clicks sounded in reply, signaling that both former Rangers understood. He stepped forward one big step and then spoke up. "Howdy, Walter. What's with bringing all of these things?"

"For starters," Walter said, "you are trespassing."

"We were actually planning on leaving," Foster said. He glanced to his left and then to his right. No one in his group seemed to have shifted their position, and the comms were uncomfortably silent. "At least, until our boat blew up. You know anything about that?"

"Don't you mean our boat?" Walter answered.

"No, it wasn't. The boat belonged to my cousin. I'll ask you again," Foster said. "Did you sabotage it?"

"Everything you see around you belongs to the Disciples," Walter said. "Everything. We will take any measure we see fit to protect what is ours."

"I think that answers the question if any of the other boats are booby trapped," Walker muttered over the comms.

"We've got to try something," Sams said softly. "Staying here is a fucking death trap."

"Three options," Walker said. "Option one, Foster sweet-talks us out of this mess. Option two, we funnel them through the marina opening and kill as many of them as we can until they're all dead or we are. Or option three, we make an escape path through these things and get to our vehicles."

"All of those options suck," Sams countered.

"Take a look around. We're already trapped," Foster whispered over the comms. "Feel free to offer a better plan, Army."

"Ah, hell." Sams groaned. "Foster, better turn the charm up to eleven, or things are going to get really ugly fast."

"Please accept our apologies," Foster said. "We are a group of survivors who are just passing through. If you grant us safe passage, we will leave in peace and never return."

"I gave you that option before, and you didn't take it," Walter said. "I need your decision, Malcolm."

"I'm not sure we can," Foster stalled. "Some of our group are still trying to reunite with lost family members in North Carolina and Florida."

"Then all the more reason to join us," Walter shouted back. "We will help you bring in your lost sheep."

"Did he just call us sheep?" Lizzy asked.

"Not now, hon," Walker said in a low voice. "Let Foster handle this."

"Let's talk trade," Foster said. "We have things to barter. Food. Medicine. If you are willing to trade one of your boats and let us leave in peace, then we'll make it worth your while."

"I'm afraid not," Walter said. His voice suddenly became more hostile-sounding. "Enough talking. Join us, or else." All of the Reapers immediately moved one step forward.

"Now, hold on," Foster protested. "This doesn't-"

"You have ten seconds to repent," Walter said. His voice began to get louder. "After that, I will give the order for our Guardians to purge your existence from our lands."

"Come on, Walter," Foster said. "Be reasonable."

"Nine, eight," Walter yelled. The other cult followers began chanting the countdown along with him. "Four, three, two-"

A single shot sounded out. A lone bullet hole suddenly appeared in the middle of the man's forehead, and he crumpled to the ground.

"What the hell did you do that for?" Foster demanded.

"Seemed like a good idea at the time," Sams answered. "The guy wouldn't shut up."

"The bullhorn was really annoying," Walker pointed out. "If he hadn't shot him, I was going to when he reached one."

"Oh hell, here they come," Foster said. He brought his rifle up into a shooting position, sighted on a charging Reaper, and fired. He heard his friends begin firing, and the fight was on.

CHAPTER FIFTY-SEVEN

A series of alarms started going off in the command center.

"What's wrong?" Vickers asked.

"We've got multiple incoming Reaper attacks on six different bases," Weindahl said. "Including Burlington Air National Guard Base, Wright-Patterson Air Force Base, and Scott Air Force Base."

"Wait, isn't that where we launched our planes from?" Vickers asked.

"Yes, it was," Weindahl said. "Wright-Patterson Air Force Base and Scott Air Force Base are where we landed our personnel afterwards."

"Those things are hitting back," Flores said. "We need to get those people out of there."

"We're trying, but we're seeing an overwhelming amount of hostiles incoming."

"Do you have camera feeds there?"

"Yes," a technician answered. "Got one for Scott Air Force Base. I'll put it on screen."

Vickers watched the screen and felt her spirits crash to the floor. There were tens of thousands of Reapers swarming from multiple directions at once. She watched as several soldiers tried to stand their ground, firing at the incoming monsters, but it was a hopeless cause.

The men were quickly overrun and taken to the ground. Vickers heard the screams of pain and anguish as soldiers were being torn apart.

The sound of machine gun fire sounded out, and a Humvee rolled into view. The vehicle's .50 caliber machine gun began to fire, and Vickers watched as the soldier opened fire on a pack of Reapers, walking the tracer rounds up their bodies, striking the creatures with dozens of bullets at once. Nearly a dozen Reapers collapsed under the machine gunner's fury. Vickers felt her spirits start to shift upward. They came crashing back to reality just as quickly. She saw a pack of Reapers attack the gunner from behind. Vickers watched in horror as the man was violently yanked backward off the top of the vehicle and dragged onto the ground. Three Reapers tore into him immediately. The president saw his legs kick twice, and then he was gone.

The camera view switched, and she saw Reapers slamming repeatedly into a building's walls.

"What are they doing?" Vickers asked.

"I'm not sure," Weindahl said. "That's a fuel storage building. I highly doubt anyone is hiding in there. Give us some more camera angles of this base."

"On it," the tech said.

Several more images appeared on the master screen. In each one, the Reapers were slamming their bodies into stationary walls.

"Very strange," Weindahl said. "I've never seen them act like this before."

"It's payback," Vickers thought out loud. "It's not enough to kill our soldiers for the bombing attacks. They're going to level our bases until there's nothing left to ever use again."

"You really think they're that clever?" Weindahl asked.

"Do you really think they're not?" Vickers countered.

"General Weindahl," a technician yelled, "The Pentagon is under attack."

"Give me satellite imagery," Weindahl demanded. "All available camera angles right now."

An overhead image of the Pentagon appeared on the screen. A strange, dark formation surrounded the iconic building.

"What is that?" Vickers said softly.

"The enemy," Weindahl answered. "That has to be hundreds of thousands of Reapers."

"My God, that's a death trap," Vickers said. "We gotta get our people out of there."

"We're trying," the tech shouted, "but communications are down for the Pentagon."

"The entire Pentagon?" Vickers yelled. "It's over six million square feet of space. You mean to tell me you can't reach anybody?"

"There's normally over twenty thousand people there," the technician added. "And I'm telling you I can't get a call through to anyone there right now."

"Keep trying," Vickers said. "We need to at least get those people to the fallout shelters."

"I'm not sure it will make much of a difference," Weindahl said softly. "It didn't for President Marshall, and he was in a state-of-the-art bunker. A fallout shelter isn't nearly as secure."

"We can't just sit on our hands," Vickers said. "What about a bombing attack to thin the herds?"

"There are limited air assets in the area. Most of them are at bases which are also under attack."

"Which means they're probably busy trying to survive and not organize a new attack," Vickers thought aloud. "We might be lucky to get someone on the comms there right now."

"I'm afraid so."

"Fine. What about launching a rescue mission?"

"For thousands of people?" Weindahl asked. "It could take days to move everyone."

"What about by air?"

"Ronald Reagan Washington National Airport is the closest airport."

"How close?"

"Less than two miles."

"Which means anyone on foot probably wouldn't make it," Vickers thought aloud. "Correct me if I'm wrong, but aren't there other ways to get to Reagan National from the Pentagon?"

"Sure. There are bus, train, and taxi options. But if people are on one of them, then why only stop two miles away? The Reapers would eventually notice and head there instead."

"Good point," Vickers admitted. "There is a helipad at the Pentagon."

"Yes, there is," Weindahl said. "But you can't fit dozens or hundreds of people on a helicopter at once. It would take numerous trips to evacuate everybody."

"Then what the hell can we do besides sit here and watch a bunch of people get slaughtered?"

"The underground Metro or bus station would be a better option to move large groups of people quickly," Weindahl said slowly. "Of course, that's assuming whatever armed personnel on the premises could repel incoming Reapers long enough to get everybody else out."

"And what are the odds of that happening?" Vickers demanded.

"Slim at best," Weindahl admitted. "They're facing an overwhelming number of hostiles. The majority of the people on the premises are not armed military."

The room grew quiet as everyone watched the screens in horror. The Reapers were pouring into the Pentagon through multiple entrances.

Several of the screens switched to cameras inside the Pentagon. As they did, they saw people hopelessly fighting and dying. Of course, not every person died, and a growing number of people were transformed into new Reapers. Monsters that would likely attack or kill their former colleagues and friends.

"We've got to find a way to stop this," Vickers said.

"Firebombing them didn't work, and bullets seem to have a limited affect," Weindahl said carefully. "Are you ready to authorize nuclear weapons?"

"No. Seeing how Operation Flashpoint failed, I'm not completely sold on the idea that a nuke would do the trick."

"There's no way those things could survive a direct nuclear strike."

"Do you know that for sure?" Vickers argued. "Or are you guessing? Because everybody was absolutely certain they wouldn't survive the firebombings, and they did."

Weindahl looked at the floor in silence.

"Until we know for certain that nukes will kill these things, that option is not up for discussion."

"With all due respect, Madam President, the only way to know for sure is to try it," Weindahl said softly. "At the rate we're losing this war, I'm not sure how much is going to be left to defend against future attacks. We're quickly reaching the point where we would be extremely vulnerable to attack from foreign countries, too."

Vickers swore under her breath. "Every being has a weakness," she said. "We need to find theirs. General, I have a new mission for you."

"Ma'am?"

"Those scientists you are supposed to be hiding away in a secure location? I want them working on this Reaper problem around the clock. Whatever it takes. Do you understand me?"

"By the time they find something, it might be too late."

"I don't care," Vickers said. "Get our best people on it. Give them the best equipment and resources they need to solve this. We either find the Reapers' weakness to kill them quickly or a way to keep people from being turned into new ones. We do this, or we die trying."

"Yes, Madam President."

CHAPTER FIFTY-EIGHT

The battle had been going heavy for minutes now, and Foster fought to hold back a growing feeling of despair. The Reapers continued to charge toward his small group from three sides. The only direction they weren't attacked from was the one which led to the still-anchored but burning boat. He glanced at his remaining ammunition and saw he was down to three magazines.

"Changing," Foster shouted a moment before he executed a combat magazine swap. He brought his rifle back into a shooting position, sighted on a closing Reaper, and fired once. The monster's head snapped back, and it crumbled awkwardly onto the ground, dead. "How much of the special ammo do we have?" he yelled over the comms.

"Not enough," Walker answered. "I didn't have a chance to make anymore."

"You think using it now would scare the rest of them away?" Foster asked.

"Do they look like they're scared at all?" Walker hollered. "We've killed dozens of them, and they're still coming."

"At least the whack jobs are retreating," Sams yelled over the comms. "I'm down to my last two magazines. If anybody has any brilliant ideas, let's hear them."

"Any of these things look like it's in charge?" Walker shouted. "Shout out its location and maybe Foster can take it out."

"Yeah, like Foster did at the farm. Good idea," Sams answered. "What about the shithead at two o'clock?"

Foster looked in the direction Sams had called out. A single Reaper stood on the back of a pickup truck, keeping its distance from the attacking packs. It didn't seem to be doing anything but watching the battle in front of it. But right now, it was the most likely candidate to be in charge.

Kill the head, and the body will die, Foster thought. "I'm going to take a shot on the possible Reaper leader," he said with a forced calmness. "Cover me."

A series of shouts erupted around him, and there was an increase in gunfire. Foster saw several Reapers in his vicinity drop as his allies scored head shots. Foster turned his attention back to the lone Reaper. He switched to his sniper rifle, a Remington 700, which was loaded with the silver-laced bullets. He sighted on his target and took a slow, calming breath. His scope was visibly moving, and he forced himself to take another breath.

Pull your shit together, Malcolm. You've made harder shots than this, Foster mentally scolded. *If Sams is right, then you can end this battle with this one shot.*

Foster took a third breath and held it. He sighted center mass on the still-oblivious Reaper and pulled the trigger like he was drawing a straight line. The rifle fired, and he watched the Reaper collapse through his scope. "Splash one," he called out. He lowered the rifle and saw the battlefield in front of him, and his heart dropped like a rock.

The Reapers were still attacking.

"Are you sure you killed it?" Sams yelled.

"Positive. I used a Reaper bullet," Foster answered. "Maybe these bastards didn't get the message."

"Switching weapons," Sams shouted. Foster saw him drop his assault rifle, letting the sling catch its weight, draw his holstered handgun, and continue firing. He quickly emptied one magazine and immediately reloaded.

Foster quickly switched back to his M4 and turned his attention back to the battle in front of him. He spotted three Reapers bearing down on Walker's blindside and unleashed a short burst of bullets. The gunfire struck the Reapers in the legs, cutting them down and halting their charge. Foster shifted his aim onto the closest Reaper and fired once, scoring a direct head shot. He immediately shifted his aim to the next Reaper and fired again. He saw the creature's nose sink inward and turned his attention to the remaining hobbled Reaper. As he did, he noticed it was already lying on the ground, a fresh head wound bleeding freely. Foster turned his attention to the surrounding area, searching for the next hostile closing in on their position.

Suddenly, a wave of screams broke out. Dozens of Reapers dropped to their knees, clutching their heads in apparent agony. The monsters fell over as one as if someone had cut a giant invisible string and began spasming uncontrollably. A moment later, all of the downed Reapers stopped moving completely. The chatter of guns firing quickly faded. Foster checked his surroundings and couldn't see any Reapers still standing.

"I'm cutting the zip ties," Walker said as he pulled out his combat knife. "Cover me."

Foster watched as his friend sliced through the bindings and opened the marina gates. Walker stepped slowly forward and stopped near an unmoving creature. He kicked it once, and the creature didn't move. Walker bent down and checked for a carotid pulse. "This one's dead," he said calmly. He scanned the Reaper bodies laying everywhere. "Looks like all of them are dead."

Sams let out a small whoop of victory. "It's because Foster took their leader's sorry ass out. Nice shot, Malcolm."

"Thanks," Foster said. "Cover me."

"Yeah, sure," Sams said.

Foster slowly moved toward where he had seen the Reaper leader collapse.

"What's wrong?" Sams asked.

"Maybe nothing," Foster replied. "I want to check something."

"Come on, man; don't bullshit me," Sams said. "What are you thinking?"

"Remember when I killed that red-eyed Reaper at Uncle Ray's?"

"Of course."

"So how come these ones didn't drop immediately, too?"

"No clue. To be honest, I really don't care, because all of them still wound up dead."

"Yeah, I hear you," Foster said. "But I can't shake the feeling that I'm missing something."

"Foster and his damn gut again." Sams chuckled. "The monsters are fucking dead. That's all that matters."

Foster had reached the downed Reaper in the pickup truck. The creature had fallen onto its back and was lying in a large pool of blood. Foster checked for a pulse, found none, and carefully lifted one of its eyelids. As he did, a lifeless yellow eye slowly appeared. Foster felt a chill run up and back his spine. He checked the other eye. It was also yellow.

"Ah, hell," Foster swore out loud.

"What's wrong?" Walker asked.

"This one has yellow eyes," Foster said.

"So this wasn't their leader?" Sams asked.

"Apparently not," Foster replied. "Which raises another question."

"If we didn't kill their leader," Walker answered, "then how did all of these Reapers suddenly die at once?"

"Fuck a duck," Sams said. "You know what? Let somebody else figure this shit out. We need to get the hell out of here while we can."

CHAPTER FIFTY-NINE

"No!" Haas screamed as Beeks continued to assault the helpless Giles.

There was a sickening crunch as Beeks's foot slammed down again and again. Haas continued to fight, trying to get free. There might still be a chance that his friend wasn't dead. If he could break free, then maybe he could still save Giles. But with each blow he saw his friend's still body absorb, the more he began to feel an overwhelming feeling that his friend was gone.

A moment later, Beeks stepped back. The Reaper leader's chest was heaving from the exertion. He spun toward Haas and roared, "Pull him up."

Haas felt dozens of arms grab him and yank him to his feet. "You'll pay for that," he roared.

"Really? Take a look around you," Beeks said. "Your friend was weak. And now he's dead. Don't make the same mistake."

Several yellow-eyes moved, and for the first time in far too long, Haas could see his downed friend's body clearly. Giles was lying face-down on the floor. There was a growing pool of blood under his head. He looked at the body once more. Giles's head and neck were off-kilter, like someone had torn the critical connections apart. It was obvious that the injuries that his friend had sustained were insurmountable. There was no way that his body would ever regenerate from the damage it had suffered.

There was more noise around him, and Haas quickly glanced around. Hundreds more yellow-eyes had entered the throne room. He turned his attention back to Beeks, who had returned to his throne.

"You killed him," Haas roared. "Why? We came in peace."

"I'm only gonna ask you once," Beeks continued. "You and I have history. It's a good history, and that's the only reason we're still talking. You have two choices. Join or die. Kneel and become part of my family. You'll become one of my loyal generals. Your pack will join mine, and you will have an even larger group of soldiers to command. Join me, and you can enjoy the spoils of war as we take over the world."

"You son of a bitch."

Beeks ignored the insult. "You have ten seconds to decide," he said coolly. "Join or die."

Haas looked around him. He was hopelessly outnumbered. Giles was dead, and there was nothing he could do about it. But as loyal as he felt toward Giles, he wasn't ready to join him in whatever afterlife waited for them.

"Three seconds," Beeks said. "Two. One-"

Haas felt his knees buckle. He slowly lowered himself onto one knee and bowed his head. "I submit," he said with clenched teeth.

"What's that? I can't hear you."

"I said," Haas said between clenched teeth, "I will join you."

"Excellent," Beeks said. He clapped his hands in an exaggerated applause. "You won't regret this."

Haas felt the hands holding him back release his limbs. A series of growls and yips sounded out as the group celebrated their newest addition.

Haas didn't share their joy. He'd been powerless to stop Beeks from murdering his best friend, and that was unacceptable. But it wasn't the right time to avenge Giles. Not against such overwhelming odds. One day he'd be able to exact his revenge, but today was not going to be that day.

CHAPTER SIXTY

Ezekiel made one final adjustment to his robes before deciding he was ready to talk to his waiting flock once more. His study's door burst open, and he heard a staffer shouting. He paused, turned to look toward the disruption, and frowned. He wasn't sure where Joseph was, but he would be sure to tell him how unacceptable it was for an ordinary staff member to come barging into his inner sanctum.

"What is it?" he said firmly.

"A big problem," the guy said, out of breath. "The people we were supposed to stop."

"What about them?"

"We did what we were supposed to and cut off their exit. But then there was one man. He had a vest on that said POLICE."

Ezekiel immediately recognized Foster's description. "I need you to get to the point already," he said impatiently. "I have to address the congregation."

"He shot one of the Chosen, and the rest fell over and died."

Ezekiel felt the hair on the back of his neck stand straight up. "That's impossible," he stammered. "No man has that power."

"B-but sir, I know what I saw. Several Chosen were also found dead in one of our stores."

"That's unfortunate. Even the Chosen can die if they are shot in the head."

"Not all of them were."

"What?"

"A few had been stabbed or shot in their bodies."

Ezekiel felt the bile rush up the back of his throat. He forced it back down. Now more than ever, it was important for him to seem calm in front of his flock. He'd have no choice but to wait for Giles to contact him and explain what the hell had happened in their attempted capture of Foster. Was it possible the man had some type of weapons that Giles had neglected to mention?

"Walk with me," Ezekiel said. "Where's Joseph or Walter?"

"Joseph is trying to calm down several members of our congregation. They aren't taking the news very well."

"What about Walter? He's supposed to handle Foster's capture."

"He didn't make it."

"What?"

"He was trying to get them to peacefully surrender when he was shot."

"Who shot him?"

"I'm not sure. It was either the man in the vest or one of his group."

Ezekiel felt a wave of sadness. He couldn't believe Walter was gone. He pushed down his grief. There would be time later to mourn the loss of his trusted guardian. A time when the guilty party could be forced to pay for taking Walter's life.

"You know in the lifetime of humanity, there's been an endless struggle between good and evil," Ezekiel said. "Heaven and hell. It seems we know what evil this man in the special vest stands for. I'm sorry, but I can't keep the congregation waiting any longer." He stepped into the room, and an immediate roar of applause and clapping began.

Ezekiel mentally counted to five and then raised his hands. The applause immediately stopped as if somebody flipped a switch.

"My children, what is the oldest struggle known to mankind?"

Ezekiel asked as he leaned slightly toward the microphone in front of him.

"Man and woman?" a congregation member shouted out.

Ezekiel let out a low chuckle. "That's a good one," he said. "But I'm thinking of one that's even older."

"Adam and Eve," another voice called out.

"Cain and Abel," a different person yelled.

Ezekiel raised both hands, and his flock immediately silenced. "All good guesses. But I was talking about the struggle between good and evil." He paused a moment for dramatic effect before continuing. "God has sent us his messengers, the Chosen to help purge this world of the evil that has taken root in so many places. I have received some very disturbing news. I'm afraid there is a group of people out there who have defiled God's messengers. Lost souls who have taken it upon themselves to kill members of the Chosen and our congregation."

A loud rumble went through the audience.

Ezekiel raised his hands again, and his flock quieted on command.

"They are led by a man named Foster. This man uses instruments of great evil. Weapons that kill the souls of the Chosen. This is something that poses a grave danger to our way of life. God has spoken to me. He has asked us to help the Chosen. We must find this man and his followers. We must force them to repent their ways. If they will not, then they must be sacrificed for the greater good of mankind."

A low rumble of voices began to form among the congregation.

"Who's with me?" Ezekiel shouted. "Who will join me in confronting these sinners? Who will give them a simple choice: Repent or die for your sins?"

A chorus of shouts and yells broke out. The volume grew louder and louder, until the entire congregation had joined in shouting, "Repent or die."

Ezekiel couldn't help but smile. He didn't know what had happened in their last attempt to capture Foster and his group. He wasn't sure if something had happened to Giles or if his transformed friend would soon make an appearance. But he had to assume that Giles was okay. And that meant when Foster was finally captured or killed, the two former partners-in-crime would be on top and in charge of everything in this area.

The flock continued to chant, and Ezekiel decided to add his voice to theirs. He couldn't wait to bring Foster to his knees and give him a simple choice: Join Ezekiel's flock, or die broken and alone.

CHAPTER SIXTY-ONE

Amanda strapped herself into the passenger seat as Foster stepped on the gas. The Suburban lurched forward and then began to gradually pick up speed as they exited the flaming ruins of the marina.

"Where are we going?" Sams said from the back seat.

"I don't know," Foster said. "Gregory's house is not secure. The marina's not an option anymore, either."

"We need a place," Sams said. "We can't just keep driving in circles."

"I know that, dammit," Foster snapped. "Let me think, okay?"

"What about any places we've already been?" Amanda suggested. "We already know what is there."

"Sporting goods store is out," Sams said. "That place was the Reapers' nighttime hangout."

"Above the gun shop," Foster said quickly. "There's a few staircases up to a second floor. It'd probably be the last place they'd look for us. We can secure it for tonight. Then, in the morning, we can worry about finding a better location."

"Yeah, that should work," Sams said. "You know those bastards are going to be looking for us."

"Which ones? The Disciples or the Reapers?"

"Both, actually."

"I'm expecting them, too," Foster said. "We'll lay low tonight and regroup."

"Yeah," Sams said. He turned and began looking out the side window.

The Suburban went silent, and Amanda felt herself drift back into her own head. It had been a close call. They could have all easily died today. It was pure luck that all of them weren't on the boat when it exploded. It was probably equal amounts of luck that all of the Reapers had suddenly fallen over dead and the remaining Disciples had chosen to flee.

She glanced over at Foster and saw the man had both hands on the steering wheel. His knuckles were white from gripping it hard. He was positively filthy from head to toe from the debris of the marina and everything that happened. As tired as he looked, she couldn't help but feel amazed that he was still able to go full force like he continued to do. The man just refused to quit fighting to protect the group. To protect her.

Amanda reached over with her left hand, touched Foster's forearm, and slid her hand forward until it touched his hand. He let go of the steering wheel and took her hand in his. He glanced at her quickly and smiled, and Amanda felt a rush of joy filling her chest till it felt like she was going to burst.

It was crazy. They were in the fight of their lives. Who knew how long they might have together? But with everything that had happened and everything that might still be yet to come, Amanda had reached a decision.

It was better to love and lose than to never love at all. Maybe it was too soon to call this love. But right now she couldn't think of another reason why the two of them couldn't take the chance and see if it truly was meant to be.

THE STORY CONTINUES...

The story continues in Wretched Aftermath

AUTHOR NOTES AND ACKNOWLEDGMENTS

Author Notes:

As of this writing, there is no Cutler Inn in Rehoboth Beach. The same is true with the Disciples of the Divine cult.

There is an actual store called Beef Jerky Outlet on Coastal Highway in Rehoboth Beach. According to their website, they offer over 100 different types. Since I'm not a fan of any kind of jerky, I haven't visited the store myself personally. Its location was a good choice for Foster to stop for information, so I created a fictional store description, including who the owner of the establishment may be. If the actual owner(s) of that business happens to read this, please accept my humble apology—no slight was intended.

The 134th Fighter Squadron are known as the "Green Mountain Boys." They are indeed part of the Vermont Air National Guard 158th Fighter Wing that is stationed at the Burlington Air National Guard Base in Burlington, Vermont. As I was writing this, they were supposed to receive F-35s in September 2019 (the same month this book was released), so I wrote it as such in the story. But as I neared completing this novel, I found out the F-35 delivery date had been pushed into early 2020. I opted to not to change this part of the story.

In other words, the "Green Mountain Boys" got their promised fighter jets a bit sooner in my book than they did in the real world.

In 2014, one of the early F-35s experienced engine failure where "pieces of the failed rotor arm cut through the engine's fan case" and eventually out "through the aircraft's upper fuselage." The problem has since been fixed, but I thought it would serve as a reasonable explanation in this story for Captain Vasquez's fighter suffering mechanical failure.

Special thanks to:

To my wife, my two children, and my mom. Thank you for everything you do and who you are. I love you.

To my editors, Pat, Jen, and Wendy. Your efforts to whip my manuscript into even better shape is often overlooked but always appreciated by me.

To my fellow indie authors Tom Abrahams, T.W. Piperbrook, Sam Sisavath, and Steve Konkoly. Thanks for your continued encouragement and suggestions about the Air Force, F-35s, and piloting in general. This book became even stronger with your help and I really appreciate it.

Last but not least, to my current and new readers. I hope you enjoyed "Wretched Retribution." If so, please take a few moments to leave a review where you purchased this book. As a self-published author, every honest review helps other people know about my books and inspires me to keep writing them.

Thanks again for reading this book. You'll also want to sign up for my email newsletter at http://www.egmichaels.com, which will alert you when the next E.G. Michaels book is ready for your enjoyment. Periodically, I'll also share news, updates, and even other books I've read that I think you'll enjoy.

<<<>>>